# ANY WAY YOU WANT IT

# ANY WAY YOU WANT IT

## MAUREEN SMITH

Recycling programs for this product may not exist in your area.

ANY WAY YOU WANT IT

ISBN-13: 978-0-373-53461-6



For questions and comments about the quality of this book, please contact us at CustomerService@Harlequin.com.



www.Harlequin.com

**Printed in U.S.A.**

## Acknowledgments

A huge, heartfelt thanks to the many readers and fans who enjoyed *Whatever You Like* and eagerly requested Remy and Zandra's story.
I truly hope that *Any Way You Want It* will live up to your expectations.

My sincere thanks to Senior Executive Editor Glenda Howard for her editorial guidance and unwavering patience and support.

# *Chapter One*

Zandra Kennedy reclined on a chaise lounge along a stretch of white sand beach sheltered by swaying palms. She'd gone out there to relax with a fruity cocktail and catch up on her summer reading. But her mai tai sat untouched, her novel completely forgotten.

She'd found something better to stimulate her imagination.

And she wasn't alone, judging by the riveted gazes of several other women lounging on the beach.

From behind a pair of dark sunglasses, Zandra watched as Remington Brand swam toward the shore, his strong limbs slicing cleanly through the shimmering turquoise waters. Though he'd been discharged from the navy three years ago, the rigorous training regimen he'd undergone as a SEAL had given him a body to rival any classic Grecian statue.

As Zandra watched, pulse thudding, his head broke

the surface of the water. And then came the rest of him, rising slowly from the waves like some mythical sea god. Massive shoulders, abs ripped with muscle, powerful thighs and sculpted calves.

His body was, indeed, a work of art. A Rembrandt. So that's what Zandra called him. Privately, of course. She'd never give Remy Brand the satisfaction of thinking he was the hottest guy she'd ever met.

Which he was. Hands down.

He smoothed water off his face, oblivious to the predatory stares of every female on the beach, many of whom would fantasize about him when they made love to their partners tonight. Their hungry eyes followed him as he sauntered across the sugary sand, brown skin glistening in the tropical sun, testosterone seeping from every pore.

Zandra realized she was gawking and quickly dropped her gaze.

Moments later Remy reached the palm-thatched hut where she lay in the shade, pretending to be absorbed in her book.

"Man, that water feels good." The deep, smoky timbre of his voice made Zandra shiver as her nipples hardened. "You don't know what you're missing, Z."

Oh, but she did. Every time she looked at him, she knew *exactly* what she was missing. Which was why she tried not to look at him very often. But it was hard not to, considering how ridiculously gorgeous he was. With sharp cheekbones, a square jaw and chin, and dark, electrifying eyes shaded by thick black brows, his face was perfect for a military recruitment poster. But it was his lush, sensual lips framed by a trim goatee that drove a woman's thoughts straight to cunnilingus. The kind of back-arching, thigh-shaking, toe-curling cunnilingus that enslaved you for life.

And therein lay the problem.

Zandra and Remy had known each other for twenty-five years, and for most of that time, she'd never seen him as more than just a friend. But something had changed over the past several months, and now she couldn't be anywhere near Remy without wanting to do all sorts of raunchy things to him. She'd tried to keep her distance from him, but he wasn't cooperating. He'd started showing up unannounced at her office to commandeer her into having lunch with him. Three weeks ago, he'd invited himself to a small dinner party she was hosting for some professional associates. He'd claimed that he was interested in networking, but he'd spent most of the night watching Zandra as she mingled with her guests.

At the end of the evening, one of her friends had pulled her aside and gushed, "You are *so* damn lucky! I'd forfeit my inheritance to have a gorgeous hunk like that completely under my spell!"

Zandra had laughed at the absurdity of the remark. Remy Brand had never fallen under *any* woman's spell. When it came to matters of seduction, *he* was the sorcerer.

And she'd do well to remember that while she was stuck on an island with him for two more days.

Grabbing a towel from the lounge chair beside hers, Remy rubbed his face and arms. "Why don't you put that book down and go for a swim?" he suggested.

"I will. Later." Unable to resist, Zandra peeked over the top of her novel to watch as lucky rivulets of water trickled down his chest, inching over the hard, sinewy muscles before disappearing into his dark swim trunks.

The wet material clung to his powerful thighs, drawing her gaze unerringly to the thick bulge at his groin.

Gulping hard, she jerked her gaze back to her book, trying to ignore her throbbing breasts and pulsing clit. No such luck.

Remy finished drying himself off, then stretched out on the lounge chair next to hers with his hands clasped behind his head. She felt him studying her, felt the heat of his eyes slowly roaming down her bare legs. She wished the cover-up she wore was longer, though something told her Remy's scorching gaze would make her feel naked even in an Eskimo suit.

"It must not be very good," he drawled.

"What?"

"Your book. Must be a snoozer."

Zandra frowned. "What makes you say that?"

"You're practically on the same page you were on when I left you over an hour ago."

Her face flushed. "How do you know that?"

Remy chuckled. "I noticed."

Of course he had. He'd always been sharply observant, a trait that had served him well as a SEAL commando. So well, in fact, that his teammates had often teased him about having eyes in the back of his head. Nothing escaped his detection.

Unnerved by the thought—and annoyed with herself for not owning a damn eReader—Zandra shifted uncomfortably on her chair. "The book's great. I'm just reading slow, savoring every word."

"Uh-huh." Remy wore a small, lazy smile that made her wonder whether he'd caught her watching him while he swam.

"I've also been enjoying the scenery," she hastened to add.

His smile deepened, but all he said was, "It *is* beautiful."

For a moment they gazed across the shimmering expanse of the Caribbean Sea, which was rimmed by lush, palm-fringed bays and towering emerald mountains. A distant sailboat drifted lazily across the horizon, and bright sunlight glinted off the frothy waves lapping the shore. To their right, perched on a cliff overlooking the water, was the luxury resort where Zandra and Remy were staying, along with several members of his family.

"Man, it feels like paradise out here," Remy murmured.

"Mmm," Zandra agreed, thinking of how she'd had to be coerced into coming on the trip.

Three weeks ago she'd been a bridesmaid for her friend, Lena, who'd married Remy's twin brother, Roderick. The couple had surprised everyone by inviting their families to join them in St. Lucia at the end of their Caribbean honeymoon. The invitation had included Zandra, who'd been excited at the prospect of spending five relaxing days on a gorgeous tropical island. That is, until she realized that she would be in close quarters with Remy—the very thing she'd been trying to avoid.

She'd regretfully told Lena and Roderick that she couldn't make it, blaming her busy workload. But Roderick, like his twin, had never learned to take no for an answer. He'd badgered Zandra for days, reminding her that she'd always accompanied his family on vacations when they were growing up. Though she'd tried to resist, he'd made her nostalgic for those boisterously chaotic road trips aboard the Brands' Winnebago. When he sensed her resolve weakening, Roderick had gone for the kill by enlisting his grandmother's help, because he knew that Zandra could never refuse the beloved family matriarch.

So there she was lounging on a sun-drenched beach beside a man who'd gone from being her childhood playmate to the star of her most illicitly erotic fantasies.

Frowning, she pushed her sunglasses off her face and set aside her book. As long as Remy was around, trying to read was absolutely pointless.

"I thought you were going sightseeing with the others," she grumbled.

He chuckled softly at her disgruntled tone. "Nah, I changed my mind."

"Why?"

One broad shoulder lifted in a shrug. "Didn't seem right to leave you here alone."

"I wouldn't have complained," Zandra muttered.

"Maybe not verbally, but you might have cried yourself to sleep at night, thinking of how I'd callously abandoned you."

Zandra couldn't help laughing. "In your dreams!"

He grinned, flashing a set of straight white teeth. He was so devastatingly handsome he took her breath away.

"Excuse me, Mr. Brand?"

A young woman had appeared, balancing a drink on a small tray. Her tropical shirt and khaki shorts easily identified her as a resort employee.

She smiled shyly as she handed the cocktail to Remy. "For you, sir. From the woman in yellow at the bar."

Zandra followed Remy's gaze across the beach to the cabana where an attractive, leggy woman sat alone at the counter watching him. When their eyes connected, she smiled alluringly and raised her own glass in a small toast.

Lips curving in a lazy smile, Remy winked at her.

Seeing the way Zandra's eyes narrowed, the resort employee gave her an apologetic look. "She assumed you two weren't together."

"Is that so?" Zandra said coolly. "And what made her assume that?"

The young woman looked uncomfortable. "Your body language, ma'am. She said you seemed to be, um, hiding yourself from Mr. Brand."

Zandra's face flamed. She shot a glance at Remy, whose dark eyes were glittering with laughter as he brought the glass to his mouth and drank.

"Mmm, that's good. What is it?" he asked the departing employee.

She smiled over her shoulder. "A Hole in One."

Remy laughed.

But Zandra wasn't amused.

"On second thought." She snatched the glass out of Remy's hand, looked toward the cabana and met the bar floozy's gaze. As the other woman watched, Zandra raised the drink to her lips and took a long sip, then deliberately licked her lips and mouthed, *Delicious. Thanks.*

The woman smirked, her eyes flashing with challenge.

Zandra should have stopped right there. She'd made her point and had nothing more to prove. But something came over her, some reckless impulse that had her jumping up and standing over Remy's chair.

He stared up at her. "What—"

"Shut up."

His eyes widened in surprise as she lowered herself onto him, straddling his hard, muscular thighs. The moment she felt the thick, rigid bulge between his legs, she knew she'd made a big mistake. But it was too late to backtrack.

"What're you doing?" Remy asked in a rough voice.

"I'm teaching your not-so-secret admirer a lesson in respect. There are some boundaries women just shouldn't cross."

"Oh, yeah?"

"Yeah."

Remy's eyes glinted wickedly. "So you're gonna show her, huh?"

"Damn straight."

Zandra reached inside the cocktail glass and removed a cube of ice, then set aside the drink. Holding Remy's dark gaze, she slowly rubbed the ice over his full, succulent lips until they glistened wetly. Unbearably aroused by the sight, she leaned down and lightly stroked her tongue over his bottom lip.

He groaned softly, sliding his big hands up her thighs to cup her ass. She gasped, scorched by his touch. Her hips slowly began to undulate, feeling his cock swell against her mound. Her clit hardened from the erotic friction, and moisture pooled in the crotch of her swimsuit.

She held the melting ice cube to her chest, shivering as Remy's hot tongue chased the stream of water that trickled down between her breasts. Her nipples tightened, straining against his palms as he slowly caressed her.

In that moment Zandra forgot about where they were, forgot about the woman watching them from the cabana. All she cared about was Remy's mouth on her burning skin, his hands on her aching breasts, the massive length of his cock between her legs. She wanted to be filled with him, wanted to feel his powerful body thrusting so deep inside her she'd have to breathe for both of them.

Lowering her head to the hard slab of his chest, she ran her tongue over his warm flesh, tasting the salty tang of the sea. His muscles quivered as she dragged her mouth over to the tattoo that curved around his chiseled biceps. She licked him slowly and sensually, her tongue tracing the intricate trident that would always identify him as a Navy SEAL.

"Mmmm," she purred as his erection thickened even more. "You are one *sexy* sail—"

"Yo, Zandra?" A large, masculine hand waved in front of her face. "Hello? You there?"

The sound of Remy's laughter-tinged voice snapped Zandra out of her trance. She blinked, staring dazedly at him.

He grinned. "Damn, what happened? You just zoned out on me."

"I did?" Zandra blushed furiously, embarrassed to realize that she'd been fantasizing about him. *Shit, shit, shit!* "Did I, um, happen to…say anything?"

"Like what?"

Her face flamed hotter. "Nothing. Don't worry about it."

Remy's grin widened. "One minute you were snatching my drink away. The next minute, you blanked out."

She glanced down at the cold glass in her hand, then looked toward the cabana. Remy's flirtatious admirer was now conversing with a guy who'd joined her at the bar. Zandra was relieved that the woman had turned her attention elsewhere—a feeling she didn't care to examine too closely.

"So," Remy said in an amused voice, "can I have my drink back?"

"No." Zandra emptied the contents of the glass into the sand. "I'll buy you another one. What're you in the mood for?"

"A Hole in One."

The suggestive timbre of his deep voice made Zandra's stomach clench. "Why don't you try something else?"

"Okay." His voice dipped indecently lower. "How about Sex on the Beach?"

When she glared at him, he threw back his head and laughed, a dark, delicious sound that heated her blood and sent thrills racing along her skin. She shifted on the chaise lounge, squeezing her thighs together to stop her clit from vibrating.

"Tell you what," Remy said, reaching for her forgotten mai tai on the table between them. "How about I just help myself to *your* drink?"

"Sure. Knock yourself out." She shoved her sunglasses back into place and closed her eyes, hoping Remy would take the hint and disappear. She couldn't relax when he was around, and what was the point of being on vacation if you couldn't relax?

"Since you're not reading anymore," Remy drawled, "why don't you go for a swim with me?"

Zandra shook her head. "No, thanks."

"Why not?"

"I don't feel like swimming right now. Not everyone is an amphibian like you, addicted to water. Besides— *Hey!*" she cried out as he suddenly plucked off her sunglasses and effortlessly swept her into his arms, unleashing just a hint of the brute male strength he possessed.

She glared up at him, instinctively clinging to his neck

as he strode purposefully from the palm-thatched hut. Trying to ignore the heat of his big body penetrating hers, she demanded, "What the hell do you think you're doing?"

"Getting you wet."

Damn if her mind didn't rush straight to the gutter!

"I don't want to get wet," she protested, absorbing the flex and glide of his hard pectoral muscles as he carried her across the beach. Several other sunbathers sat up quickly and peered at them over the rims of their sunglasses. The women's envious expressions told Zandra they would gladly trade places with her in a heartbeat.

"This is ridiculous, Remy," she complained as they reached the foaming shore. "You can't make me go swimming if I don't want to."

"Aw, don't be such a spoilsport, Z. You haven't gotten in the water since we arrived on Monday. It's downright unnatural, if you ask me."

"Well, no one asked you," she retorted.

He slanted her a lazy grin.

Looking at his sensual mouth just inches from hers, Zandra wanted to kiss him so badly she ached. When their eyes caught and held, a current of pure sexual awareness sizzled between them.

After a long, supercharged moment, Zandra averted her gaze and gruffly commanded, "I'm serious, Remy. Put me down *this instant*."

His dark eyes glinted with mischief. "If you insist."

And without further ado, he tossed her unceremoniously into the water.

Remy Brand had a secret.

Not the kind of secret he'd been sworn to keep in his former life—secrets involving classified intelligence and covert operations in dark, treacherous jungles. Secrets that were matters of national security.

No, *this* secret was far more personal.

Far more dangerous.

Because while the revelation of this secret might not get him hauled before a military tribunal or put him at the mercy of a ruthless dictator, it could *definitely* cause some serious damage if it were revealed too soon.

Damage to his longtime friendship with Zandra.

Damage to his ego.

Damage to his heart.

So what was the deep, dark secret he'd been guarding with his life for the past two years?

He was in love with Zandra.

Madly, deeply, hopelessly in love with the woman.

And it was killing him. *Killing* him.

It was crazy.

He'd survived the most brutal training to gain passage into the elite brotherhood of Navy SEALs. He'd engaged in the most dangerous combat missions in the most dangerous places in the world. He'd experienced the exhilaration and horror of taking lives.

He'd seen the bowels of hell and lived to have nightmares about it.

But nothing—absolutely nothing—could have prepared him for the sweet agony of losing his heart to a woman.

As he watched, Zandra surfaced from the cold water gasping and sputtering indignantly. "I can't believe you just did that!"

Remy laughed. "You told me to put you down."

"You know damn well what I meant," she shrieked,

swiping water from her eyes so she could glare at him. "I swear, Remy, you drive me crazy sometimes!"

*I know the feeling,* he thought, his mouth running dry at the sight of her nipples outlined sharply against the wet fabric of her cover-up. When she arched her neck back to smooth water from her black hair, blood rushed straight to his groin and made his dick throb.

"I don't know why you have such a hard time accepting no for an answer," she ranted. "It's so damn annoying."

Remy grinned unabashedly. "I got you in the water—mission accomplished."

She rolled her eyes. "Whatever."

As she spun away and began wading toward the shore, Remy reached out and caught her around the waist.

"Hey!" she protested as he playfully dragged her backward. Squirming out of his grasp, she turned and shoved ineffectually at his chest with both hands. "Will you stop trying to manhandle me!"

Remy smiled. *God, she's beautiful when she's all riled up. Hell, she's beautiful, period.*

And *that* was an understatement. Zandra Kennedy—with her sultry dark eyes, high cheekbones, erotically plump lips and luscious body—was a walking wet dream. With a seductive sway of her hips or the flash of a sexy smile, she could have any man she wanted.

Remy was determined to prove *he* was the only one she'd ever need.

"Do you know what this reminds me of?" he asked her.

Zandra just crossed her arms and glowered at him, drops of water clinging to her long lashes like diamonds scattered over black velvet.

"It reminds me of the first summer we went to Lake Carroll," he said quietly. "Do you remember?"

He watched as her expression softened. "Of course I remember," she murmured. "You taught me how to swim during that trip."

Remy smiled reminiscently. "You were so scared to get in the water."

"And *you* weren't very sympathetic," she reminded him. "You called me names and taunted me mercilessly."

Remy chuckled. "It was reverse psychology. I knew if I made you mad enough, you'd want to prove me wrong by showing that you *could* learn how to swim."

"And you were right," Zandra grudgingly conceded.

*"What?"* Remy exclaimed, cupping a hand to his ear with an expression of exaggerated shock. "Did I just hear you say that I was *right* about something?"

She laughed. "Yeah, and that was over twenty years ago!"

Remy guffawed. "Are you suggesting that was the last time I was right about something?"

Her eyes glimmered. "I'm not *suggesting* it. I'm stating it as fact."

Without realizing it, they had drifted closer together, nudged by the gentle waves lapping at their bodies.

Beads of water shimmered on Zandra's skin, and her hair lay in thick, silken strands upon her shoulders. Unable to resist, Remy reached out and twined a wet lock around his finger, watching as Zandra's lips parted on a soft intake of breath.

As desire coiled in his groin, he murmured, "I'm pretty sure I've been right about other things over the years."

She bit her lush lower lip, making it glisten. "I don't think so."

"No?" Remy stared at her mouth, wanting to kiss her so badly he shook with it. "What about the time I told you to dump that accountant because he seemed shady as hell? Did he, or did he not, get busted for tax evasion and money laundering four months later?"

Zandra heaved a breath. "Fine. You were right *that* time. But only because you ran a background check on him without my knowledge or consent," she added, uncrossing her arms to jab a finger into his chest. "And I'm still convinced *you* were the one who reported him to the feds."

Remy chuckled. "I'll never tell," he drawled, his gaze dipping to her voluptuous breasts. Her nipples were still hard, thrusting brazenly against the thin cover-up. It was all he could do not to lower his head and suck one into his mouth like a ripe cherry.

Seeing the naked hunger in his eyes, Zandra shivered, goose bumps rising on her skin. Her nipples tightened even more.

Licking his lips, Remy lifted his gaze slowly to hers.

They stared at each other, the air between them seething with the kind of raw heat that led to hard, grinding, primal sex.

Pulse pounding, Remy took a step toward her. "Zandra—"

Something like panic flared in her eyes before she blurted, "Let's race."

He stopped, brows furrowing. "Race?"

"Yeah. You know, like we used to when we were kids." She pointed to a distant white buoy bobbing in the water. "That'll be our finish line."

Remy chuckled softly. "I don't think racing is a good idea."

"Why not?"

*Because I don't want to swim anymore. I want to carry you back to your hotel room, strip you naked, lick every inch of your beautiful body and bury myself deep inside your wet heat until you scream and beg for mercy.*

Aloud he drawled, "As I recall, you used to throw temper tantrums and sulk for hours after I beat you at anything."

Zandra sniffed. "That was then. I'm thirty-two years old now. I think I can handle losing a friendly little race—*especially* to a former SEAL. So are you game or not, sailor?"

"Sure." A lazy smile curved Remy's mouth. "I'll even give you a head start."

"Oh, please. I'm not a helpless little girl. I don't need any charity from you."

Remy eyed her knowingly. "Then why are you—What the hell?" he called as she took off suddenly with a bewitching peal of laughter.

He grinned as he watched her swim away, her arms and legs gliding through the water with the grace of a mermaid.

He knew she'd only suggested the race as a diversion tactic. She'd felt the powerful attraction between them and it terrified her. So she'd invented an excuse to flee, just as she'd been doing for the past several months.

But if Zandra thought she could keep running from him, she underestimated the depth of his feelings for her.

Underestimated his determination to have her.

Underestimated him, period.

He patiently waited until she'd put enough distance between them, and then he started after her.

*Ready or not, here I come.*

# *Chapter Two*

Dinner that evening was held beneath a canopy erected on a private area of the beach. Candles flickered and glowed on the linen-covered table, which was long enough to accommodate the festive gathering of twenty-one. Fragrant platters of grilled fish, lobster, conch, curried chicken and plantain were passed around for sharing as a steel drum band serenaded the diners with calypso music.

Zandra swayed her shoulders to the melodic island beats as she enjoyed her meal and tried her damnedest to ignore Remy, who sat across the table from her. But no matter how hard she willed herself not to look his way, she found her eyes straying to him, unable to resist the magnetic pull of his presence.

He looked incredible in a black polo shirt and white linen trousers. She couldn't help staring at the hard angles of his face, the breadth of his wide shoulders and the strength of his powerfully muscled arms. His potent masculinity was an assault on her senses, leaving her breathless and aching in places she'd nearly forgotten existed.

Every time she glanced across the table, she found him already watching her, his midnight eyes glittering with a fierce, possessive hunger that made her feel branded. Claimed.

It should have angered her. She didn't belong to him, or any other man. But trapped in the smoldering beam of his gaze, with her heart thumping and her womb clenching, she felt no anger. Only lust. The kind of lust that could tempt her into doing something utterly stupid, reckless and dangerous.

Like having sex with Remy.

"I need to move that candle out of the way," murmured an amused voice beside her.

Snapped out of her trance, Zandra tore her gaze from Remy to stare at his youngest sister, Racquel, who sat to her right. "Hmm? What'd you say, Rocky?" she asked, calling her by the childhood nickname she'd earned for the feisty temper that had frequently gotten her into fights at school.

"I said," Racquel repeated, her dark eyes glinting with amusement, "I need to move that candle out of the way before you and my brother start a fire. You think I haven't noticed the way you two have been staring at each other across the table?"

Zandra's face flamed. Reaching for her rum cocktail, she mumbled, "I don't know what you're talking about."

Racquel laughed. "Yeah, right. And I'm a world-famous supermodel."

"You could be."

Racquel snorted. An award-winning photographer,

the tall, slender, exotic beauty could just as easily have made her living *in front of* the camera as behind it—a fact acknowledged by everyone but her.

As Zandra sipped her drink, Racquel eyed her speculatively. "Did something happen between you and Remy this afternoon while the rest of us were gone?"

Zandra shook her head quickly. "Of course not."

It was true. After their race—which she'd lost, of course—she and Remy had spent the next couple hours swimming, splashing and frolicking in the water like they'd done as children. By the time they returned to shore and collapsed upon their lounge chairs, Zandra had been too worn-out to do more than shove her sunglasses onto her face and close her eyes. She'd dozed off, awakening a short time later to find Remy kneeling beside her, gently easing her sandals onto her feet.

He'd looked up at her, and their eyes met and held for a breathless moment before Zandra glanced away, mumbling something about needing to wash and dry her hair in time for dinner. They'd gathered their things and walked back up to the hotel without speaking. When they reached the door to Zandra's room, Remy had brushed her cheek lightly with the back of his knuckles and mouthed, *See you soon,* before sauntering down the hall to his own room.

Long after they parted ways, the warmth of his touch had lingered on her skin.

Technically nothing *had* happened between them. Yet something had definitely changed. Zandra sensed it, like a tremor running beneath the ground before an earthquake erupts.

It scared her shitless.

Racquel sighed, the sound breaking into Zandra's reverie. "Too bad."

Zandra glanced at her. "Too bad what?"

"Too bad nothing went down between you and Remy." Racquel grinned, snagging the last plantain from Zandra's plate and forking it into her mouth. "But there's always tomorrow."

Which was the *last* thing Zandra needed to think about.

Gulping down more rum, she hazarded another glance at Remy. He was laughing and conversing with his eldest brother, Royce, whose dark good looks, charming personality and healthy bank account made him irresistible to every woman but the one who'd divorced him three years ago.

When Remy suddenly turned his head and met Zandra's gaze, a rush of heat flooded her loins.

As they stared at each other, she realized that the only way she could keep herself out of trouble was to cut her trip a day short and catch the first thing smoking back to Chicago.

"May I have everybody's attention?"

Silence fell over the table as everyone turned to look at Remy's twin brother, Roderick, who wore a broad smile of satisfaction that matched the one worn by the gorgeous woman seated beside him.

"Lena and I just wanted to thank all of you for joining us in St. Lucia—"

"Yeah, it was a real hardship," a deep voice joked, drawing a round of laughter.

Roderick chuckled, shaking his head at his younger brother, River. "Wiseass."

*"Roderick!"* chided their big sister, Robyn, clapping

both hands over the ears of the pigtailed little girl sitting next to her. "Have you forgotten that there are small children around?"

"My bad." Roderick winked at his niece. "Sorry, Mackenzie."

She gave him a huge, dimpled grin. "It's all good, Uncle Rod."

Everyone laughed.

When the humorous moment passed, Roderick continued warmly, "As I was saying, Lena and I are glad all of you could be here this week. At the risk of repeating what was already expressed at our wedding reception, we truly appreciate the love and support all of you have given us over the past four months. From helping with wedding preparations to dispensing marriage advice to knowing when we needed space to be alone together, everyone at this table played an important role in making our special day the most unforgettable day of our lives."

Turning to Lena, Roderick picked up her hand and laced their fingers together, gazing at her with such tender adulation that a wave of soft feminine sighs wafted around the table. Zandra was pretty sure she sighed, as well.

"As you all know," Roderick continued, "the way Lena and I came together was by no means typical. But then, there's nothing remotely typical about the way I feel about her. I wanted her from the moment we met, and I have no regrets about going after her and not taking no for an answer. Now that we're married, I fully intend to spend the rest of my life making sure that *she* never regrets giving her heart to me."

"Oh, baby," Lena whispered tearfully. "I won't regret a thing. I love you so much."

Roderick gently stroked her face. “I love you, too, sweetheart.”

Beaming with pride and satisfaction, Lena’s grandfather, Cleveland, lifted his glass and called out jubilantly, “Here’s to the bride and groom!”

A chorus of cheers swept around the table as everyone raised their drinks to toast the newlyweds, who shared a deep, passionate kiss that left the women fanning themselves.

“*That’ll* get me some more grandchildren soon,” predicted Roderick’s mother, Bernadette.

Everyone laughed.

“Not to be greedy,” added Eleanor Brand, the indomitable family matriarch, “but I’m ready to start planning the next wedding.”

“Me, too,” Bernadette agreed.

As several pairs of eyes turned and settled—inexplicably—on Remy and Zandra, a slow flush crawled up her neck and spread over her cheeks.

Grandma Eleanor gave Remy and Zandra an indulgent smile. “Did you two have a good time this afternoon?”

“Yes, ma’am, we did.” Lips twitching, Remy met Zandra’s gaze. “Didn’t we?”

She couldn’t help smiling. “Yes. We did.”

“That’s good,” Grandma Eleanor said approvingly. “I’m so glad you were able to come on this trip, Zandra. I would have been sorely disappointed if you couldn’t make it. You know you’ve always been a cherished member of this family.”

“I know,” Zandra said with warm sincerity. “And I’m very grateful for that, Grandma Eleanor.”

The old woman’s dark eyes twinkled. “Well, if you’d *really* like to show your gratitude—”

"Oh, my God!" Racquel suddenly exclaimed, pointing toward the sky. "Would you guys just *look* at that!"

Everyone turned to watch as the golden glow of the setting sun illuminated the horizon with breathtaking hues of pink, lavender and blue.

As the others admired the view, Zandra leaned close to Racquel and murmured, "Thanks for the bailout."

Racquel chuckled, her eyes glimmering with amusement. "As someone who's been on the receiving end of Grandma's uncensored advice more times than I care to recall, I considered it my duty to intervene on your behalf."

Zandra grinned. "God bless you."

Not everyone was preoccupied with the spectacular sunset.

As Zandra turned and reached for her drink, she noticed Remy and Roderick looking at each other from opposite ends of the table, silently communicating in their secret twin language.

As her eyes narrowed suspiciously, the two brothers tipped their glasses to each other and shared the slow, cunning smile of coconspirators.

After dinner, everyone lingered on the beach to enjoy the live music and the gentle trade winds wafting off the Caribbean Sea.

Grabbing a cold bottle of Piton beer, Remy walked to a large boulder jutting out of the sand and nimbly climbed to the top. From his elevated perch he could see the entire beach, a glittering oasis rimmed by lush green mountains and cliffs.

Sipping his beer, he surveyed the tranquil scene below him, mentally adding it to the collection of images that had gotten him through the darkest days of battle and bloodshed, when he'd succumbed to rare moments of wondering whether he would ever see his family again.

He watched as his nieces and nephews chased one another up and down the beach, their squeals of laughter like music to his ears. He smiled at the sight of his older sister and her husband strolling along the shore holding hands, while the image of his mother and grandmother with their heads bent close together made him wonder what they were plotting.

He chuckled at the sounds of raucous laughter and banter coming from the table where his older brother, father, grandfather and Cleveland Morrison were playing gin rummy.

Farther down the beach, Racquel danced with one of the dreadlocked cabana boys who'd caught her eye during dinner, while River put the moves on Lena's younger sister, Morgan, his hands spanning her slender waist as they gyrated to the pulsing soca beats.

Zandra and Lena stood by the water letting the foaming waves wash over their bare feet as they laughed and talked. Wearing white halter dresses with red hibiscus flowers tucked behind their ears, they looked like some artist's rendering of beautiful island nymphs romping through a tropical paradise.

Captivated, Remy watched as Zandra arched her head back and closed her eyes, savoring the ocean breeze that tossed her hair about her face and shoulders.

He stared at her, his heart knocking against his ribs.

"Damn, boy," drawled a deep voice laced with amused sympathy. "You got it *bad.*"

Remy dragged his gaze from Zandra to watch as Roderick climbed up the boulder and sat beside him.

Ignoring his brother's teasing remark, Remy took a

swig of beer and grunted, "Where'd *you* disappear to after dinner?"

"I went to see the hotel manager. Had to confirm some details for a surprise I'm planning for Lena tomorrow night." Roderick grinned. "Don't change the subject. I saw the way you were staring at Zandra just now."

Remy flashed a narrow, insolent smile. "How do you know I wasn't staring at your wife?"

Roderick snorted. "Because you don't have a death wish. Not anymore anyway."

Remy chuckled grimly, remembering the words Roderick had spoken to him the day he came home and announced that he was headed to Coronado Island to undergo BUD/S training to become a Navy SEAL. Upon hearing the news, Roderick—who knew Remy better than anyone and had always supported his dream of joining the SEALs—looked him in the eye and stated half seriously, "You must have a death wish."

Remy had escaped death, but only by the grace of God.

"Oh, yeah," Roderick said now, "I have something for you." Reaching into the pocket of his linen pants, he removed a small white napkin and handed it to Remy.

"What's this?"

"A booty call from some woman who approached me in the lobby. She told me to stop by her room later if I wanted another Hole in One." Roderick chuckled. "She obviously thought I was you."

Remy glanced down at the lipstick-marked napkin, his mind flashing on an image of the attractive woman who'd sent him a drink earlier while he and Zandra were lying on the beach. He remembered the way Zandra had reacted, snatching the glass out of his hand and dumping the contents into the sand. If he didn't know better, he would have sworn she was jealous.

Observing his private smile, Roderick cocked a brow. "You interested?"

Remy hesitated, contemplating the napkin. Beneath the red lipstick kiss, the woman had written her name, cell phone and room number along with the words *Come see me.*

Why shouldn't he? He was on an exotic Caribbean island surrounded by beautiful women. It'd be a damn travesty if he went home in two days without getting laid. But there was only one woman he wanted to make love to, and *she* bolted every time he went anywhere near her.

Scowling at the thought, Remy balled up the napkin and shoved it into his pocket.

Roderick eyed him sympathetically. "So the self-imposed drought continues, huh?"

Remy grunted, tipping back his bottle to drain the last of his beer. It had been four months since he'd had sex—an eternity for a guy with a healthy libido who'd always enjoyed the pleasures of the female flesh. But since making the discovery that Zandra was his soul mate, he'd lost his appetite for meaningless affairs with women whose names and faces tended to blur together. His last hookup had been with a leggy bank manager he'd met at a bar. After doing the unpardonable—groaning Zandra's name during sex—he'd decided it was time to take a step back and get his shit together before his obsession with Zandra got him stabbed by the wrong woman.

"So when are you going to tell her how you feel?" Roderick asked him.

Remy stared across the beach to where Zandra and his niece Mackenzie knelt by the water picking up seashells that had washed ashore. The sweetly poignant image made his chest ache.

"I'll tell her when she's ready," he murmured.

"How do you know she isn't ready now?" Roderick countered.

"Because I know her. And she isn't."

Roderick pondered that for a moment. "I think you should tell her anyway. Get it out in the open."

Remy grimaced. "So she can run even further away from me? No, thanks."

"You might be surprised. Look, Rem, you and Zandra have been in each other's lives forever. You know her better than any other guy, and she knows you better than any woman you've ever been with. Is it *really* so hard for you to believe that she just might return your feelings?"

Remy was silent, his eyes wandering back to Zandra. She and Lena were strolling away from the water, their sandals dangling from their fingertips.

As if sensing Remy's gaze, Zandra suddenly lifted her head and looked right at him, as though she'd been aware of his location the whole time.

His pulse thudded as they stared at each other.

After several beats, Zandra shifted her gaze to Roderick and gave him the winsome smile that should have been Remy's. When Roderick grinned back at her, Remy felt homicidal.

Following the line of Zandra's vision, Lena beamed and blew a kiss at her husband, who pretended to catch it, tip back his head and drop it into his mouth. Lena laughed.

Remy rolled his eyes.

As the two women moved on, he muttered to Roderick, "I don't know what nauseated me more. That little exchange, or your sappy speech over dinner."

Roderick grinned, hooking an arm around Remy's neck and giving him a noogie before Remy laughingly shoved him away.

Though identical twins, the two brothers were so different that friends and family members humorously referred to Roderick as the "more civilized version" of Remy. Roderick was polished, charming and debonair, favoring a dirty martini with three olives while Remy's drink of choice was a good lager that put hair on your chest. Roderick smoked premium Cuban cigars, while Remy had been known to chew tobacco and light up a blunt to calm his jagged nerves. Roderick wore expensive Italian suits and loafers, while Remy was most comfortable in battered leather jackets, camouflage pants and combat boots. Roderick was *GQ* to Remy's *Guns & Ammo,* James Bond to his Rambo.

Though their personalities were as opposite as night and day, what they both possessed in abundance was confidence, an iron will and the innate swagger of alpha males who were accustomed to getting whatever they liked, any way they wanted.

Roderick had gotten the woman of his dreams.

Now it was Remy's turn, damn it.

"You've been pining over Zandra for the past two years," Roderick drawled, as if he'd read Remy's mind. "Sooner or later you're gonna have to make your move."

Remy grunted. "Tell me something I *don't* know."

Roderick chuckled. "Seriously, man. You should listen to me. I'm older and wiser."

Remy snorted. "You're two minutes older."

"Ah, but two minutes can be a lifetime."

Remy smirked. “Is that what you tell Lena every night?”

“Ha ha. Very funny.”

Remy grinned. “You have to admit you walked right into that one.”

“Maybe,” Roderick conceded with a lazy smile, “but I’ll let it pass this time because I know you’re just jealous.”

Remy cocked a brow at him. “Jealous of who? You?”

“Yup. ’Cause I’m getting some—and you ain’t.”

Remy scowled, incensed because his brother was right. “Screw you,” he grumbled.

Roderick laughed, clapping him on the shoulder. “Anyway, I did my part by getting Za-Za here. The rest is up to you.”

Remy sighed. “I know. And…thanks for everything.”

“Hey, what are twins for?” Roderick grinned, his dark gaze traveling across the beach. “Look at Papa Dez getting down with your woman.”

Remy turned his head, grinning when he saw their grandfather dancing with Zandra. Desmond Brand—a tall, broad-shouldered, eighty-year-old man with meticulously groomed white hair and mustache—drew cheers and applause from the gathered crowd as he shuffled his feet and swayed his arthritic hips to the calypso music. When he dipped Zandra low, Remy and Roderick roared with approval and laughter and high-fived each other.

“I wanna be *just* like that old man when I grow up,” Roderick proclaimed.

“Hell, yeah.” Grinning broadly, Remy stood. “Come on. We’re missing the party.”

They climbed down from the boulder and sauntered across the beach. As they reached the others, the band struck up a slow number that lured the couples onto the dance floor.

As Grandma Eleanor teasingly reclaimed her husband, Remy approached Zandra. Her face was flushed and her eyes were glowing.

He held out his hand to her. "Dance with me."

She hesitated, biting her lip. She'd had the same panicked look when he'd asked her to dance at Roderick and Lena's wedding reception. But as a bridesmaid, she'd known that she couldn't refuse to dance with the best man without raising some eyebrows.

Thankfully she didn't refuse now.

As Remy pulled her into his embrace, she slipped her arms around his neck. As her soft, luscious breasts melted into his chest, he stifled a groan of pleasure and closed his eyes. His arms circled her waist, his hands resting just above the plump curve of her ass. She was the perfect height for him—not too short or tall. Just right.

Like everything else about her.

As they began swaying together, he bent his head to murmur in her ear, "I bet you made my grandfather feel thirty years younger."

Zandra smiled. "Grandma Eleanor already does that for him."

"True," Remy agreed, following the direction of her gaze. He smiled when he saw his grandparents grinning affectionately at each other as they slow danced. "They're amazing. Married sixty years and still going strong."

"I know," Zandra marveled softly. "Your parents are pretty remarkable, too, going on forty years. I can't even imagine what that's like."

"Neither can I," Remy murmured, "but I hope to find out someday. Don't you?"

Zandra met his probing gaze for a long moment, then glanced down, her black lashes shadowing her high cheekbones. She didn't answer him.

They danced in silence, their bodies moving as one to the rhythmic purr of steel drums. A gentle breeze blew tendrils of Zandra's hair across Remy's face, a soft caress. He could feel the heat of her skin beneath her lightweight dress. And the scent of her, exotic fruit and sultry woman, was an intoxicating aphrodisiac.

His hands tightened around her hips, tilting her closer. He heard her breath quicken, felt her nipples pucker against his chest. Blood rushed to his groin. If his family hadn't been around, he would have palmed her curvy butt cheeks and ground himself against her.

All too soon the slow song ended, melting into an uptempo soca number.

Zandra backed out of Remy's arms, but to his immense relief she didn't walk away or look for another partner. Holding his gaze, she stepped right into the dance, rolling her hips with a mesmerizing sensuality that took his breath away.

They moved rhythmically together, rocking from side to side, grooving and winding as the music pulsed between them.

When an electronic chord sizzled through the song, Remy dipped Zandra backward, then twirled her around. The hem of her dress flew up, teasing him with a glimpse of her smooth bare thighs.

He licked his lips, his dick hardening painfully when he thought of those luscious thighs wrapped around his back as he thrust into her. Blood pumping, adrenaline soaring, he grabbed her around the waist and hauled her into his arms.

When she felt his erection against her belly, Zandra's eyes widened in surprise.

And then came the panic.

When she tried to step away from him, Remy pulled her closer, trapping her against his aroused body.

Lips tightening with anger, she raised her arms and pushed at his chest.

This time he let her go, reluctant to cause a scene.

They stood staring at each other, chests rising and falling rapidly, heat and need throbbing between them.

"I want you," Remy said, low and husky. "And you want me, too."

Her eyes darkened. She knew better than to deny it.

But as the music ended, she turned and hurried away.

Clenching his jaw, he glanced around, encountering the sympathetic stares of his siblings, parents and grandparents.

*Be patient,* his mother mouthed encouragingly.

Remy just nodded.

But patience was something he was losing—and fast.

Zandra tried to keep her distance from Remy for the rest of the evening.

She had to.

Because the more time she spent in his presence, the more her resistance eroded, to the extent that she'd begun inventing rationalizations for why he would make a better partner than a stranger for an island fling.

He was her closest friend, she reasoned, so she didn't have to worry about him giving her an STD, robbing her or lying to her about not having a wife and kids stashed somewhere. And since he knew her so well, he might have a better idea of how to please her sexually than a complete stranger would.

It was madness. Absolute madness.

Around ten o'clock, nearly everyone retired to their hotel rooms for the night. Zandra stayed on the beach, having drinks with Racquel and Morgan. Remy and River stood outside the tent, smoking cigars and shooting the breeze with one of the friendly resort employees, who invited all of them to accompany him to a popular island nightspot. Zandra declined the invitation, joking that she'd done enough dancing for one night.

When Remy agreed to go to the club, she told herself she didn't care that he would be dancing with other women, sensually grinding against their undulating bodies as sweat glistened on their skin. She told herself it wouldn't matter to her if he met an exotic island beauty and chose to spend the night with her, or if he fell hard for her and convinced her to return to Chicago with him.

She told herself these lies as she assured everyone that she'd rather stay behind, then watched them depart for the club, smiling as Racquel playfully hopped onto Remy's back and looped her arms around his neck.

When one of the cabana boys sidled up to the table and began flirting shamelessly with Zandra, she decided it was time to leave. But instead of returning to her room, she struck out across the beach, hoping that a moonlit stroll along the shore would help clear her mind before she went to bed.

As she walked, she passed more than a few couples holding hands and gazing into each other's eyes as they enjoyed a leisurely romantic stroll. It was hard for Zandra not to envy them, harder still to pretend that she didn't long for the company of someone special. Someone who would hold her hand and make her feel warm inside as he walked close beside her.

*You could have had that someone,* an inner voice taunted. *But you pushed him away.*

Shaking off the unnerving thought—and an accompanying pang of regret—Zandra quickened her stride. As she ventured farther from the hotel, she saw lights glowing from the windows of cozy cottages nestled into the cliff side. She decided that the next time she visited St. Lucia, she'd find a rental property so that she could stay longer and enjoy the beautiful island.

"Zandra."

The sound of the low, deep voice had her leaping from her skin before she whirled around, her feet spinning in sand. She was stunned to find Remy standing there, seemingly materializing out of thin air.

"Damn it, Remy!" she screeched, staring wildly at him as her heart pounded against her ribs. "You scared the shit out of me!"

"Sorry." One corner of his mouth quirked upward. "I was trying *not* to scare you, which is why I called your name first."

"Well, it didn't work," Zandra snapped.

"Apparently not."

As Remy stepped closer to her, the heat of his body invaded hers, sending electric currents through her blood and raising the fine hairs on her skin. Her body had been calling out for him ever since she'd abruptly ended their dance, which had been nothing more than a prelude to seduction. She'd known it, and so had he.

She pulled in a shaky breath and tucked her windblown hair behind one ear as Remy watched her quietly. "How long have you been following me?"

"Long enough to wonder how much farther you plan

to walk. Or haven't you noticed that you've gone pretty far from the hotel?"

Zandra glanced down the beach, surprised to see that he was right. She shrugged nonchalantly. "What's your point?"

"My point," he drawled wryly, "is that it's not safe for you to go wandering off alone at night on a strange island. You should stay closer to the hotel where it's well lit."

Zandra heaved an exasperated sigh. "Yes, Daddy."

Remy chuckled, the sound drifting through the moonlit darkness like tendrils of smoke. "Mock all you want, but you know I'm right."

She rolled her eyes. "What I know, Remy, is that you see danger lurking in every shadow."

"Not every shadow." He sounded faintly amused. "More than enough, though."

Zandra shook her head, turning to watch as whitecapped waves danced close to the shore, as if beckoning them to wade in and frolic.

"I thought you were going to the club with the others," she said.

"I was," Remy murmured.

"So what happened?"

"I changed my mind."

Zandra looked at him. "Why?"

"I wanted to be here." He moved closer. "With you."

Zandra's heart beat triple time as she gazed up at him. "Remy..." she said softly. Just his name. Nothing more.

He reached out and gently cupped the side of her face, his thumb stroking her lower lip.

She shivered, swallowing hard. "You...you should have gone to the club."

"Why?"

"You could have had fun. Met someone."

His dark eyes glittered with challenge. "Is that what you really want? For me to meet someone?"

Zandra opened her mouth to respond, but no sound emerged.

"I didn't think so," he growled.

She shook her head at him, feeling more confused and frustrated than ever. "What are we doing, Rem? We came here to relax and have a good time, not destroy our friendship."

He frowned. "How are we destroying our friendship? By admitting that we're attracted to each other? By accepting the fact that we want to sleep together?"

Heat flooded Zandra's cheeks. "That's not going to happen."

Remy laughed softly. "I don't think you believe that any more than I do, sweetheart."

She held his gaze another moment, then abruptly sidestepped him and started back toward the hotel.

Remy followed her, his long-legged stride making it impossible for her to outpace him.

They walked without speaking for several minutes, the only sound between them coming from the ocean.

As they neared the hotel, Remy broke the silence. "What are you so afraid of, Zandra?"

"I'm not afraid of anything." But that was a lie, and they both knew it.

"Zandra—"

She sighed, staring up at the moon. "Look, you're right, okay? I'm attracted to you. And yes, damn it, I want to sleep with you. More than you can imagine."

"Now we're getting somewhere," Remy murmured.

Zandra shook her head at him. "But just because we're

attracted to each other doesn't mean we should act on those feelings. There's a lot at stake here."

"I know," Remy agreed.

"Do you?" Zandra stopped, prompting him to do the same. As they turned and faced each other, she said earnestly, "I cherish your friendship, Remy. I don't want to do anything that would jeopardize the good thing we've had all these years."

"Neither do I," he said quietly. "But believe me when I tell you that there's absolutely nothing you could ever do to jeopardize our friendship. I'm not going anywhere. Ever. So you're stuck with me whether you like it or not."

For the first time in hours, Zandra smiled. "You promise?"

His lips curved. "I promise."

"Good." Zandra sighed, closing her eyes as he stroked her windswept hair off her face. "In the meantime, if it's an island fling you're looking for, you should have no problem—"

"Don't."

She opened her eyes, bewildered by the sudden change in Remy's demeanor. She stared at him. "I was just going to suggest—"

"I know what you were going to suggest," he growled, "and I already told you I'm not interested in meeting someone else. But if I were, I sure as hell wouldn't need your assistance."

Zandra scowled. "I never implied—"

"If it makes you feel better to pretend that you're unfazed by me going out with other women—"

Zandra bristled. "I'm not pretending anything. What you do in your personal life is none of my business."

Remy shook his head at her, his lips twisted sardonically.

Averting her gaze, Zandra glanced around the beach and belatedly noticed that they'd come upon the cabana, where several people sat at the bar nursing drinks and enjoying the warm tropical night. Zandra's eyes narrowed at the sight of Remy's flirtatious admirer seated at the counter, her head thrown back in laughter as an attractive man whispered in her ear.

Zandra frowned. *Seriously? This chick again?*

No sooner had the thought crossed her mind than the woman suddenly glanced around. When her gaze landed on Remy, the look of unadulterated pleasure that swept over her face set Zandra's back teeth on edge.

She turned to look at Remy, but he'd already made eye contact with his leggy admirer. As they smiled at each other, Zandra's fingers curled into her palms until her nails dug into the flesh.

She watched as the woman murmured something to her companion, who frowned deeply, then picked up his drink and shuffled away with the slumped shoulders of a rejected suitor. Raising her glass to her lips, the woman winked invitingly at Remy, completely ignoring Zandra.

"Come on," Remy murmured, turning back to Zandra. "I'll walk you to your room."

"No need," she said coolly. "I can find my way back on my own."

He frowned. "That's not the p—"

"Besides," she continued, "I wouldn't want to keep you from your date, especially after she took the liberty of clearing the path for you to join her."

Remy regarded Zandra for a long moment, a knowing gleam entering his eyes. "You're not sounding very unfazed right now."

Heat stung her face. "Like I was trying to explain before," she said, striving for a neutral tone, "you should have no problem finding a plethora of partners for an island fling." She paused, then couldn't resist adding, "Maybe that's what we both need. A hot island fling—with other people, of course."

Something lethal flashed in Remy's gaze.

He nodded curtly to her, then turned and sauntered across the beach toward the waiting woman, leaving Zandra to stew all the way back to the hotel.

# *Chapter Three*

Three hours after Zandra returned to her hotel room, showered and crawled into bed, sleep eluded her.

She was burning up, her skin damp with perspiration as she tossed and turned restlessly against the cotton sheets.

When she couldn't take it anymore, she lunged from the bed, padded to the French doors and flung them open, thinking that the ocean breeze would cool her down. But the night air was sultry, wrapping around her heated body like a lover's embrace.

Closing her eyes, she stood on the balcony bathed in moonlight as her blood pumped hotly through her veins.

Suddenly there was a low, rough knock at the door.

She spun around, her heart vaulting into her throat.

She didn't have to wonder who it was.

Her body had been calling out for him ever since she'd abruptly ended their dance, which had been nothing more than a prelude to seduction. She'd known it, and so had he.

And now he'd come for her.

Before she could stop herself—not that she would have—Zandra rushed across the room, unlocked the door with trembling fingers and swung it open.

Remy loomed in the doorway, his shoulders nearly spanning the opening, his eyes blazing fiercely in the shadows. His chest and feet were bare and he wore dark pajama bottoms, as if he'd rolled right out of bed and snuck to her room like a thief in the night—or a man on a mission.

They stared at each other.

No words were spoken as Remy stepped forward, cupping her face between his big hands and crushing his mouth to hers. Gasping with shocked pleasure, Zandra threw her arms around his neck and pressed her swollen breasts against his hard, powerful chest.

His hungry mouth devoured hers in a deep, scorchingly erotic kiss that left her aching with need as wetness dripped from her pussy. She whimpered his name, her hips writhing feverishly against the huge erection bulging from his pants.

Parting her lips, he plunged his hot, silky tongue into her mouth. She captured it and sucked it hard, making him groan hoarsely.

He backed her into the room and kicked the door shut behind him, then lifted her effortlessly into his arms and carried her over to the nearest piece of furniture, a sturdy bamboo table.

When he set her down and reached for the lamp, she whispered self-consciously, "No, leave it off."

"Keep it on," he growled savagely. "I need to see you."

The light clicked on, spreading a warm glow around the luxurious room.

With a feral gleam in his dark eyes, Remy reached down and ripped her nightshirt in two. She shivered as the flimsy halves fell away from her body, leaving her naked and exposed to his fiercely ravenous gaze.

"I knew it," he rasped. "You are so beautiful. So *fucking* beautiful."

Looking like a starved man who'd been invited to a lavish smorgasbord, he reverently touched her knees, then ran his callused hands up her thighs and past her flat stomach before he cupped her plump breasts, pushing them together.

She trembled hard, watching through heavy-lidded eyes as he lowered his mouth to her erect nipples. They were unbearably sensitive, exploding with sensation as he blew lightly over them, then sucked them into his mouth.

She groaned and arched backward as his tongue flicked over one nipple then the other, shooting spasms of pleasure from her areolas down to her pussy.

Through the intoxicating haze of passion and lust suffusing her brain, a tiny voice reminded her that this was *Remy,* her childhood friend and tormenter—the *last* man on earth she should become intimate with.

But she didn't care. What he was doing to her felt so damn good, she couldn't have stopped him if a hurricane was tearing the hotel apart.

He stroked his hands down the front of her body, caressing her heated skin. She arched into his touch, gasping when he slipped one hand between her legs and palmed her throbbing mound. Watching her face intently, he used his blunt fingers to spread her labia while his thumb rubbed the tight nub of her clit.

*"Mmm,"* she moaned, writhing desperately against him.

Face hard, nostrils flaring, he pushed two fingers inside her creamy wetness. She cried out and flung back her head as he stroked her cunt, probing deeper as her inner muscles clenched around his fingers. She was on fire, burning up from the inside out as she bucked her hips against his hand, craving sweet release.

"I'm sorry, sweetheart," he growled, giving her a look of savage lust as he withdrew his fingers from her wet clasp. "I have to be inside you the first time you come."

With that, he swept her up from the table and carried her to the bed. He lowered her to the mattress, then stepped back to yank down his pajama pants.

She gasped, her eyes widening at the sight of his long, thick cock rearing from a trim patch of black pubic hair. Her mouth watered as she watched a bead of precum emerge from the narrow slit.

Remy lowered himself onto her, both of them shuddering as their naked flesh met. He shoved his fingers into her hair, slamming his mouth over hers as she wrapped her legs around his broad back. They rolled across the bed kissing hungrily, tongues twining, hands stroking and exploring until Remy pinned Zandra beneath his heavy body and gazed down at her.

"Zandra," he whispered softly. *"Zandra."*

The way he said her name made her shiver. His voice was awed and husky, achingly reverent, as if she were the embodiment of a dream he'd never expected to come true.

Shaken, she stared into his eyes. "Remy?"

"What, baby?"

"Fuck me. *Please.*"

He groaned. "You have no idea how long I've waited to hear you say that."

Before she could comprehend his meaning, he wrapped his hands around her hips and pulled her tight against him, driving his cock inside her with one long, brutally erotic stroke.

Arching her back, Zandra almost wailed at the intensity of the pleasure that ripped through her.

Remy shuddered deeply, his eyes slamming shut as he threw back his head, the tendons straining in his neck and shoulders.

Zandra stared up at his face, his features contorted in ecstasy. She'd never seen anything so profoundly beautiful. So stunningly powerful.

*"Ahh,"* he groaned, as if he were in acute agony. "You feel so… I can't… *Oh, God...*"

Zandra understood. This joining was like nothing she'd ever experienced before. The way he felt inside her, his cock filling her, stretching her unbearably… Words couldn't begin to describe it.

After several moments, Remy opened his eyes and lowered his head. They stared at each other as he slowly began thrusting into her. He was so big, so thick, that she could feel every inch, every vein, every ridge of his shaft sliding into her. Tears welled in her eyes, white-hot pleasure scorching her insides.

She moaned as his strokes came harder and faster, her fingernails scoring his back and the flexing muscles of his ass. He whispered erotic endearments as he drove into her, reaching a part of her no man had ever touched. Desperately she arched against him, hearing their flesh slap at each furious joining.

And then suddenly her whole body was shaking. She screamed as she came, racked by spasms so staggeringly intense she thought she must be dying.

Moments later Remy went rigid against her, then exploded with a shout that was raw and hedonistically primal. He jerked out of her and fisted his hand around his cock, white spurts of cum shooting out of him and splashing onto her stomach.

Purring with breathless satisfaction, Zandra reached down and smeared his hot semen into her sweat-slicked skin. Then, as he watched her through hooded eyes, she slid her sticky fingers into her mouth and sucked them dry, savoring his clean, salty taste.

Remy gave a husky groan, then slanted his mouth over hers and kissed her. It was a soft kiss, slow and tender, infused with an emotion she couldn't define.

Her lips clung to his as he slowly lifted his head and stared into her eyes.

"That was lovemaking," he murmured, his midnight-velvet voice sending shivers through her. "Now…we fuck."

Remy meant what he'd said.

After two long years of torturing himself with erotic fantasies about Zandra, he'd finally, *finally,* made love to her. It had far surpassed anything he could have ever imagined.

And he was just getting started.

Kissing his way down to the curving mounds of her breasts, he latched onto a dewy nipple that hardened against his tongue. As he pressed the nipple to the roof of his mouth and sucked, Zandra whimpered with pleasure.

"Are you still on the Pill?" he murmured, all after the fact.

Her breath caught. "H-how did you know I was?"

"Sweetheart, I know almost everything about you." He licked his way to her other breast. "So yes or no?"

"Yes." Her voice was shaky. "I'm…I'm still on the Pill."

"Good. I wanna come inside you from now on."

She gasped as he rolled her over and pulled her onto all fours. Grabbing her hips, he rubbed his throbbing erection against the smooth, shapely swell of her ass. Zandra shivered, looking over her shoulder to watch as he nudged his dick between the swollen folds of her slit.

As he thrust into her, she arched backward with a high-pitched cry. All the breath left his body in a harsh groan as her pussy clamped around him like a vise. She was so hot, so tight and honey-wet, sheathing his cock with a perfection unmatched by any other woman he'd ever been with.

Tightening his grip on her waist, he began a hard, pounding rhythm that rocked the entire bed. Zandra gasped and moaned, her hands clenching in the rumpled covers beneath her. Reaching under her body, Remy cupped her swaying breasts and rubbed her taut nipples, making her moan louder and longer.

Perspiration sheened their skin as he hammered into her, his pelvis slapping her ass until the sound drowned out the roar of the pounding surf below. This wasn't sweet or gentle lovemaking. This was raw sex. Pure fucking.

As he jacked her hips into the air, she nimbly wrapped her long legs around his back, giving him an even deeper angle of penetration. Growling with savage satisfaction, he pummeled her harder and faster, ramming his swollen balls against her pussy as sweat dripped from his forehead and spattered her back.

*"Remy..."* Zandra keened with ecstasy. *"Oh, fuck... fuckkk!"*

He felt her inner muscles contracting. Then she wailed, long and hard, as her juices spilled around his thrusting flesh.

Throwing back his head, Remy exploded in a searing burst of pleasure that tore through his balls and shot out of his cock. He shuddered and groaned Zandra's name as he ejaculated, hot and violently, into her pulsing womb.

Closing his eyes, he limply dropped his head forward.

When he could move again, he gently lowered Zandra's legs to the bed, wrapped his arms around her and pulled her down with him. They were both panting, her slick breasts heaving against his chest as he held her close.

For several minutes neither spoke, lulled by the sounds of the ocean and the warm breeze wafting through the open balcony doors.

Remy had never felt more relaxed and content in his life. He hoped Zandra felt the same, hoped she didn't already regret what they'd done.

When the silence stretched between them, he stroked a hand over her tousled hair and murmured, "What're you thinking about?"

She sighed languorously. "I don't think I'll have the energy for ziplining and sailing and horseback riding tomorrow."

Remy chuckled, relieved. "We could always just stay here."

"And skip out on your family a second day?"

"I'm sure they won't mind." He *knew* they wouldn't mind.

Zandra chuckled dryly. "Um, no, that's okay."

"You sure?" His lips nuzzled her damp temple. "We could have plenty of fun on our own."

"That's what I'm worried about," she muttered under her breath.

Remy grinned.

"You don't think anyone heard us, do you?"

His grin widened. "I don't know…we *were* kind of loud."

"Oh, God." She groaned, covering her face with her hands.

Remy laughed. "Relax, sweetheart. These rooms are so big, and the walls are nice and thick. So I'm sure no one heard us."

"You're just saying that to make me feel better," Zandra grumbled.

"Did it work?"

"No."

"Okay. What if I tell you that we're probably not the only ones getting busy tonight? Would *that* make you feel better?"

"No." She grinned wryly. "Nice try though."

"Can't blame a guy, right?"

"Guess not." She sighed.

He waited.

"This is such a beautiful island," she said appreciatively.

"It certainly is," Remy agreed.

"And this hotel is amazing. Very scenic and romantic."

"Very." Remy knew where she was going.

"It's not hard to understand how people could come here and…you know, lose their inhibitions."

*Bingo.*

"No," Remy said silkily, "it's not hard to understand at

all. But I also think if two people are already attracted to each other, it's only a matter of time before they're going to act on those feelings—tropical island or not."

He felt her swallow. Hard.

He smiled with satisfaction.

She remained silent.

"Nothing to say?"

"Shut up," she grumbled.

Remy laughed, then reached down and smacked her on the ass.

*"Ow!"* She angled her head back to glare at him. "What was *that* for?"

He grinned. "For what you did earlier. Smiling at Rod and not me."

She rolled her eyes. "Jeez, Remy, I never knew you were so sensitive."

He kissed her forehead. "Only when it comes to you. You've always known how to push my buttons. And don't pretend you didn't know what you were doing when you dissed me like that."

As Zandra tried unsuccessfully to hide her smile, Remy chuckled.

"But that's all right," he drawled, pushing her onto her back and covering her body with his. "I've got something for you."

Anxious eyes stared up at him. "Remy, I don't want your family to know—"

He put his finger to her soft lips. "I'll leave before anyone else wakes up."

"You promise?"

"I promise." He captured her wrists in one hand and held them over her head as he guided his engorged shaft to her wet opening.

She shivered, her breath quickening.

Watching her intently, Remy parted her swollen pussy lips, slid through the thick cream that covered them and slowly entered her.

Zandra moaned, her eyes slitting closed.

Staggered by the look of ecstasy on her face, Remy thought of the endless days and nights he'd dreamed of this moment.

And then he got busy making up for lost time.

# *Chapter Four*

When most people learned that Zandra was the owner of an escort agency, they usually assumed that she was a madam who peddled prostitutes, therefore, by extension, she must have a wild sex life.

In reality Zandra had never promoted prostitution. She'd always enforced a no-sex policy for her escorts, which they'd adhered to—with few exceptions.

As for her personal life, she rarely dated, and prior to her recent island tryst, it had been several months since she'd been penetrated by anything other than her vibrator.

She should have kept it that way. Because now that she'd experienced Remy's lovemaking, it'd be an eternity before she could even think about sleeping with another man, and getting off on her vibrator would only be a cruel tease.

Zandra groaned, leaning her forehead against the warm glass window of her downtown Chicago office.

Since returning from St. Lucia two days ago, she'd been consumed with thoughts of Remy and the explosive night of passion they'd shared. He'd done things to her no man had ever done, making love to her with a ferocious insatiability she would never forget.

With his thick shaft embedded so deep inside her she couldn't tell where she began and he ended, she'd forgotten who they were, forgotten that he was only supposed to be a friend.

But when she awoke the next morning—alone, thankfully—she was so shocked and embarrassed by her reckless behavior that she'd avoided being alone with Remy for the rest of the trip.

If only she believed that was the end of what they'd started.

With a deep sigh, Zandra lifted her head from the window to stare out at the glistening Chicago skyline.

For the past five years, she'd owned and operated Elite For You Companions, an upscale escort agency patronized by some of Chicago's richest, most powerful men. Her clients included chief executives, industrialists, philanthropists, foreign diplomats and Arab sheikhs, all of whom came to her because she had the best escorts in town—beautiful, intelligent, classy women who knew how to handle themselves in any social setting.

With two degrees in economics, Zandra prided herself on being a shrewd businesswoman. Everything about the way she ran her agency—from hiring escorts to catering to clients—was intended to protect her business interests and ensure maximum profitability.

Instead of using a booking agent to set up client appointments, she delegated the task to her efficient receptionist, who was the soul of discretion. Zandra set the hourly rates and fees, which were unapologetically high and unapologetically nonnegotiable.

Though her escorts were hired as independent contractors, Zandra treated them like employees and took her cut off the top, because she'd only needed to be burned once to remember that she could trust no one.

She didn't accept credit cards for payment because even though she was running a legal business, she believed her clients were entitled to their privacy, and accepting their plastic hardware established a paper trail that could later be used against them *or* her.

She ran complete background checks on clients to ensure their financial solvency and to weed out criminals and undercover cops, because she didn't have time or patience for bullshit. If prospective clients were married, she politely referred them to other agencies, because she wasn't in the business of wrecking homes.

Thanks to her shrewd professionalism and eye for quality, Zandra was now worth a small fortune that afforded her a luxury penthouse on the Gold Coast and the loyalty of a personal chef and chauffeur.

Not bad for a girl from the South Side.

Just then the phone on her desk buzzed.

"Zandra?" Her receptionist's voice came through the intercom.

She glanced over her shoulder. "Yes?"

"Sorry to disturb you, but Enid Roche is on the line. She wanted to confirm your RSVP for the museum fundraiser gala on Sunday."

In addition to running a successful escort agency, Zandra was also a patron of the arts who served on the board of various arts councils, hosted fundraisers at her own home and promoted the works of local artists.

She smiled. "Tell Enid I'll definitely be there."

"Yes, ma'am," Christine chirped.

Zandra stared out the window another moment, then sighed and smoothed down the front of her Chanel shift dress, turned on the heel of her Louboutin snakeskin pumps and sat behind a custom-designed glass-top desk with a sleek leather base.

*Enough daydreaming about Remy,* she told herself. *You have work to do.*

No sooner had she completed the thought than her cell phone rang. When she picked it up and saw Remy's number, her heart pounded into her throat.

Taking a deep breath to summon her composure, she pressed the answer button and spoke as calmly as possible. "Hello."

"You. Me. Lunch at noon."

Her stomach pitched at the sound of his deep, dark voice. Leaning back in her chair, she murmured, "Good morning to you, too, Remington."

"Good morning, Zandra." She could hear his smile. "How are you?"

"I'm fine." Her lips curved wryly. "It seems that we're making progress."

"How so?"

"Instead of calling, you usually just show up unannounced and make me go to lunch with you."

Remy chuckled, low and husky. "I couldn't wait that long to hear your voice again."

Zandra closed her eyes, heat curling from the base of her skull to the bottom of her spine. "Well, um, I'm not free for lunch today."

"Why not?"

"Because I've been out of the office, and I have work to catch up on."

"And it will be there when you get back from lunch."

"That's not the point—"

"Listen."

Never had one word conveyed such quiet authority.

Zandra snapped her mouth shut, her pulse thudding as she waited for him to continue.

"I let you ignore me for the rest of our trip because I knew you needed time to process what had happened between us. For that same reason I didn't come to your room the next night, even though it killed me to stay away, and I couldn't sleep worth a damn because my dick was so hot and hard for you—"

*Oh, God,* Zandra thought as a ripple of lust shot to her groin, making her cross her legs tightly.

"On the flight back home," he continued, "I let you get away with sitting next to Royce instead of me, and I didn't say a word when you insisted on having your driver pick you up from the airport, even though you'd previously agreed to let *me* take you home." He paused, his voice turning dangerously silky. "Under the circumstances, I think I've shown remarkable patience and restraint. But if you think I'm going to keep my distance and pretend that nothing has changed between us, you obviously haven't met me."

Zandra was silent, heart thumping, hand pressed to her quivering belly.

"So what time should I pick you up for lunch?"

Zandra dragged in a shaky breath, then exhaled on a sigh of defeat. "Be here at twelve-thirty."

Remy chuckled low. "Atta girl."

Incensed at the dark satisfaction in his voice, Zandra

scowled. "I'm in the mood for Mirage," she said peevishly, knowing how much he hated the modern fusion cuisine served at the trendy downtown restaurant.

But instead of balking at the suggestion, Remy merely drawled, "Whatever you want, babe. See you soon."

"Fine." Zandra hung up, then swiveled toward the window and glared at the cerulean summer sky as if it were to blame for her problems.

*It's just lunch,* she assured herself. *It's not like he can debauch me in public.*

But then again…

The phone on her desk buzzed a second time.

"Zandra?" Christine spoke through the intercom. "There's a gentleman here to see you."

Zandra frowned, swiveling back toward her desk. She wasn't expecting anyone that morning. "Who is it, Chris?"

There was a pause. "Landis Kennedy."

Zandra froze, her spine stiffening in shock as the blood drained from her head.

Staring at the phone as if it were a venomous snake poised to strike, she said tightly, "I don't have an appointment with Mr. Kennedy."

"I know, but he says it's important that he see you."

Zandra closed her eyes, her fingers curling on the arms of her chair. After all these years, what could he possibly want from her?

"Zandra?" Christine prompted. "Should I send him back?"

*I'd rather you send him to hell where he belongs,* Zandra thought darkly.

"Yes," she relented through gritted teeth. "Show him to my office."

Releasing her death grip on the chair, she took a slow, deep breath and prepared to face her past.

Moments later Landis Kennedy strode through the door of her office as if he had every right to be there, every right to intrude.

He wore an expensively tailored suit, and his short black hair was wisped with gray at the temples. His face was broad and handsome, with shrewd dark eyes and a square chin.

He seemed shorter than Zandra remembered, not the hulking monster of her childhood nightmares. But a monster he was and always would be.

When she deliberately didn't stand to greet him, he sat without invitation and smoothly crossed his legs. His pants were meticulously pressed, and his dark Italian loafers were polished to a high gleam.

"What do you want?" Zandra asked coldly.

He gave her a chiding smile that made her skin crawl. "Now is that any way to greet your long-lost father?"

The word curdled in Zandra's stomach. *Father.* What had Landis Kennedy ever known about being a father? He'd terrorized her from the day she was born until she turned sixteen and left home to live with her grandmother. The last time she'd seen him had been at her mother's funeral ten years ago, after which she'd told him to stay the hell out of her life. Years later, she'd boycotted his lavish wedding to a widowed socialite, and when he became a city alderman, she'd tossed away the invitation to his swearing-in ceremony.

"Why are you here?"

He met her icy glare, his eyes raking over her face before he glanced away. A muscle jumped in his jaw.

"You look just like your mother." It was an accusation. A bitter indictment.

Zandra swallowed hard, fighting to keep the painful memories at bay. "You still haven't answered my question."

His gaze swept around the tastefully furnished room before returning to hers. "First, I wanted to inform you of my decision to run for mayor of Chicago."

Zandra leaned back in her chair and crossed her legs, offering no congratulations or words of encouragement.

"Once I announce my candidacy," he continued, "every facet of my life will come under intense scrutiny by the media and my opponents. I can't afford to have any skeletons in my closet that could be a liability to my campaign. Which brings me to you and your—" he paused, lips thinning in distaste "—brothel."

Zandra arched an amused brow. "You mean my escort agency?"

He smirked. "If that's what you prefer to call it. The point is that your line of work will be a liability to my campaign once the public learns that you're my daughter. And that's why I'm here." He looked her in the eye. "I want you to relocate your agency to another state."

Zandra didn't even blink. "No."

He frowned. "Hear me out—"

"I don't need to. What you're suggesting is out of the question."

"I'm prepared to write you a check—"

"I don't want your damn money," Zandra spat. "I'm not going anywhere, so you wasted your time coming here."

Landis's face hardened, a malicious gleam filling his eyes. "You seem to forget that I'm a member of the city council. I have friends in high places. All it would take is one phone call for the state's attorney to launch an investigation that would put your brothel out of business."

"Do your worst," Zandra dared him. "I'm not worried about being investigated because I know I'm running a legitimate business."

"Since when did peddling prostitution become legitimate?"

Zandra clenched her jaw. "You know nothing about me or my agency—"

"I know plenty." He sneered at her. "I've seen you being chauffeured around town, showing up at all the ritzy parties and rubbing elbows with the rich and famous. You think those people admire you? Respect you?" He snorted contemptuously. "Everyone knows you're nothing but a high-priced whore masquerading as an entrepreneur."

Zandra let out a caustic laugh, refusing to give him the satisfaction of knowing how deep his words cut. "I can't believe you have the audacity to lecture *me* about respectability when you slithered your way into society by seducing an heiress just days after she'd buried her husband. You may not approve of the way I make my living, but at least *I* earned everything I own. It seems to me that the only whore in this room is—"

Landis shot from the chair, banging his fist on top of her desk.

Suddenly the years evaporated, transforming Zandra into that terrified little girl who'd cowered in the kitchen doorway watching as he brutally punched and kicked her sobbing mother.

"You ungrateful little bitch," he snarled, his face twisted with hatred and fury. "Who the hell do you think you are? You should be down on your knees *thanking* me for everything you have. *I'm* the one who went out every day and worked my ass off to provide for you while your pathetic excuse for a mother could never keep her head out of the clouds long enough to tend to our home. You and that goddamn woman robbed me of the best years of my life! The only thing *she* ever did right was tie a belt around her neck and hang herself."

Zandra gasped. As grief and fury seared her from gut to throat, she lunged to her feet and screamed, "*You bastard!* Get out of my office and don't ever come back, or I swear to God I will *kill* you!"

He sneered. "Your empty threats don't scare me, little girl."

As he took a menacing step around the desk, Zandra snatched open the top drawer, reached inside and grabbed the pearl-handled pistol she'd received as a gift from Remy.

Her father blanched as she pointed the gun at his face, her eyes narrowed with lethal promise.

"Does this look like an empty threat to you?"

He stared at her, nervously licking his lips. "I always knew you were as crazy as your damn mother."

"Take one more step," Zandra warned, lowering the nozzle to his chest, "and I will blow your fucking heart out. Assuming you ever had one."

Landis hesitated for a moment, then jabbed a trembling finger at her. "This isn't over," he vowed before turning and storming from the room.

Zandra stood there frozen, her heart knocking painfully against her ribs.

Distantly she heard the rapid staccato of high heels on the tiled floor, then her receptionist appeared in the doorway. Her brown eyes widened with alarm when she saw the gun clutched in Zandra's hand.

"Oh, my God, Zandra. Are you okay?"

She jerked her head in a nod. "I just need a minute."

"Do you want me to call Rem—"

"No," Zandra said sharply. "Don't call anyone. Just close the door."

Christine frowned, eyeing her worriedly. After another moment, she pulled the door shut behind her.

Slowly, finger by finger, Zandra released her grip on the butt of the pistol, then set it down on her desk and took a step backward, then another, until her back hit the window.

That was when the tremors began, starting deep in the pit of her stomach and spreading outward until she shook all over.

Closing her eyes, she wrapped her arms around her midsection, bowed her head and wept for the mother she'd lost, and the innocence she could never reclaim.

# *Chapter Five*

Remy roared down West Grand Avenue astride a sleekly powerful MTT Turbine motorcycle, weaving through Monday morning traffic with a reckless aggression that would have made Zandra curse and shriek at him if she were riding shotgun.

He grinned at the thought. He couldn't wait to meet her for lunch that afternoon. With any luck, they could just skip the meal and feast on each other instead.

At the next traffic light, he whipped the motorcycle around the corner and sped down a narrow street that ran through the warehouse jungles of Chicago's manufacturing district, an area untouched by the gentrification efforts that had shined up the West Loop.

As Remy reached a nondescript brick building perched at the end of the block, he slowed down and swung onto the ramp that led into the underground parking garage.

Pulling up to the security gate, he lifted his helmet shield to have his retinas scanned.

As the metal garage doors slid open, a smoky female voice intoned from the speaker panel, "Welcome back, Mr. Brand. You were missed."

"Thanks, Magna," Remy drawled with a lazy smile. "Who needs Siri when we have you?"

The simulated voice responded with warm laughter as Remy rumbled through to the parking garage. Swerving his motorcycle into his reserved spot, he silenced the ignition, removed his helmet and climbed off the bike.

As he strode to the elevator, the camouflage-clad security guard pressed the call button for him and offered a deferential "Good morning, sir. Welcome home."

"Thanks, Erwin," Remy said, clapping the man on the shoulder. "It's good to *be* home."

*Though I wouldn't have minded another week in paradise with Zandra, just the two of us.*

Remy smiled to himself as he entered the elevator.

Once the doors closed behind him, his thoughts shifted to the busy day that awaited him as head of Brand Security Solutions, a multimillion-dollar global corporation that provided executive protection and investigative services to government, military and corporate sector enterprises. His itinerary for today included a series of meetings and consultations that would hopefully result in new contracts.

When he reached the top floor, his assistant was waiting for him. She had her Bluetooth headset in place and held a steaming cup of black coffee, which she handed to him as soon as he stepped off the elevator.

In her late twenties, Mona Fay Yancy had dark hair that she always scraped back into a severe ponytail, square shoulders and wide childbearing hips, though she swore she'd yet to meet a man who could sweet-talk her into "birthing his melon-head babies." She was a sassy Southern girl whose tough, no-nonsense demeanor would have made Remy's tobacco-chewing, ball-busting BUD/S instructors gush with pride. She kept Remy on track, ran a tight ship and suffered no fools.

"Good morning, boss. Nice to have you back." She gave him one of her rare smiles, which faded the moment her eyes landed on his combat boots. "Good Lord, *what* are you wearing?"

Remy grinned, sipping his coffee. "I took the Turbine today."

"Whatever for?" Mona demanded, falling into step beside him as he started from the lobby with long, ground-eating strides. "You're supposed to be meeting with the top executives of a major pharmaceutical company. You can't show up wearing an Armani suit with *combat boots*."

"I'm not showing up anywhere," Remy corrected. "*They're* coming to me. So why the hell should they give a rat's ass what I'm wearing? They're interested in the services I provide, not my fashion sense."

"Or lack thereof," Mona muttered under her breath.

"I heard that."

"Good morning, Mr. Brand. We missed you."

Remy smiled and winked at the attractive young receptionist manning the phone from behind a futuristic-looking glass desk.

While the exterior of the old warehouse resembled every other warehouse on the block, the interior featured an ultramodern design with exposed steel beams, sleek leather furnishings and glacial white walls that formed a dramatic contrast to gleaming black granite floors.

Given his military background, Remy would have gone for something stark and functional, but when he brought Zandra to the empty warehouse and gave her the grand tour, she'd seen so much potential that she'd urged him to commission one of her interior designer friends to renovate the space. Even if Remy hadn't been pleased with the results—which he was—it would have been worth it just to see the girlish delight on Zandra's face as she'd rushed from room to room oohing and aahing over everything.

As Remy and Mona headed toward his office, they came upon a pair of tattooed, rough-looking ex-marines, one sporting a blond Mohawk while the other wore long dreadlocks. Their beefy hands were wrapped around coffee cups and powdered beignets that they'd just pilfered from the kitchen.

They nodded to Remy. "Wassup, Chief."

"Gentlemen. How's it going?"

"Need to talk to you about that assignment in Abu Dhabi."

"It'll have to wait until later," Mona interjected before Remy could open his mouth. "He has important meetings all day, and y'all aren't leaving for Abu Dhabi till Wednesday."

As the two marines walked past, Remy made eye contact with them and subtly gestured to indicate that he'd be available in ten minutes.

"Nice try," drawled Mona, who missed nothing, "but I don't think so."

The men could only chuckle and shake their heads. "Catch up with you later, Chief."

When Remy and Mona reached his office, he sauntered to the black granite desk, sat down in the leather executive chair and propped up his booted feet as he drank his coffee.

Mona arched a brow at him. "*Someone's* feeling mighty relaxed this morning."

Remy grinned. "Five days of fun and sun in the Caribbean will do that for you. You should try it sometime."

Mona snorted. "This place would fall apart if I went on vacation."

"Probably, but that shouldn't stop you from going anyway."

She made a face. "I will, but not now. Things are too busy around here." Which, of course, she'd been saying for the past two years. "Anyway, I know you're already familiar with Hospira Pharmaceuticals, but I prepared some additional notes for you to review before your meeting at nine. The file is on your desktop."

"Thanks, Mona. Oh, and I brought you something."

She eyed Remy curiously as he reached inside his breast pocket, removed a narrow envelope and leaned forward to pass it to her.

When she opened the envelope and saw what was inside, her eyes widened in shock. "Oh, my Lord. Are these plane tickets to *St. Lucia?*"

"Yup. One for you and your mother, or whoever else you want to take. The hotel accommodations have already been arranged."

Mona stared at him, shaking her head in disbelief. "This is too much. I can't—"

"Yes, you can. Besides, you don't have much of a choice. I'm disabling your access to the building that week—"

*"What?"*

"—so you might as well take your country ass down to St. Lucia and enjoy your birthday."

Mona glowered at him for a moment, then contemplated the plane tickets in her hand. Remy could see the corners of her mouth quirking as she fought a smile.

"You couldn't just bring me back a souvenir like normal people?" she grumbled.

"You couldn't just squeal for joy and jump up and down like a normal girl?"

The smile broke through, but only for a moment. Briskly clearing her throat, she straightened her shoulders and gave Remy a stern look. "You have a meeting to prepare for, and I have work to do."

"Aye aye, sir," Remy teased, watching as she pivoted on her heel and marched across the room.

Reaching the doorway, she paused and glanced over her shoulder at him. Her expression was soft. "Thank you."

Remy smiled. "Don't mention it, kiddo."

After Mona left, he set aside his empty coffee cup, then swung his legs down from the desk, rose from the chair and moved to the windows. Standing with his feet apart and his hands folded behind his back, he stared out over the industrial landscape.

As a SEAL he'd operated in the shadows, attacking where he wasn't expected and vanishing before the enemy could strike back. He'd adopted that same mentality when scoping out territory for his new company, searching for areas that wouldn't announce his presence to the world. He'd chosen the warehouse district for the obscurity of its location, which was also important since his firm housed millions of dollars' worth of high-tech equipment and computer systems programmed with military applications.

Remy closed his eyes for a moment, his mind traveling back to three years ago.

After getting discharged from the navy, he'd struggled to adjust to life as a civilian. He'd spent nine years as a member of SEAL Team Three, and he'd lived for every moment of it. He'd always expected to retire on his own terms, but when his insubordination during a gruesome combat mission landed him in the crosshairs of the whitewashed bureaucrats at the Pentagon, he'd been bounced out on his ass.

For months afterward he'd felt adrift, angry and depressed. He became surly and withdrawn from his family and friends, and he'd often wandered out alone on frigid winter nights to walk the streets for hours, haunted by memories of what he'd seen and experienced.

Over lunch one day with Roderick, his twin had given him an ultimatum: find a new purpose in life, or move to Outer Mongolia to spare everyone from having to watch his continued descent into self-destruction.

Roderick's dose of tough love was just what Remy had needed. That same day, the idea for Brand Security Solutions was born.

Though Remy would always miss serving his country as a Navy SEAL, he enjoyed running his own company and answering to no one.

Well, *almost* no one.

At the sudden knock on his door, he turned from the window, prepared to explain to Mona why he was daydreaming instead of preparing for his nine o'clock meeting.

The words died in his throat at the sight of the man standing in the doorway behind his assistant.

Lieutenant Commander Sam Keegan.

In the flesh, as if he'd been conjured by Remy's trip down memory lane.

Mona looked slightly aggrieved. "Sorry to intrude, boss, but you have a visitor."

"I'll be damned." Recovering from his shock, Remy rounded the desk and crossed the room to greet his former commanding officer. "It's good to see you, sir."

"Likewise, Lieutenant Brand," Keegan said, strong fingers grasping and pumping Remy's hand. "You look good, son. And I see you haven't lost your grip."

"On reality or…?"

They laughed at the old joke.

"I apologize for just barging into your office," Mona told Remy, "but Mr. Keegan was too impatient to wait in the reception area."

Remy grinned. "That doesn't surprise me."

Sam Keegan was tall and robust, with piercing green eyes and the erect bearing of the decorated war veteran he was. Before retiring from the navy two years ago, he'd had a reputation for being a formidable, ass-chewing leader who was both feared and revered by the men of SEAL Three. A fellow Chicagoan, he'd mentored Remy from the time he joined the Teams until he was discharged, earning Remy's undying loyalty and respect.

"Hope I'm not catching you at a bad time," Keegan said.

"Actually—"

"Not at all," Remy spoke over Mona. He gestured to the chair across from his desk. "Please have a seat."

As the commander strode toward the proffered chair,

Mona pointed to her watch to remind Remy of his nine o'clock meeting. He nodded before closing the door in her face.

As he rounded his desk and sat down, Keegan observed with wry humor, "She's a pistol, isn't she? Ex-military?"

Remy laughed. "No, believe it or not."

"Too bad. She'd have made one hell of a drill sergeant."

"I know. Uncle Sam's loss is my gain."

Keegan huffed a gravelly laugh.

He'd grown out the military buzz cut, but his steel-gray hair was still meticulously groomed, and he wore a well-tailored charcoal suit with the same air of authority he'd once worn his navy blues.

"It's really good to see you, sir," Remy said again. "How's Mrs. Keegan?"

"She's doing great. Glad to be back home with her family and friends for good. And we just learned that our eldest is expecting her first child."

"That's wonderful," Remy said warmly. "Congratulations, Grandpa."

"Thank you." Keegan smiled, beaming with pride. "And how's your family?"

"Everyone's doing really well."

"Good. Glad to hear it. Give them my best, will you?"

Remy smiled. "I sure will."

Keegan gestured around the office. "This is quite an outfit you got here. I'm impressed."

"Thank you, sir," Remy murmured, leaning back in his chair. "It's not the same as being in the Teams, but it'll do for now."

Keegan snorted. "Who're you fooling? Between you

and your billionaire brother, Roderick—not to mention Royce and River—some folks are predicting that the Brand boys will be running the Windy City before too long."

Remy chuckled wryly. "I don't know about all that. And speaking of running the city, how are things going at Mayor Norwood's office?"

"Good, good." After retiring from the service, Keegan had returned home to Chicago and gone into politics, becoming a trusted senior advisor to the mayor. "We're gearing up for his reelection campaign, so I've been scouting the field, assessing the strengths and weaknesses of the other candidates."

Remy nodded. Of course Keegan would approach politics as if he were preparing for a combat mission—gathering intel on the enemy, checking the maps and charts, doing the necessary reconnaissance before planning an attack strategy.

"What can you tell me about Landis Kennedy?"

Remy frowned, his gut tightening at the mention of a name he hadn't heard in years. "Is he running for mayor?" he asked, answering Keegan's question with a question.

"He's expected to throw his hat into the ring any day now," Keegan replied. "And so far, he's the one we're most worried about. He has the financial resources and name recognition as an alderman, and he's been gunning for the black vote by cozying up to church leaders on the South Side. Hell, he even has the support of some Teamsters who're soured on the mayor after that whole city budget fiasco last year."

Remy's frown deepened at the idea of Zandra's estranged father becoming the next mayor. Though Remy generally regarded politicians as scum-sucking bottom feeders, Landis Kennedy was particularly abhorrent. He was a cold, sadistic motherfucker who'd tormented his wife and daughter for years, robbing Zandra of her childhood and warping her perception of men. Some of Remy's most violent fantasies involved him cornering Kennedy in a dark alley and dragging the blade of his KA-BAR knife across the man's throat. Slowly, so the bastard would see the promise of his own death in Remy's eyes before he took his last breath.

Yeah, he hated the guy *that* much.

Watching the play of emotions across his face, Keegan observed dryly, "I take it there's no love lost between you and the alderman."

"Let's just say I'd sooner vote for Osama bin Laden than Landis Kennedy," Remy muttered darkly.

"I see." Keegan eyed him knowingly. "Your animosity wouldn't have anything to do with your long-standing friendship with Kennedy's daughter, would it?"

Remy regarded Keegan for a long moment, then leaned forward in his chair and asked in a very low voice, "What's this about, Lieutenant?"

The air crackled between the two men as they stared at each other.

Keegan was the first to glance away, his lips pressed into a thin line. "The reason I came here today is to tell you that the mayor knows about Zandra Kennedy, and he's planning to use her escort agency against her father."

Remy scowled. "That's ridiculous. Zandra has nothing to do with the old man. She hasn't seen or spoken to him in ten years."

Keegan gave a snort of grim laughter. "Since when has that ever mattered in politics? Look how they tried to crucify Obama over his illegal immigrant aunt. It didn't matter that he really didn't know that poor woman. She was fair game, and so is Zandra Kennedy."

Remy clenched his jaw, his gut churning with dread. The last thing he wanted was Zandra's good name and reputation being dragged through the mud of Chicago politics. She'd be savaged by her father's campaign rivals and the media, who would cast her in the same sleazy tabloid light as Heidi Fleiss and the D.C. Madam.

"The mayor wants me to hire a private investigator to find out if Zandra's escorts are engaging in prostitution," Keegan explained. "He wants the smoking gun that will torpedo Kennedy's candidacy. That's why I came to you."

Remy glared at him. "If you think I'm going to investigate Zandra's agency behind her back," he growled, "think again."

Keegan gave him a level look. "If you turn me down, Norwood *will* hire another firm. Can you guarantee that no illegal behavior will be uncovered?"

Remy frowned, remembering how Roderick and Lena met. She'd been one of Zandra's escorts, and she'd slept with Roderick on their first date. Though they wound up falling madly in love and getting married, their relationship demonstrated that it *was* possible for any of Zandra's girls to break the rules on any given night.

"I'm giving you an opportunity to protect Zandra from potential scandal," Keegan continued. "If you investigate her agency and uncover any wrongdoing, then you can warn her to get her house in order before it's too late. But you have to do it by the book, Brand," he added sternly. "You can't tip her off about the investigation. You need to get legitimate results—good or bad. Covering up the truth will only hurt Zandra in the long run."

The knot in Remy's gut pulled tighter. He knew Keegan was right, but damn it, he *hated* the idea of going behind Zandra's back to investigate her agency. It was the ultimate breach of trust, and she'd never forgive him if she found out.

"I can't do it," he said flatly.

Keegan frowned. "Brand—"

"If my investigation reveals that her escorts are having sex with clients, then what? You'll report back to the mayor, he'll go public and Zandra will suffer the repercussions." Remy shook his head. "I can't do that to her."

Keegan looked him in the eye. "You have my word that I won't report any damaging information to Norwood."

Remy frowned in confusion. "Then what the hell is the point of all this?"

"To appease the mayor. When he's got his sights set on something, there's no moving the target." Keegan's expression softened. "Look, son, I know how much Zandra Kennedy means to you. Whenever you talked about home, her name came up as often as any of your family members—sometimes more. I have no desire to cause her any trouble, but if the mayor hires another firm to investigate her agency, all bets are off. And we both know there's nothing to stop any of the other candidates from going that route. If I were you, I'd want to know what kind of ammunition the enemy can use against me."

Remy held the commander's intent gaze for a moment, then shoved to his feet and stalked to the windows. He rubbed a hand down his face, rasping the short whiskers of his goatee.

Behind him, he heard the soft creak of leather as Keegan rose from the chair. "I've heaped a load onto your shoulders, so I'll give you till this evening to get back to me with your decision."

Remy nodded tightly.

Not only had Keegan been one of the best mentors he could have ever asked for, but when the shit hit the fan, he'd put his neck on the line for Remy, intervening with the brass to spare Remy the ignominy of a dishonorable discharge. And now he'd come through for him again.

Remy turned from the window. "Sir."

Keegan stopped at the door, meeting his gaze.

"Thank you for bringing this to my attention. You didn't have to. You could have gone to another firm, and I'd have been none the wiser. I really appreciate you looking out." His lips twisted ruefully. "Of course, if I go through with this and Zandra finds out, she'll never speak to me again."

Keegan gave him a smile of sympathetic understanding.

"'Cheat if you must,'" he said, quoting an old Navy SEAL expression, "'but don't get caught.'"

# *Chapter Six*

Landis Kennedy's unexpected visit left Zandra shaken for the rest of the day.

On her way home from the office that evening, she mentally replayed the painful confrontation until her insides churned with anger and her eyes burned with fresh tears.

After all these years, and after everything she'd done to put her traumatic past behind her, she should have been immune to her father's cruelty and hatred. But she wasn't.

And something told her she never would be.

Closing her eyes, Zandra let the memories wash over her, pulling her deeper under.

Fifteen years ago when she'd graduated from high school as class valedictorian, she'd had her choice of any college or university to attend. Determined to get as far away from home as possible, she'd stunned everyone by accepting admission to Oxford University in England.

She'd majored in economics and spent the next four years studying rigorously while working odd jobs to help pay her tuition. She'd loved living abroad, and had only returned home every summer to look after her mother, who remained trapped in an abusive marriage.

No matter how often Zandra implored Autumn Kennedy to leave her husband, to run away and start over someplace new, Autumn had insisted on staying. She was afraid to do anything else. And after her mother passed away, she seemed to cling even more to Landis.

But when Zandra graduated from Oxford, Autumn had made the trip overseas without her husband, who couldn't be bothered. After the graduation ceremony, she and Zandra had celebrated over lunch. Autumn's face had held the serene glow of someone who was at peace with herself, a memory that would haunt Zandra years after her death.

When she announced her decision to remain at Oxford for graduate school, Autumn had reached across the table and taken Zandra's hands between hers. She'd told Zandra that she loved her and was very proud of her, which Zandra already knew. But hearing it again, on that day, had meant the world to her.

Over dessert, Autumn had opened up and spoken poignantly of her own dreams of living the artist's life in Paris, painting masterpieces inspired by the beauty and romance of the city.

So for the next seven days, she and Zandra had lost themselves in Paris. They'd visited museums, gone for long strolls, sipped coffee at cozy sidewalk cafés, enjoyed the simple pleasure of breaking the crust on a crème brûlée while watching pedestrians dash across a busy street.

And Autumn had painted to her heart's content. She'd painted people at a market, a red dress hanging in a boutique window, a bridge overlooking the Seine.

And she'd painted Zandra, a tender smile on her face as she'd quietly stroked her brush across the canvas.

It would be the last time Zandra saw her mother alive.

Shortly after Autumn returned home, Zandra received the phone call from her father that would change her life forever.

In a voice devoid of emotion, he'd told her, *Your mother's dead. Come home.*

Reeling with shock and grief, she'd rushed back to Chicago, where she learned the unspeakable details of her mother's suicide.

After washing and folding a load of laundry, Autumn had walked into the bedroom closet and hung herself with one of her husband's belts. He'd found her there when he came home from work that evening.

Zandra was so absorbed in her dark reverie that she didn't notice when her driver, Norman, pulled up outside the luxury high-rise on East Delaware and climbed out to open the back door for her. She woodenly thanked him and wished him a good night, then walked into the building, nodded abstractedly to the concierge and rode the elevator to her floor.

As soon as she entered her penthouse, she set down her purse and attaché case, stepped out of her heels and headed straight to her custom-built wine cellar off the kitchen. She needed a drink. The more, the better.

She'd just selected a bottle of merlot when her doorbell rang.

She frowned, wondering who it could be.

*Not Remy,* she prayed. After the emotionally trying

day she'd had, she couldn't deal with his overwhelming masculinity or the dangerous feelings he aroused in her.

She'd called him earlier to cancel their lunch date, citing an appointment that came up unexpectedly. In the heavy silence that followed, she'd sensed Remy's skepticism and displeasure. But to her surprised relief, he'd accepted her excuse and told her he would see her later.

She hoped *later* didn't mean *tonight*.

The doorbell rang again.

With a sigh, she set down the corkscrew and went to answer the door.

She was surprised to find one of her new neighbors standing there holding a bottle of wine.

He smiled, green eyes crinkling at the corners. "Hi. I hope I'm not intruding. I moved into the building a couple weeks ago, and I've been meaning to stop by and introduce myself. My name's Colin."

Zandra hesitated, then shook his proffered hand. "Nice to meet you. I'm Zandra."

"I know." His smile turned sheepish. "I saw you heading out for a jog one morning and asked the doorman your name. He couldn't say enough wonderful things about you."

"Oh, I pay him to do that."

Colin laughed, a warm, easy sound. He was a very attractive man, with dark brown hair, olive skin and the rangy build of a casual athlete.

He held out the bottle to her. "This is for you."

"Oh, how thoughtful." Accepting the wine, Zandra glanced at the distinctive label.

"It's a Napa Valley rosé. I spent a day at the vineyards during my recent business trip to San Francisco."

Zandra smiled at him. "I appreciate the gift, but I'm

afraid you have me at a disadvantage. You just moved here. *I'm* supposed to bring *you* something to welcome you to the neighborhood."

His eyes twinkled. "Well, you could always invite me inside for a glass of wine," he suggested.

"I could." Zandra gave him an amused, considering look. She didn't make a habit of welcoming strange men into her home, but Colin seemed harmless enough. She'd glimpsed him around the building once or twice, and judging by the way he'd been staring at her, she'd known it was only a matter of time before he would make his move.

Deciding she could use some company—if only to keep her mind off the troubling events of the day—Zandra opened her door wider. "Please come in."

Colin smiled with pleasure, stepping into the apartment. As Zandra closed the door behind him, he cast an appreciative look around the spacious living room, taking in the glossy wood floors, luxurious crown molding, richly painted walls, eclectic collection of art and photography, and the plush sofa and chairs strikingly accented with red, chocolate and blue quartz.

He gave a low whistle. "I know we just met, but I need the name of your interior designer. This place is stunning."

"Thank you." Zandra smiled, accustomed to the reaction from new visitors. "She's an old friend. I'd be more than happy to refer you."

"That'd be great. I'm still settling into my apartment, but you've definitely given me something to strive for."

"That's good. Have a seat, and I'll be back with the wine."

As Zandra headed from the room, Colin went from

admiring her decor to blatantly checking out her ass. That, too, was nothing new to her.

Inside the chef's kitchen, she returned her unopened bottle of merlot to the wine cellar, then uncorked the rosé and filled two glasses.

When she reentered the living room, Colin was standing at the row of windows that boasted spectacular lakefront views. He turned and smiled warmly as Zandra handed him a glass.

"To beautiful new neighbors," he toasted her.

She smiled. "And neighbors who come bearing gifts."

They chuckled softly and clinked glasses.

Colin watched as Zandra nosed the aromatic wine, then took an experimental sip. It was delicious, bathing her palate with flavorful notes of strawberry and raspberry with a hint of citrus. "Mmm."

"Good?"

She sipped again, sighed. "Very good."

Colin looked as pleased as if he'd fermented and distilled the wine himself.

As he drank from his glass, Zandra noticed that he had the smooth, manicured hands of a man who made a living pushing paper. She couldn't help comparing them to Remy's much larger hands, dusted with black hair and callused from years of combat. At the memory of those hands masterfully stroking her body, she flushed all over.

*Stop it,* she ordered herself. *Don't think about Remy. What happened in St. Lucia was a huge mistake, one that shouldn't—won't—be repeated.*

As she and Colin moved to the sofa and sat down, she asked conversationally, "So are you new to Chicago, or just this building?"

"New to Chicago," he answered. "I'm from Phoenix,

but I was recently transferred here to head my company's research and development division."

"What kind of company do you work for?"

"Software."

Zandra nodded, crossing her legs. She didn't miss the way his gaze roamed from the curve of her thighs down to her French-pedicured feet.

His eyes glinted with appreciation. "I'm starting to think this job transfer was the best thing that could have ever happened to me."

She smiled, sipping more wine.

"So what about you, Zandra? What do you do for a living?"

*You're nothing but a high-priced whore masquerading as an entrepreneur.*

She met Colin's gaze, her chin lifted a defiant notch. "I own an escort agency."

His eyes widened in surprise. "An escort agency?"

"Yes."

"Wow." He shook his head slowly. "I don't think I've ever met a mad—" He caught himself, stopping just short of calling her a madam.

After an awkward pause, he eyed her curiously. "What made you decide to open an escort agency?"

Zandra didn't feel like getting into the multilayered reasons, so she merely responded, "Escorting is one of the most profitable businesses in the world. Wealthy men will always seek the company of beautiful women, so I'm more than happy to bring them together."

She'd spoken with such cool, clinical detachment that Colin raised his brows. "But don't you ever worry about… you know, getting in trouble with the law?"

Zandra gave him a look of amused indulgence. "You're

assuming that all escorts are prostitutes and all escort agencies are in the business of prostitution. I won't deny that many are, but contrary to what moralizing politicians and overzealous cops would have you believe, there *are* exceptions. A business that books clients and sends them to a woman's home or hotel room isn't an escort agency. My escorts accompany clients to social and business functions. They're paid for their time and companionship, not sexual favors. Just because the public has been trained to believe that every professional escort is a hooker doesn't make it so."

When she'd finished speaking, Colin held up his hands, looking thoroughly abashed. "I'm sorry. I didn't mean to offend—"

"You didn't offend," Zandra said mildly. "You asked a question based on a common misconception, so I took the opportunity to enlighten you."

Colin smiled, staring at her. If he'd been merely interested before, he was now fascinated, as evidenced by his next words.

"I've never met anyone like you before."

Zandra chuckled. "So you've already said."

"No, I don't mean because of what you do for a living. You're an incredibly beautiful woman, Zandra, and you have this really seductive aura of mystery. Honestly, I've spent the past two weeks just working up the nerve to introduce myself to you."

Zandra smiled, touched by his sincerity. "Well, I'm glad you came by. I always enjoy making new friends. Especially ones who have excellent taste in wine."

Colin grinned. "I have to fly back to San Fran in two weeks. Maybe you could go with me, and we could pack a picnic lunch and spend a day in Napa Valley—"

Zandra laughed. "Or maybe we could just start with dinner first. In Chicago," she added pointedly.

His grin deepened. "That works, too. Are you free on Friday night?"

Before she could respond, the doorbell rang.

Zandra automatically tensed. Because this time she *knew* who was at the door.

Colin eyed her curiously. "Are you expecting some-one?"

"No." *But that's never stopped him before.*

Setting down her glass, Zandra rose and walked to the front door.

Sure enough, Remy stood there in shirtsleeves with his hands tucked into his pockets, the hem of his dark suit pants folding over huge combat boots.

Zandra's pulse hammered at the way he was looking at her from beneath the thick veil of his lashes.

"Hey," he murmured.

She swallowed dryly. "This isn't a good time."

"I need to talk to you."

"Not tonight," she said, wedging herself in the door-way so he couldn't see inside the apartment. "We can talk tomorrow."

His eyes narrowed. "Why not tonight?"

"Because I—"

"Zandra, I'm going to get some more wine."

At the sound of Colin's voice behind her, Remy's ex-pression darkened. "Who the hell is that?"

Bristling at his possessive tone, she snapped, "None of your damn business."

As she moved to close the door, his arm shot out, quick as lightning. She gasped as he put his hand to the door and shoved it open, forcing her backward as he barged inside.

His eyes swept over the living room, homing in on the two wineglasses sitting on the coffee table. "You have company?"

She hated that his accusatory tone made her feel guilty, as if she'd been caught cheating.

She scowled. "As a matter of fact—"

She broke off as Colin returned from the kitchen holding the bottle of wine.

He pulled up short at the sight of Remy looming in the foyer. The look that came over his face reminded Zandra of someone who just realized that he'd wandered into the path of a grizzly bear.

Not only did Remy *look* capable of tearing Colin apart with his bare hands, Zandra knew he was.

Closing the door, she deliberately cleared her throat. "Remy, this is my new neighbor, Colin. He stopped by to introduce himself. Colin, I'd like you to meet Remy."

The two men nodded tightly to each other, making no move to shake hands.

"Remy and I are old friends," Zandra added to cover the tense silence.

Colin divided a speculative glance between them. "How old?"

Zandra met Remy's simmering gaze. "I've known him since I was seven and he was ten."

*"Really?"* Colin shot an incredulous look at Remy. "And you haven't put a ring on her finger yet? What's wrong with you, man?"

When Remy made a growling sound in his throat, Zandra put a hand to his rigid chest and smiled sweetly at Colin. "Would you excuse us for a minute?"

"Sure," he agreed, green eyes glinting with amusement. "I'll top off your glass while you're gone."

"Great. Thanks."

Clenching a fistful of Remy's shirt, Zandra led him from the room. As soon as they reached the kitchen, she jabbed a finger into his chest and hissed, "What the hell is your problem?"

He scowled. "I told you I needed to talk to you."

"And *I* told you this wasn't a good time for me."

"Because of *that* guy?" he growled, jerking a thumb toward the living room. "He's not even your type."

"How the hell do you know what my type is? Besides, it's none of your damn business!"

Remy's nostrils flared. "So are you gonna sleep with him?"

Heat rushed to her face. "Like I said—"

"Because if not, you'd better hope he's not out there slipping something into your damn drink."

*"Are you serious?"* Zandra sputtered incredulously. "Do you realize you said practically the same thing to me the night I was leaving for my prom? In case you haven't noticed, I'm not seventeen anymore."

"I know that," he snapped.

"Coulda fooled me. Anyway, Colin doesn't need to drug me to get me into bed." She smirked. "*You* didn't."

Remy flinched, clenching his jaw so hard she thought his teeth would break.

"Now if you don't mind," she said levelly, "I'd like to get back to my guest. Feel free to see yourself out."

As she turned and marched from the kitchen, Remy growled, "I'm staying."

She whirled around. "No, you're—"

"We need to talk."

"Like I said before," Zandra bit out, "we can talk tomorrow. I have company."

"Then I'll just wait until he leaves." He shot her a dark look. "I'm not giving you another chance to blow me off like you did earlier."

Zandra glared at him. He wanted to be a third wheel? Fine, she'd treat him like one.

As she returned to the living room, Colin glanced up from perusing the glossy pages of a coffee table book. "Is everything all right?"

"Everything's fine," she said brightly, rejoining him on the sofa.

He looked unconvinced. "Maybe I should just go. I don't want to cause any trouble."

"You're not causing any trouble," she assured him. "Remy's just being his usual overprotective self. Old habits die hard. Anyway, I want you to stay. I was enjoying your company."

Colin smiled, looking pleased. "And I was enjoying yours."

"Good." She picked up her glass. "Now where were we?"

"I believe we were setting up our date for—" He broke off with a frown, watching as Remy sauntered into the living room swigging from a bottle of beer.

When he plopped down in a nearby chair and grabbed the remote control, Colin looked at Zandra and mouthed, *Is he staying?*

Rolling her eyes in exasperation, she mouthed back, *Just ignore him.*

Of course this was easier said than done with Remy just a few feet away, pumping more testosterone and aggression into the air than a feral lion staking his territory.

Setting down the coffee table book, Colin remarked offhandedly, "I thought this building had tighter security."

Zandra sipped her wine. "What do you mean?"

"Isn't the front desk supposed to call tenants when they have visitors?"

Zandra wished he hadn't gone there. Instead of heeding her advice to ignore Remy, he seemed determined to needle him. "I've never had a problem with the front desk." She paused. "That said, I think they're, ah, intimidated by certain visitors. And that's why they might give those visitors a pass."

Colin frowned and looked over at Remy, who was sprawled insolently in the chair with his long legs stretched out as he flicked through TV channels.

Trying to redirect Colin's attention, Zandra said cheerfully, "Since you're new in town, I'll choose the restaurant for dinner on Friday night."

Meeting her gaze, Colin smiled. "Sounds good. I can't wait."

Out of the corner of her eye, Zandra could see images flashing rapidly across the LCD screen as Remy clicked faster through channels.

"Speaking of dinner," Colin said conversationally, "what kind of foods do you like, Zandra?"

She laughed. "Oh, I eat everything."

He gave her a slow, appreciative once-over. "I find that hard to believe."

"It's true," Remy lazily confirmed. "She eats like a horse. Always has."

As Zandra sputtered indignantly, he drawled with wicked satisfaction, "But that's okay. I don't mind helping her burn off all those calories."

Her face flamed at the unmistakable implication.

Colin frowned, glancing from Zandra to Remy. "I thought you two were just friends."

"Well, see, that's the interesting thing—"

Zandra abruptly set her glass down on the table and blurted, "You know, it's getting late, and I have an early appointment tomorrow. So we should probably call it a night."

Ignoring the flash of triumph in Remy's eyes, she got up and ushered Colin to the door, thanking him for the wine.

"Are we still on for Friday night?" he asked hopefully.

"Of course. I'm looking forward to it."

He smiled. "Me, too. Good night."

"Good night." Closing the door, Zandra rounded furiously on Remy. "I can't *believe* you just did that!"

He bounded to his feet. "And *I* can't believe you expected me to sit here and watch you cozy up to that asshole!"

"You wouldn't have had to 'watch' anything if you'd gotten the hell out like I told you to!"

"And leave you alone with loverboy?" Remy gave a harsh snort. "I don't think so."

Zandra glared at him, trembling with anger. "You just don't get it, do you? It's none of your damn business who I sleep with!"

"The hell it isn't!"

*Where the hell have you been, woman? Who you been screwing?*

*No one—*

*Don't lie to me!*

*Not in front of Zandra. Please, Landis, not—*

WHAP!

*Lying whore!*

Shaking off the painful memory, Zandra turned and yanked the door open. "Get out."

Remy didn't budge. "I'm not going anywhere."

*"Get out!"*

His eyes blazed. "So this is how it's gonna be, Zandra? After everything we shared last week?"

She sneered. "We had sex, Remy. You weren't my first. You won't be my last."

He scowled ferociously. "We didn't just 'have sex.' We made love—"

"We *fucked*," Zandra spat crudely. "There's a big difference."

His face contorted with wounded outrage. "You little liar," he snarled, advancing dangerously on her. "You know *damn* well it was more than that!"

Zandra stared at him, her insides quaking at the waves of heat and fury rolling off him. If she'd been in her right mind, she would have thought better of antagonizing someone his size. But her emotions were in turmoil. She was angry and hurting, so like a wounded animal cornered by a savage predator, all she could do was lash out at him and hope to inflict as much damage as possible before he devoured her.

Reaching her, Remy shoved the door shut, then seized her upper arms and hauled her roughly against him.

"Don't manhandle me," Zandra warned, trying to wrench herself free.

He tightened his hold. "Look—"

Something snapped inside her, and she roared into his face, "Did you hear what I just said? *DON'T. FUCKING. MANHANDLE. ME!*"

Taken aback by the force of her anger, Remy released her arms and stepped backward.

Chest heaving, nostrils flaring, Zandra glared at him.

After such an outburst, she expected him to leave, to slam out of her apartment without a backward glance.

What he did was something she never would have expected.

Holding her gaze, he slowly dropped to his knees.

Zandra stared, stunned speechless by the sight of this big, brawny, domineering male kneeling before her.

It broke her.

As tears rushed to her eyes, she covered her mouth to smother a choked sob.

Remy looked up at her, his gaze so earnest, so achingly tender and vulnerable, that her own knees nearly buckled.

"You have to know," he said, husky with emotion. "You have to know I would *never* hurt you."

*Oh, God,* Zandra silently moaned, squeezing her eyes shut as tears spilled down her cheeks.

Remy pulled her into his arms and buried his face in her abdomen, murmuring raggedly, "I don't wanna fight, Z."

God, neither did she. She was tired of fighting—him, herself, ghosts from her past. She was exhausted. But fighting was the only way to survive, and one thing she knew was survival.

Still, she didn't resist as Remy stood and swept her up into his arms and carried her over to the sofa. He sat down and settled her on his lap. Her head found a familiar place on his shoulder as his arms curved around her waist, gathering her close.

She shouldn't have felt so safe and protected, like nothing and no one could ever harm her as long as he was holding her. It shouldn't have felt so good. So damn perfect.

She closed her eyes, savoring his heat, the strength of his chest and arms, the hard muscles of his thighs beneath her bottom.

He brushed the tears from her cheeks, his touch gentle. "Talk to me," he murmured, his deep voice rumbling against her ear. "What's going on with you? Hmm?"

Zandra swallowed tightly. She was so tempted to tell him about her father's visit and the devastating things he'd said. But she wasn't a child anymore, running to Remy's house and crying on his shoulder after one of Landis's violent outbursts. She was an adult now, more than capable of handling her problems on her own.

"It's been a long day," she answered without opening her eyes. "I'm still interviewing girls to replace Lena. I'm planning a showing for a new artist that I'm sponsoring. I had a ton of paperwork to catch up on. Like I said…long day."

"So nothing else is bothering you?" Remy probed.

She shook her head.

She knew, even without seeing his face, that he didn't believe her. He'd always been able to read her like a book.

She waited, hoping he wouldn't press the issue.

"Things have changed between us, Zandra," he said quietly, "and our relationship will never be the same again. But I hope you know that no matter what happens from this day forward, I'll always be here for you. Do you believe me?"

Zandra hesitated, then nodded. She did believe him.

"Good." He kissed her forehead.

Snuggling closer to him, Zandra slid her hand up his chest, soothed by the strong, steady thud of his heart beneath her palm. Even after a long day, she could still smell soap on his skin. He smelled clean, warm and masculine. He smelled like Remy.

"Do you remember the first time we met?" he murmured against her temple.

She smiled, opening her eyes to stare at the rugged curve of his jaw. "Of course I remember. Do you even have to ask?"

His lips curved. "Tell me what you remember."

She sighed. "Hmm, let's see. I had just moved into your neighborhood at the end of the summer. On the first day of school, I was walking home when some knuckleheads from my class started following me and taunting me just because our teacher had made a big deal about me skipping the second grade."

Never one to back down from a fight, Zandra had thrown down her backpack and put up her fists, knowing she was outmatched but not caring. Just as the ringleader shoved her, Remy had appeared—materializing out of nowhere, it seemed.

Even then he was tall, towering over her and the other kids. His dark eyes flashed with fire as he stepped between Zandra and her adversary.

*"Aw, man, you gonna fight a* girl?*" he demanded, his raspy voice filled with disgust. "What a punk."*

*"I ain't no punk," the ringleader protested. His comrades had grown silent, watching the exchange from a safe distance.*

*"Then fight* me,*" Remy challenged, leaning down until his nose nearly touched the boy's. "Whatsa matter? You scared?"*

*"Nah, man," the bully insisted, the denial contradicted*

*by the tremor in his voice. "This ain't none of your business."*

*"It is now."*

*The boy hesitated, casting a furtive glance to his friends for support.*

*They shuffled uncomfortably, regarding Remy with wide, fearful eyes. "Come on, man, let's just go. It's not worth it. He's in the fifth grade!"*

*The ringleader frowned, torn with indecision. He was afraid to look cowardly in front of his friends, but even more afraid of getting beat up by an upperclassman.*

*Finally he relented, shoving his hands into his pockets and backing away with a mumbled, "She's just a dumb girl anyway."*

*"Who're you calling dumb?" Zandra demanded, starting after him as he and his friends crossed the street. Halted by Remy's hand on her arm, she yanked herself away and scowled up at him. "What'd you do that for? You don't even know me!"*

*He seemed taken aback by her reaction. While he stood there gaping at her, Zandra snatched her backpack from the ground and stomped off.*

*He caught up to her. "You're welcome," he grumbled irritably.*

*Zandra whirled on him. "For what? I didn't need your help."*

*"Sure looked like it to me," he retorted. "That fat kid woulda whipped your butt, little girl."*

*"What's it to you?"*

*"Nothing, except I didn't wanna see you get blood on your pretty dress."*

*Zandra instantly melted. Because even though she'd resented her mother for making her wear a dress to school, and even though she had a reputation as a tomboy to protect, she secretly enjoyed girly things. The frillier, the better.*

*"You think it's pretty?"*

*"Sure." Remy shrugged, as if it were of no consequence to him. "So are you."*

Watching the poignant childhood memory unfold across Zandra's face, Remy drawled wryly, "Twenty-five years later, and you're *still* an ingrate."

Zandra stuck her tongue out at him, and he laughed.

Kissing her forehead, he tightened his arms around her and rested his chin on top of her head. "Just think. If I'd stayed after school with Roderick to help our teacher clean the classroom, I wouldn't have been there to rescue you from those little punks."

Zandra smiled. "Yeah, yeah, yeah."

Remy chuckled softly. "Ingrate, like I said."

"Whatever." She rubbed her cheek against his chest and sighed, enveloped in the cocoon of serenity he'd spun around them. "Have you had dinner yet?"

"Nah." His voice was as lazy as she felt. "You?"

She yawned and shook her head. "Cora left something warming on the stove," she murmured, referring to her personal chef.

"Are you inviting me to stay for dinner?"

"Mmm." Zandra closed her eyes, her words slowing. "Just to prove…I'm not an ingrate."

She felt Remy's lips curve against her temple. "In that case…I'll stay."

"Mmmkay." She shifted in his arms, burrowing closer as he leaned his head back against the sofa and let his eyes drift shut.

Within minutes, they were both asleep.

# *Chapter Seven*

It was the heat of Remy's touch that awakened her.

Slowly opening her eyes, Zandra stared down at his large hand resting on her thigh, where the hem of her dress had risen sometime during their nap. The warmth of his skin had penetrated the fabric to set off a tingling ache between her legs.

Drawing a shaky breath, she carefully tugged down her dress and squeezed her thighs together. Then she stared at Remy's face, marveling at how sleep softened his hard, masculine features and made him boyishly beautiful.

As if sensing her gaze, he suddenly stirred. She watched as his black lashes fluttered and swept upward to reveal hazy dark eyes. He stared at Zandra for a moment, then smiled a lazy smile.

"Hey, pretty girl." His sleep-roughened voice made her shiver.

"Hey." She smiled almost shyly. "Guess we both needed a power nap."

"Mmm. Guess so." He stretched his back, thick muscles taxing the seams of his fine broadcloth shirt.

Zandra swallowed hard and looked around the lamplit living room. "I wonder what time it is."

Remy glanced down at the black TAG Heuer watch adorning his thick wrist. "Almost nine."

"Goodness," she murmured. "We should eat dinner before it gets any later."

"Probably," he agreed.

But neither moved.

As they stared at each other, Remy took Zandra's chin between his thumb and forefinger and lowered his head. She felt his breath across her face, and then he kissed her. His lips were incredibly soft and warm, sliding slowly and sensually over hers. She shivered, keeping her eyes open so that she could see herself in his as they kissed.

As his hot tongue flicked out to tease the seam of her lips, her nipples tightened. She opened her mouth, and his tongue stole inside to stroke hers. She moaned with pleasure, need pulsing between her thighs.

She wrapped her arms around his back and pulled him closer. He groaned softly against her mouth, his thick shaft hardening beneath her bottom. Even through their clothes, the heat of his body was enough to scorch her.

Cradling her head between his hands, he deepened the kiss, his lips devouring hers with a searing intensity that left her breathless and intoxicated. The man could kiss like no other.

Closing her eyes, she managed to whisper, "Are you ready to eat?"

"Yeah." He sucked her tongue. "But not food."

Her breath escaped her in a shaky rush as he lifted her from his lap and set her down on her feet. Holding her gaze, he reached beneath her dress, making her shiver as his callused palms caressed her thighs and buttocks. Gripping her silk panties, he dragged them down her legs. When she stepped out of them, he stood and picked her up, carrying her to one of the upholstered chairs.

She stared up at him as he set her down and spread her legs, hooking them over the curved arms of the chair so that her sex was completely bared to him.

She trembled hard, feeling vulnerable and deliciously aroused. "Remy…"

He swore gutturally, his eyes nearly black as he stared at the pink, glistening tulip of her cunt. "You have such a pretty pussy, Zandra. So damn pretty."

She blushed as he sank to a crouch between her legs and licked her, one swipe that sent shards of pleasure stabbing through her.

She groaned, arching into his mouth as he growled hoarsely, "And you taste *so* fucking good."

His tongue flayed the sensitive nub of her clit with slow, hot licks that felt so incredible, tears stung the backs of her eyes. No guy had ever eaten her out the way Remy did, stroking her clit and sucking the swollen flesh of her labia with just the right amount of pressure.

She moaned with pleasure, her fingers gripping the arms of the chair, her hips rocking against his mouth. The man could teach a master class on the art of cunnilingus, and she'd gladly volunteer to be his test subject every time.

"Remy," she sobbed as he lapped at her cream, his tongue chasing the moisture down to her anus. When he licked the small hole, her hips bucked off the chair.

He caught and gripped her thighs, holding them apart as he stabbed his tongue into her pussy, bringing her to a hard, shuddering climax that made her scream.

Her body was still shaking from the aftershocks when he lifted her from the chair and sat down with her legs straddling his lap. His nostrils were flared, his lips glistening with her juices.

He pulled her dress up and over her head and tossed it aside. When the cool air hit her skin, she shivered.

He stared at her breasts spilling over the lacy cups of her black bra. Her pulse pounded as she watched him unhook the front clasp and slide the scrap of lingerie from her body.

Murmuring with husky appreciation, he lowered his head and closed his mouth over one breast. She gasped, her nipples elongating into tight, aching points as he suckled her. She closed her eyes and arched her head back as he cupped her breast and lifted it higher, deeper into his hungry mouth.

She shuddered, the hot stroke of his tongue sending jolts of pleasure to her womb. His mouth moved from one tit to the other, leaving her nipples wet and throbbing for more.

She ground against his thick erection, the soft cloth of his pants rasping against her clit and the sensitive flesh of her inner thighs. He raised his head from her breasts and took her mouth, kissing her deeply and ravenously. Sucking his tongue, she reached down and began unbuttoning his shirt. She got only halfway before impatience made her yank the rest open, popping and scattering buttons across the floor.

"Sorry," she breathed against his mouth, ripping the shirt off his broad shoulders. "I'll buy you another one."

His low chuckle dissolved into a groan as she flicked her tongue against a flat, dark nipple that instantly hardened. She licked his other nipple, then kissed her way down his muscular torso as he quickly unbuckled his belt and unzipped his fly. Rising from his lap, she knelt between his legs and tugged his pants and briefs down to his ankles.

As his heavy shaft jutted free, saliva pooled in her mouth. She wrapped her fingers around the thick base and leaned down, stroking her tongue over the plump head.

Remy jerked and swore hoarsely as pearly beads of precum leaked out. She lapped at the wetness like candy, then opened wide and took his engorged length down her throat. He growled with pleasure, his dick impossibly thickening inside her mouth.

She breathed deep, inhaling his heady masculine scent. And then she relaxed her jaw and began sucking him, hollowing out her cheeks to intensify the suction.

"Zandra," he groaned, shoving his hands into her hair. "Ah, *fuck,* that feels good."

She glanced up his body to meet his eyes, trembling at the raw hunger she saw in his gaze.

She took his shaft deeper, scraping her teeth along the edges just enough to make him shudder and moan at the resulting sensation. His fingers bit into her scalp as she sucked him harder, her hand massaging his swollen balls until they tightened to bursting.

Remy thrust his hips forward, fucking her mouth as saliva and precum dripped from the corners.

Suddenly he tensed and fisted his cock, pumping his hot seed down the back of her throat. Zandra swallowed every drop, savoring his clean, salty taste.

Gasping for breath, Remy closed his eyes and let his head fall back against the chair.

Pulse racing, clit throbbing, Zandra rose from her knees and climbed back into his lap. She knew it wouldn't take him long to regroup. The man possessed the kind of stamina that belonged in a world record book.

Straddling his thighs, she licked his goateed chin and rubbed her drenched cleft against the short, springy curls covering his groin.

Sure enough, his cock swelled and sprang to attention.

Her heart thundered as he lifted his head and met her hungry gaze. He smiled seductively and licked at her lips, then grasped her hips and impaled her on his hard shaft.

Her breath hissed out of her as her muscles clenched tightly around him, making him groan. She bit her lip and gripped his shoulders as he began rocking inside her. Slowly, languorously. Taking his time.

She stared into his eyes in dazed fascination, marveling at his complete mastery of her body. How could she have thought that she was done with him? Done with *this?* She must have been out of her mind.

Needing him to move faster, she squeezed her muscles around his cock. His eyes flashed and he smacked her ass, sending spikes of tingling heat to her womb that almost made her come.

She heeded the silent rebuke, and before long he was moving deeper and faster, each stroke searing the sensitized flesh of her pussy. Her pulse soared as she caught his rhythm and began riding him, breasts bouncing up and down, hips pistoning back and forth on his thighs.

"Fuck, Zandra," he panted as he licked and sucked her bottom lip, then coiled his tongue around hers. "Can't get enough of you, baby."

She moaned. “I don’t want you to. Ever.”

The chair creaked and rocked as he slammed into her, thrusting so hard she half expected the seat to collapse beneath them. And they would have kept going without missing a beat.

“Oh, shit,” she mewled as spasms of raw pleasure shafted through her. “Remy…ohh…Remy…”

“What, baby?” he whispered roughly against her parted lips. “What do you need?”

“You. Just…you.”

“You got me.” His eyes blazed fiercely into hers. *“You got me.”*

She shuddered and leaned back on his muscular thighs, so far back that her hair hung almost to the floor.

Remy groaned, his hands cupping her ass as he drove his shaft harder, deeper, drilling into her until she arched her spine and came with a primal cry.

He shouted her name as he climaxed, hot jets of semen spurting out of him to flood her pussy. She shivered as his cock pulsed and throbbed inside her for several moments.

As he slowly pulled her back up, her eyelids drooped and she slumped against him, spent and boneless.

“I can’t move,” she croaked.

He chuckled softly. “Then don’t. I like you just where you are.”

*That makes two of us,* she thought languidly as his hands stroked up and down her back, a soothing caress.

Neither spoke for several minutes, their hearts beating heavily against each other’s ribs, sweat cooling slowly on their skin.

Zandra found herself gazing at one of her mother’s paintings, a piece entitled *Three Peas in a Pod* that featured Zandra flanked by Remy and Roderick. The painting had been inspired by a photo Autumn had taken of the three children one summer as they sat licking Popsicles on the Brands' front porch. Zandra was pouting as Remy and Roderick, sporting mischievous grins, tugged on each of her pigtails, a favorite pastime of theirs.

As warm nostalgia curled through her, Zandra sighed and lifted her head from Remy's shoulder to smile at him. "Now that we've worked up an appetite, let's eat."

They dined outside on her balcony with the glittering expanse of Lake Michigan spread before them. Candles glowed on the small table, the flames flickering and dancing in the gentle summer breeze.

Zandra sat on Remy's lap as they took turns feeding each other from the same plate of spicy crab linguini. Zandra had always enjoyed Cora's cooking, but tonight it tasted even better than ever, the rich flavors enhanced by the experience of sharing the meal with Remy.

She twirled a few strands of linguini around the fork and slid it between his lips, watching as he chewed, then closed his eyes and groaned with husky satisfaction. "I think this is the best damn meal I've ever had."

Zandra smiled, licking a dab of sauce from the corner of his mouth and purring, "I was just thinking the same thing."

"Great minds think alike," he murmured, kissing her softly. "But as much as I'm enjoying this meal, I can't wait for dessert."

"You'll enjoy it. Cora made her truffle tart with strawberries. It's delicious."

"I'm sure it is, but that's not what I had in mind for dessert."

"No?" Zandra raised a brow at him. "What'd you have in mind?"

A purely carnal gleam lit his eyes. "You."

Her stomach quivered, and she smiled demurely. "I'm not on the menu."

"Then we'll just have to create a new one, won't we?"

As he leaned close to recapture her lips, she pulled back with a soft laugh and reached for the glass of Chablis they were sharing.

To her dismay, Remy had poured the rest of Colin's rosé down the drain. When she'd protested, he'd reminded her of what she'd done to the drink he'd received from the woman in St. Lucia.

That shut her up.

As she sipped the Chablis, Remy took the fork from her other hand and twirled it into the linguine noodles. When she set the glass down, he held the fork up to her and she opened her mouth. He slid it inside, watching the way her lips closed around the warm tines.

Before she could stop him, he leaned over and stole another kiss flavored with spices, succulent crab and white wine.

"Umm," he rumbled appreciatively. "Delicious."

Zandra licked her lips. "Indeed."

Setting the fork down, Remy folded her into his arms, brushed her hair over one shoulder and nuzzled the nape of her neck. She shivered at the warmth of his lips and the soft scrape of his goatee on her skin.

Gazing out across the moonlit lake, she sighed contentedly. "Do you realize that I've spent most of this evening on your lap?"

Remy nibbled her ear. "You don't hear me complaining."

She smiled, closing her eyes. "No, I don't."

"And you won't. I love having you on my lap." As he

reached inside her robe and gently cupped her breast, Zandra gasped and swatted his hand away.

"Stop that," she laughingly scolded, clutching her robe together and knotting the sash. "I'm trying to enjoy a civilized meal here."

"Sweetheart," Remy drawled, "I've never claimed to be civilized—"

Zandra snorted. "*That's* an understatement."

"—but I'm evolved enough to know that the meal's over when there's no more food."

Zandra glanced down at the table, surprised to see that their plate was empty. When had that happened?

Remy chuckled. "Time flies when you're having fun."

"Apparently so." Zandra dragged her finger through a puddle of garlic sauce and licked it off, then sighed. "I'll definitely have to ask Cora to add this to the rotation."

"Hmm. Well, speaking of rotating…" Remy's tongue swiped the shell of Zandra's ear and she trembled, unintentionally squirming in his lap. His dick hardened, pushing against the cleft between her butt cheeks. As heat shot to her groin, she bit back a moan and picked up the empty plate.

"Time for dessert."

Before Remy could grab her, she sprang from his lap and laughingly darted back inside the apartment.

He followed her, sauntering into the kitchen where she stood at the sink running water to wash the plate and fork. With his SEAL tattoo stretched over his thick biceps and his dark pants slung low on his hips, he looked so rakishly sexy that her knees went weak. And that was before he came up behind her, pressing her against the counter until she could feel the heat of his naked chest burning through her silk robe.

She swallowed tightly. "I took the tart out of the fridge before dinner," she told him, her voice breathy. "It can be served cold, but I prefer room temperature."

"That's fine," Remy murmured against her neck, sending sensual shivers down her spine, "but I already told you what I want for dessert."

She trembled as he slowly dragged her robe up her bare thighs. "Cora went to the trouble—"

"Oh, we can have the tart. Strawberry, right?"

Zandra gave a jerky nod.

"Good. I like strawberries." Sucking her earlobe, he reached between her thighs and touched her drenched, throbbing sex. "Mmm. All this cream. More than enough to drizzle over some plump strawberries."

Zandra whimpered as he stroked her hard clit while grinding his erection against her ass.

He whispered in her ear, "I'm gonna lay you down on this countertop, spread your legs wide open and eat those strawberries right out of your sweet, dripping pussy."

Zandra groaned, the plate clattering into the sink as she lost her grip. "Remy—"

The sudden blast of a phone made her jump.

Remy tensed against her, swearing under his breath.

After a few moments, he reluctantly pulled his hand out from beneath her robe and stalked over to the center island, where he'd left his cell phone earlier. He picked it up and checked the caller ID. Although his expression betrayed nothing, Zandra instinctively sensed that the caller was someone he didn't want to speak to in her presence.

Which meant it was probably a woman.

He glanced at Zandra. "Be right back."

She nodded, watching as he turned and strode from

the kitchen. Moments later she heard the balcony doors open and close, and she frowned.

If Remy felt the need to step outside to take the call, it *had* to be a woman. Why else would he require such privacy?

*Don't jump to conclusions,* a small voice reasoned. *He could be discussing work. Given the sensitive nature of his profession, it'd make perfect sense for him to want privacy to speak to an employee or a client. You of all people should understand that. Besides, why should it matter if he's talking to one of his bimbos? He doesn't belong to you any more than you belong to him.*

Gritting her teeth, Zandra finished washing the plate and fork, then stood there debating whether to cut into the strawberry tart or put the damn thing back into the refrigerator.

She still hadn't decided by the time Remy returned to the kitchen carrying the bottle of wine and the glass they'd shared over dinner.

"Sorry about that," he murmured.

"No problem." Zandra strove for aloofness. "Is everything okay?"

He nodded, setting down the bottle and empty glass.

She hesitated, then couldn't resist asking casually, "Who was on the phone?"

Pause. "Work."

Though Remy had always been frighteningly adept at hiding his emotions, Zandra knew him well enough to detect when he was lying.

He was lying now.

As a knot of jealousy unfurled inside her, she walked over and picked up the covered glass dish containing the strawberry tart.

Remy frowned, watching as she shoved the dessert back inside the refrigerator. "What're you doing? I thought we were gonna eat that."

"Not anymore."

"Why not?"

"It's late," she said curtly, "and I need to be up early."

His eyes narrowed on her face.

She stared back defiantly.

After another moment, he nodded slowly. "All right."

His acquiescence further incensed her, confirming her suspicion that he'd been talking to another woman. A woman who was probably waiting for him this very moment.

As he turned and left the kitchen, Zandra followed him, her bare feet slapping against the hardwood floor.

She watched as he crossed to the chair where they'd made love and picked up his shirt, which she'd folded and draped neatly over the back. His muscles flexed as he shrugged into the ruined shirt, then sat down and shoved his feet into those humongous combat boots he'd worn with his suit—a look only *he* could pull off.

"I have to go out of the country on business for a few days," he told her. "You can reach me on my cell if you need anything."

Zandra folded her arms across her chest. "I'm sure I'll be fine."

He nodded, tying his boots. "You still going to that fundraiser on Sunday?"

"Yes. Why?"

"I thought we could go together."

Zandra sniffed. "Actually, I already invited Colin to go with me," she lied.

Remy glanced up sharply. His expression was so ominous she took an unconscious step backward. "I suggest you uninvite him," he growled.

Her temper flared. "I suggest you go to hell."

He glared at her, a muscle throbbing in his jaw.

She returned the glare.

"Fine," he muttered darkly. "I'll go with one of your girls, then."

Zandra froze, staring at him. "What the hell are you talking about?"

"Set me up on a date with one of your escorts."

Her jaw went slack. *"I beg your pardon?"*

"You heard me." He pushed to his feet. "I was invited to the fundraiser. Since you won't go with me, I'd like to take one of your escorts."

Zandra was outraged, though she realized she probably had no right to be. "Why can't you take one of your girlfriends?"

Remy gave her a small, grim smile. "Let's just say we're not on the best terms right now."

"Oh, please," Zandra scoffed. "We both know you could step out that door right now and have thirty women scratching and clawing one another to go out on a date with you."

He cocked a brow. "Only thirty?"

Zandra wasn't amused. "I'm not setting you up with one of my girls."

"Why not?"

*Good question.* "Because I'm not."

His lips twitched. "That's not an answer."

She swallowed hard as he sauntered toward her, his unbuttoned shirt exposing his beautiful bare chest.

"We're friends, Remy. I don't set up friends and acquaintances with my escorts."

He smirked. "You had no problem setting up Roderick and Lena."

*Busted. Damn.*

"Is that what you're worried about?" he taunted. "That I might fall for one of your girls and make her my wife?"

The blood drained from Zandra's head.

"Of course not," she managed to croak out. "Don't be ridiculous."

Remy stopped before her, those penetrating dark eyes searching her face. "Is it ridiculous, Zandra?" he challenged softly.

She couldn't breathe. She held his gaze for one heart-stopping moment, then turned away and stalked to the door, appalled by how badly her legs were shaking.

"It's time for you to leave," she said coldly.

He regarded her in silence another moment, then shook his head and met her at the door.

"Set up that date, Zandra." It wasn't a request, and she knew it.

She glared up at him. "Go to hell."

A sliver of some emotion flickered in the molten depths of his eyes. "I probably will," he murmured.

With that, he walked out the door.

# *Chapter Eight*

Three days later, Zandra met Lena for lunch at NoMI, an upscale restaurant perched high above Michigan Avenue inside the Park Hyatt. When Zandra arrived, Lena was already seated at one of the tables that overlooked downtown and Lake Michigan.

"Hey, girl." Lena stood and hugged Zandra, then drew back to admire her eyelet linen skirt worn with an ivory button-down top and Gianvito Rossi sandals. "You look gorgeous. As usual."

"So do you," Zandra said warmly. "Not only are you wearing the hell out of that pantsuit, but you've still got the glow of a blushing bride."

Lena grinned, her dark eyes twinkling. "Well, there might be *another* reason for that glow."

"What do you mean?"

As Lena reached down and coyly rubbed her flat

stomach, Zandra's jaw dropped. She stared at Lena. "Are you…?"

"Preggers?" Lena beamed. "You betcha."

"Oh, my God!"

The two women squealed excitedly and hugged, drawing curious stares from the other patrons.

As they pulled apart, Zandra gently cupped Lena's cheek in her hand. "I'm so happy for you and Roderick. You're going to make wonderful parents."

Lena's expression softened with gratitude. "Thank you, Zandra."

"I meant every word. Now sit, sit. I want details. Not *those* details," Zandra snorted at the wicked look Lena sent her. "Everyone already knows you and Roderick can't keep your hands off each other. Hell, it's a miracle you didn't get knocked up sooner."

Lena tipped back her head and laughed.

When the waiter appeared, they ordered their meals—niçoise salad for Zandra, chilled buckwheat soba salad with prawns for Lena, and the signature sushi platter for both.

"Excellent choices, Mrs. Brand and Miss Kennedy." The waiter beamed, clearly delighted to be serving two customers who frequently appeared on the society pages of the *Chicago Tribune.*

After he departed, Zandra draped her linen napkin across her lap and smiled at Lena. "So when did you find out you were pregnant?"

Lena grinned. "I just got the results yesterday, but I've suspected for the past two weeks now. It was *so* hard for me not to tell Roderick during our honeymoon, but I wanted to wait until I knew for sure. You should have seen how ecstatic he was. He picked me up and swung me around, and he actually got teary-eyed. Can you believe it?"

Zandra smiled. "I can believe it. Beneath their tough-as-nails exteriors, the Brand brothers are big ol' softies, every last one of them. So have you and Rod told the family yet?"

"Not everyone. I've only told you and my sister, and of course Roderick had to call Remy and tell him."

Zandra nodded, sipping her water. Remy had traveled to Abu Dhabi to provide security services to a group of Emirati businessmen who'd specifically requested his presence. He'd be gone until Saturday, which should give Zandra enough time to come up with a rational excuse for not setting him up with one of her escorts.

Lena continued, "Roderick wants to share the good news with everyone else at the same time, so we're taking the family out to dinner this evening. I can't *wait* to see their faces, especially my Poppa, Roderick's mom and Grandma Eleanor."

Zandra grinned broadly. "They won't be able to contain themselves."

"I know," Lena said with a chuckle. "Every time they mentioned our future children while we were in St. Lucia, I just smiled to myself and kept quiet." She sighed, gazing out the window at the glistening skyscrapers that bracketed the downtown skyline. "I'm so happy, Zandra. So ridiculously happy. It seems surreal considering the way Roderick and I came together. I know some people would have called me crazy for agreeing to his indecent proposal. Hell, some might have even called me a whore—"

"Stop right there." Zandra reached across the table, covering Lena's hand with her own. "I don't like that word, and I have no tolerance for anyone who uses it to denigrate others. *Especially* when the name-calling is done by women. You and Roderick are absolutely perfect for each other. Anyone who'd have a problem with your relationship can go fuck themselves—which they'd probably be too uptight to do anyway."

Lena laughed, shaking her head at Zandra. "You are a mess."

"Just sayin'."

Lena smiled, gently squeezing her hand. "I owe you everything for introducing me to Roderick. If you hadn't set me up on a date with him, we never would have met. How can I ever repay you?"

*"Well,"* Zandra said, drawing out the word, "since you *were* one of my top escorts, you can help me find someone just as great to replace you."

They both laughed.

Moments later the waiter returned with their meals. He set the plates on the table with an elegant flourish, topped off their sparkling water and asked them if they needed anything else before he glided away.

As they dug into their salads, Lena asked casually, "So what's going on between you and Remy?"

Heat washed over Zandra's face. She speared a cherry tomato with her fork, then took her time chewing and swallowing it. "What do you mean?"

Lena gave her an amused look. "I think you know what I mean. Something happened between you two in St. Lucia."

"What makes you say that?"

"Oh, come on, Zandra. It was so obvious from the way you and Remy were dirty dancing on the beach—which, by the way, was *totally* hot. The next morning you guys were the last to arrive for breakfast, and then you went out of your way to pretend he didn't exist for the rest of the trip." Lena's eyes glimmered. "Did you think no one noticed? We all did, and we all speculated about it."

Zandra flushed uncomfortably.

"So what happened?" Lena persisted. "Did you and Remy sleep together?"

Zandra hesitated another moment, then heaved a resigned breath and mumbled, "Let's just say we did everything *but* sleep."

Lena laughed. "I *knew* it!"

Zandra's cheeks burned hotter at the memory of Remy's stamina-defying lovemaking in St. Lucia and at her apartment. "It wasn't supposed to happen."

"Says who?"

"Says me."

"Why?"

Zandra shook her head. "Even if I were interested in a relationship—which I'm not—Remy is the *last* man I'd choose to become involved with. I know him too well, yet I don't know him at all, if that makes any sense."

"Hmm." Lena pursed her lips. "Could you elaborate?"

Zandra sighed, picking at her salad. "Ever since he was discharged from the navy, he's been different. Secretive. Don't get me wrong. I'm no Pollyanna who's naive about the realities of war. Remy was a SEAL, so I know he must have seen and done things over the years that'd give most people nightmares. But I can only speculate, because he's never told me very much."

"For what it's worth," Lena said quietly, "I think Roderick is the only one who knows the full story behind Remy's discharge."

"I know, and I'm not saying that I expect Remy to confide in me. But that part of him that he keeps locked away…" Zandra trailed off, grimly reflecting on her own demons and the emotional battle scars she bore. "He's too intense and unpredictable. We'd consume each other if we ever became involved."

"Do you really believe that?"

"I do." Zandra frowned. "Besides, if he really wants to have a relationship with me, he sure has a funny way of showing it."

"What do you mean?" Lena asked, deftly picking up a piece of salmon sushi with her chopsticks and popping it into her mouth.

Zandra's frown deepened. "Before he left for Abu Dhabi, he asked me to set him up with one of my escorts."

Lena stared at her. "Are you serious?"

"Very." Zandra stabbed at a green bean. "I couldn't believe it. He's never shown the slightest bit of interest in dating any of my girls. Why now?"

Lena smiled. "Maybe he's trying to make you jealous."

Zandra snorted. "As if."

An intuitive gleam entered Lena's eyes. "So you're *not* jealous?"

"Of course not. Remington Brand is a grown man, and I'm a businesswoman. If he wants to go out with one of my escorts and he can afford to pay for the pleasure of her company, who am I to stop him? Am I baffled by his sudden interest in my girls? Of course. But am I jealous? Hell, no."

"Well," Lena drawled, "that poor legume on your plate might beg to differ."

Following the direction of Lena's amused gaze, Zandra saw that she'd totally pulverized the green bean with her fork. As an embarrassed flush crawled up her neck and spread across her face, Lena grinned knowingly.

"If that's what you do to food when you're *not* jealous..."

Zandra scowled, then reached for her glass and took a gulp of water. Needing something stronger, she signaled for the waiter. When he bustled over, she ordered a margarita, heavy on the tequila.

Lena watched her with amused sympathy. "If it bothers you this much for Remy to go out with one of the girls, why don't you just tell him how you feel?"

"Because it doesn't bother me," Zandra stubbornly insisted.

Lena looked skeptical. "Doesn't it?"

Zandra sniffed. "Not at all."

And she knew just how to prove it.

Remy stared out the tinted passenger window of the armored vehicle transporting his clients to the secret location of their business meeting. His eyes were shaded by mirrored sunglasses as he watched the heavily trafficked streets of Abu Dhabi pass by. In deference to UAE etiquette for Westerners, he wore a dark business suit and impeccably polished loafers. The expensive cut of his jacket concealed his shoulder piece, a Sig Sauer reinforced by a KA-BAR knife hidden between his shoulder blades and a .45 strapped to an ankle holster, not to mention the MP5 machine gun stowed beneath his seat.

From the backseat of the vehicle, the Emirati businessmen spoke quietly in Arabic, their conversation peppered with fervent utterances of *In'shallah,* which meant "God willing." Even if Remy hadn't been fluent in Arabic, he would have sensed that his clients were nervous. Since forging a lucrative partnership with an American energy conglomerate, the four oil executives had received kidnapping and death threats from an underground group of highly trained religious extremists who opposed any alliance with Westerners. Not knowing whom to trust, the distraught businessmen had turned to outsiders for protection.

Remy glanced from the window when his driver suddenly swerved to avoid being clipped by an aggressive cabbie switching lanes. Swearing under his breath, Dutch ran a hand over his dreadlocks and muttered, "And I thought Chicagoans were lousy drivers."

Remy chuckled, watching as the silver taxicab roared off down the busy street.

Just then his cell phone vibrated with an incoming text message. Keeping his gaze trained on the passing scenery, he reached inside his breast pocket and removed the phone.

His pulse thudded when he saw that the message was from Zandra.

It was brief, deliberately cryptic.

You're all set. Sunday at 8.

A grim smile curved the edges of Remy's mouth. He didn't know whether to be relieved or disappointed that Zandra had capitulated to his demands. Without realizing it, she'd just cleared the way for him to investigate her beloved agency.

After agonizing over Keegan's proposal, Remy had gone to Zandra's apartment on Monday evening to warn her that she and her escorts were in the mayor's crosshairs. But he'd gotten sidetracked when he found her with another man, and when they'd argued afterward, she'd seemed so troubled and vulnerable, he didn't have the heart to cause her any more distress. By the time Keegan called him, he'd made his decision. Sealed his fate.

Dutch threw a glance at Remy, observing his grim expression. "Everything okay, Chief?"

"Yeah." Tucking the phone back into his breast pocket, Remy resumed staring out the window.

Even in the peaceful emirate of Abu Dhabi, he and his entourage faced the threat of ambush and violence from heavily armed zealots.

But Remy wasn't concerned.

This assignment would be a cakewalk compared to the unpleasant task that awaited him at home.

# *Chapter Nine*

When Zandra first opened Elite For You Companions, a trusted mentor had advised her to keep her escorts apart to prevent them from competing with one another or comparing notes. She was told horror stories of shady escorts skimming profits and colluding to steal clients to start their own agencies.

She'd received the cautionary advice, filed it away, then formulated her own approach to dealing with her escorts. Even though they were independent contractors, she considered them employees. And as any smart employer knows, happy employees are the key to a successful and highly profitable business. From the very beginning, Zandra understood that if she treated her escorts with decency and respect, then they would be happy. Happy escorts produced satisfied clients, and satisfied clients were repeat customers.

So once a month, Zandra booked a private room at an

upscale restaurant and treated her escorts to dinner. Attendance was not mandatory. She knew that the women led busy lives that had them juggling the demands of a career, college and, in two cases, single motherhood. So she never required their time beyond their availability to clients. But in the five years she'd been hosting the dinners, no one had ever canceled. The women looked forward to getting together.

Over dinner, they didn't discuss clients or dates or anything that would breach confidentiality. It was simply an opportunity for them to unwind, become better acquainted, and draw strength and support from one another.

It was through these monthly gatherings that Zandra learned how much she had in common with the women who worked for her. Relaxed by good food and wine, they often let down their guards and opened up to one another. Secrets were shared and commiserated over—the sense of loss and regret after an abortion; righteous anger caused by a nasty divorce; the pain and despair suffered in an abusive relationship.

The women were ethnically and physically diverse, came from different backgrounds and ranged in age from twenty-five to forty-two. But that didn't prevent them from being able to relate to one another, a bond strengthened by the shared experience of working as an escort.

Seven months ago, Zandra had changed the venue of their outings to a luxury day spa, where the women could be pampered with manicures and pedicures, lavish massages and sauna treatments. It seemed a fitting reward for women who made a living catering to the needs of others.

That Saturday afternoon, they sat soaking in the spa's thermal whirlpool as they sipped champagne and luxuriated in the soothing fragrances of jasmine and lavender wafting up from the steamy water.

"I finally did it," announced Yana, a Russian college student who'd immigrated to America two years ago in pursuit of a modeling career that never panned out.

"Did what?" the others asked.

"I finally called home and told my mother that I'm an escort."

Everyone stared at the dark-haired young beauty. "How did she react?"

Yana grimaced. "She said she didn't raise me to be a *blyadischa*."

"Ouch. Sounds bad. What does it mean?"

Yana sighed. "Whore."

A chorus of groans swept around the pool.

"It's really a shame that she said that to you, Yana," Zandra said, her voice laced with sympathy and anger. "It's hard enough hearing that word from strangers. It has to be worse coming from your own mother."

"It was," Yana admitted forlornly. "She's been asking me if I've found any modeling work. I was tired of lying to her, so I just decided to tell her the truth. I knew she wouldn't be happy, but I never expected her to call me a whore."

"I'm truly sorry about that, kiddo," Zandra consoled, gently rubbing Yana's shoulder. "She's just concerned for your welfare. Give her time to come around and accept what you're doing."

Yana nodded despondently, sipping her wine.

Claudia—a petite, voluptuous blonde and single mother—glanced around the circle. "Angry mothers aside. Is it just me, or does that word hurt more coming from other women than men?"

There were nods and murmurs of agreement.

Claudia frowned. "Why do you think women seem so quick to use it against others?"

"Spitefulness," Yana proposed.

"Jealousy."

"Insecurity."

"Ignorance," Zandra contributed. "I think it's easy to be judgmental of something you don't understand. When most people hear that a woman is an escort, they naturally assume that she gets paid for having sex." She shook her head ruefully. "I went to college in the UK. I think Americans are way more uptight about sex than Europeans."

More echoes of agreement went around the pool.

"That's because Americans tend to have more conservative religious values," opined Laurel, a black beauty pageant veteran. "I belong to a large Methodist church on the South Side. I would *never* tell any of the members that I moonlight as an escort, or they'd run me out of there so fast my heels would leave skid marks."

"Damn," some of the others lamented, and chuckled. "That's a shame."

"I know. Now, I'm not saying congregations everywhere would be so judgmental," Laurel added. "That's just my personal perception of my own church."

"That's why I don't tell anyone that I'm an escort." This was from Noelani, an exotic beauty from Hawaii. "I know they wouldn't understand or approve, especially my family. They're very traditional and conservative. Hell, my parents just want me to hurry up and finish my doctorate so I can get married."

"Mine, too," Laurel commiserated.

Claudia grinned crookedly. "This conversation we're having would be great material for a show on Oprah's network."

The others laughed.

"Seriously," she insisted. "We should invite Oprah to one of our spa days. I don't think she's ever gone inside the lives of professional escorts who *don't* have sex with their clients."

Zandra chuckled dryly. "Tell you what, Claude. The next time you're at a party with Oprah, feel free to pitch the idea to her."

"I think I will," Claudia declared, drawing a chorus of amused groans. Given the wealthy status of their clientele, it wasn't uncommon for any of the escorts to find themselves at the same glitzy event as Oprah, and Claudia was just bold enough to proposition the famous media mogul.

Noelani sighed, gazing up at the tiled ceiling of the bathhouse. "Maybe it's just the romantic in me, but I *do* sometimes catch myself fantasizing about meeting Mr. Right—a dashing prince who will sweep me off my feet and carry me off to his castle in the forest."

Laurel snorted humorously. "I already found *my* Mr. Right. Met him at the Castle adult megastore, and he only cost me about forty bucks. He vibrates, he can't knock me up, and he takes me *anywhere* my imagination can go."

As the others shrieked with laughter, Noelani blushed self-consciously and murmured, "I guess I'm the only sap around here."

"No, you're not," Claudia laughingly assured her. "Though some of us would never admit it, we've all fantasized every now and then about getting swept off our feet by a handsome tycoon like Julia Roberts did in *Pretty Woman*."

"And don't forget Lena," Yana added.

This elicited envious sighs and murmurs at the memory of Lena and Roderick's breathtakingly romantic waterfront wedding.

"Doesn't get any more fairy tale than meeting and falling in love with a gorgeous billionaire," Claudia said.

"I know." Laurel smiled fondly. "Couldn't have happened to a sweeter person."

"Hear, hear," the others chorused, raising their glasses in a toast to Lena.

As they drank, Noelani sighed deeply. "Who knows? Maybe *my* next client will be Mr. Right."

Zandra sure as hell hoped not, considering that Noelani's next client would be Remy. She'd already had serious misgivings about setting up the date. Learning that Noelani was a hopeless romantic didn't exactly put her mind at ease.

"So what about you, boss lady? You ever fantasize about meeting Mr. Right?"

Zandra's face heated as nine pairs of eyes settled on her. "Me?"

Claudia chuckled. "Yeah, you."

"Hmm." Zandra sipped her wine, stalling as she pretended to ponder the question. She didn't share many personal details with her escorts. Not because she didn't like or trust them, but because she'd always been fiercely private, and as their employer, she felt it was necessary to maintain some professional boundaries.

During their monthly gatherings, she often assumed the nurturing role of counselor as they bared their souls, and they never seemed to mind that she knew more about them than they knew about her.

"I wouldn't say I've fantasized about it," she responded, even as her mind flashed traitorously on sensual images of Remy. His eyes…his lips…the cut of his biceps…the hardness of his thighs…the thickness of his cock. Her body heated so fast she half expected the steamy water to start boiling.

Clearing her throat, she delicately dabbed at her flushed cheeks. "I wouldn't say I fantasize about finding Mr. Right, but I *will* admit that one of my all-time favorite movies is *An Officer and a Gentleman.* That ending scene where Richard Gere goes to the factory, sweeps Debra Winger into his arms and carries her out while her coworkers cheer…"

A chorus of dreamy feminine sighs and squeals swept around the pool.

"Oh, my God," Noelani breathed, her hand fluttering to her heart. "*That* is definitely a classic."

Zandra grinned. "I was only four when the movie came out, but my mother used to watch it all the time. When I was old enough to appreciate it, we'd watch it together and cry every time at that sappy ending."

The others laughed and nodded, reliving similar experiences.

"Sentimentality aside," Zandra murmured, "I've never really been a happily-ever-after type of girl. So I don't spend a lot of time looking for Mr. Right."

"But if he comes along?" Noelani prodded.

Zandra smiled. "Then hopefully he won't make it hard for me to recognize that he's the one."

"Amen to that." Laurel grinned, holding up her glass. "In the meantime, here's to a satisfying relationship with our battery-operated Mr. Right. Even when he takes a licking, he keeps on ticking!"

The women clinked glasses, then dissolved into hysterical laughter.

# *Chapter Ten*

"Have I told you how absolutely stunning you look tonight?"

Zandra smiled indulgently at Colin as camera bulbs flashed wildly around them. "You may have mentioned it once or twice."

He chuckled. "Well, it's true. You look amazing. I can't take my eyes off you in that dress."

The dress he spoke of was a Herve Leger original—an electric blue strapless number layered with romantic ruffles that flowed sensuously over her hourglass curves. Diamonds glittered at her ears and wrist, and towering stiletto heels accentuated her long, shapely legs. She wore her hair down, parted on one side and glamorously swept over her shoulder. Her eyes were smoky and dramatic, and her lips were lusciously red.

Already considered a fashion trendsetter among her peers, she'd wanted to look her absolute best tonight. And she'd apparently succeeded, judging by Colin's response and the admiring stares and whistles that greeted her as she stepped from her limo.

"Who are you wearing, Miss Kennedy?" reporters called out eagerly to her.

She only smiled enigmatically, setting off another flurry of flashbulbs.

For tonight's fundraiser gala, the entrance to the art museum resembled an Academy Awards ceremony with a red carpet and photographers snapping pictures of arriving guests. Hundreds of well-heeled Chicagoans had shelled out two grand per ticket to enjoy a glitzy evening of fine dining and dancing, and to celebrate the highly anticipated opening of the newly renovated museum.

Colin's hand rested possessively at Zandra's waist as they climbed the grand staircase and entered the elegant lobby to join the milling crowd. Jeweled flesh wrapped in the expensive silk of designer gowns created a dazzling kaleidoscope of color. Waiters circulated among the guests offering canapés and glasses of champagne. Orchestra music from a string quartet wafted over the hall.

Zandra knew the moment Remy arrived.

Not because she saw him walk through the doors, but because her pulse quickened and her skin erupted in goose bumps.

She glanced around the crowded lobby.

And there he was.

Tall, dark and devastatingly handsome in a Brioni tux that fit his powerful body like a dream. Her mouth went dry as she stared at him, a Rembrandt who deserved his very own exhibit in any museum.

It was only belatedly that she noticed Noelani on his arm.

There was a reason the Hawaiian woman was one of Zandra's most popular escorts. Not only was she exotic and drop-dead gorgeous, but she'd perfected the art of treating each client as if he were the best date she'd ever had. The way she was staring at Remy made it clear that she wouldn't have to do much faking tonight.

As if sensing Zandra's gaze, Remy glanced up, his eyes locking on her from across the room.

She trembled as his dark gaze blazed a path from her face down to her bare shoulders, the swell of her cleavage and past her flat stomach. He lingered at the juncture of her thighs, as if he could sense the slick moisture he'd just coaxed from her body.

The eyes that slowly returned to hers glittered with a possessive satisfaction that made her shiver. Her nipples hardened, craving the heat of his touch, the stroke of his tongue.

As an electric hum of arousal crackled in the distance between them, Zandra swallowed hard and looked away.

But she felt him watching her as she worked the room—smiling beguilingly, fluttering her lashes, touching an arm here, patting a cheek there, coyly drumming up funds for one of her favorite causes, which was keeping art programs alive in Chicago's public schools.

Remy's smoldering gaze tracked her every move. But he kept his distance, because he knew Zandra had a thing about not socializing with her escorts when they were working. And given the way he'd felt about Colin accompanying her to tonight's function, it was best for all involved if he stayed as far away as possible.

Zandra and Colin were conversing with Enid Roche and her husband when a laughter-tinged voice whispered in her ear, "Oh, my God. He's doing it again."

Zandra turned and smiled at the petite, curvaceous brunette who'd appeared beside her. "Hey, Skylar."

"Hey, yourself." Skylar Blake pressed a chaste kiss to Zandra's cheek, then smiled congenially at Enid. "Everything looks fabulous. And *what* a turnout."

"Isn't it wonderful?" The gala committee chairwoman beamed with pleasure. "I was just telling Zandra that we raised over two million dollars from ticket sales. Seems that a lot of people wanted to be the first to see the renovated museum before we open our doors to the public next week."

"*Two mil?* Wow, that's awesome." Skylar shifted her smile to Colin, her hazel eyes twinkling with undisguised interest. "And you are?"

Chuckling at her friend's forthrightness, Zandra made the introductions.

"Pleasure to meet you, Skylar," Colin said easily, shaking her hand.

"The pleasure's mine. Would you excuse us a minute?" Without waiting for Colin's assent, Skylar grabbed Zandra's hand and steered her out of earshot.

"Oh, my goodness," she breathed excitedly. "I just *had* to come over here and find out what the hell is going on between you and Remy Brand."

Zandra feigned ignorance. "What do you mean?"

"Remember how he showed up at your dinner party last month and spent the whole evening devouring you with those bedroom eyes?"

Zandra nodded reluctantly. Of course she remembered.

Skylar grinned. "Well, in case you haven't noticed, he's doing it again. And this time he's eye-fucking you so hard, you're probably already pregnant."

Heat scalded Zandra's face. *"Skylar!"*

She laughed. "I'm just speaking the truth, Zandra. The way that man looks at you..." She trailed off, fanning herself with elegantly manicured fingers.

Shaking her head, Zandra lifted her champagne glass to her mouth. "You're crazy."

"Not crazy," Skylar corrected. "Jealous. Insanely jealous. Remy is hot as hell, Zandra. And even though women have been practically throwing themselves at him since he got here, he only has eyes for you. Not that anyone could blame him," she added, her eyes glinting as she looked Zandra over. "I'm as straight as they come, and *I* wanna fuck you in that dress."

When Zandra nearly spit out her champagne, Skylar threw back her head and pealed with laughter.

Zandra dabbed at the corners of her mouth with her fingertips. "You are in rare form tonight."

Skylar sighed. "I know."

They paused to smile and pose for a photographer from the *Tribune.* As soon as the man moved on, Skylar grinned mischievously at Zandra.

"So give up the goods. Did something happen between you and Remy during your trip to St. Lucia?"

Sipping her wine, Zandra glanced over her shoulder at Colin. He was nodding and smiling politely as Enid Roche told him all about the museum's two-year expansion project.

She smiled wryly. "I should probably go rescue my date."

Skylar gave her a knowing look. "Nice evasion. But I'll let you off the hook *this* time. Speaking of your date..." She paused, lips pursed as she appraised Colin through narrowed eyes. "He's a cutie. But he's not your type."

Zandra scowled, because Remy had made the same remark to her. "Why isn't he my type?" she challenged.

Skylar snorted. "He's not alpha enough for you. You'd chew him up and spit him back out."

Zandra couldn't deny it. As much as she'd enjoyed Colin's company over dinner on Friday, she'd known by the end of the date that they could never work as a couple. Which was a shame, because he really was a nice guy.

"You need a bad boy," Skylar told her. "Someone with an edge. Someone dangerous."

Zandra frowned, naturally thinking of Remy. They didn't come any more dangerous than him. He'd been a street fighter for as long as she'd known him. The U.S. Navy had sharpened his rough edges and honed him into an elite assassin who could kill with lethal precision. He had the medals to show for it, along with commendations for covert operations the public would never know about.

For the nine years that he'd been away fighting wars and doing God only knows what else, Zandra had secretly worried about him. She'd lived in fear of receiving a phone call from Roderick—it would have to be Roderick—telling her that Remy had been killed in the line of duty. Even now, whenever he traveled for business, she didn't breathe easy until he was back home, safe and sound.

Two days ago, when she'd tuned into BBC news and heard reports of a gunfight in Abu Dhabi, her heart had plummeted into her stomach. She'd only calmed down after she made some phone calls and talked to Roderick, who was always the first to know what was going on with his twin. According to Roderick, Remy and his men had taken out a group of extremists who'd tried to ambush them as they escorted their clients to a business meeting. All of the terrorists had been killed.

Zandra had calmly thanked Roderick for the information, hung up the phone, then choked back a sob of relief.

"You need someone who's bossy and unpredictable," Skylar was saying. "The kind of man who'd grab you without warning, bend you over and fuck you senseless, then chain you to a wall and have his wicked way with you until you passed out."

Zandra laughed. "Don't project your BDSM fantasies onto me," she teased, even as her body heated at the memory of her scorchingly erotic encounters with Remy. Even when she was on top, he'd dictated the pace of their lovemaking. But he wasn't a selfish lover. Far from it. He was fiercely attuned to her needs and desires, and he gave her more pleasure than she'd ever thought her body could experience.

As her clit tingled, Zandra let her gaze wander through the crowd until she located Remy. He and Noelani were laughing and chatting with two other couples. Noelani had her hand tucked into the crook of Remy's arm, her head resting coquettishly on his broad shoulder.

As Zandra observed them, she felt an irrational stab of annoyance. Under normal circumstances, it would have pleased her to see one of her escorts getting along so well with a client. But Remy was no ordinary client.

Following the direction of her narrowed gaze, Skylar asked, "Isn't that one of your girls?"

Zandra nodded shortly.

Skylar chuckled, shaking her head. "You're a better woman than me, Zandra. I know you trust your escorts, but there's no way in hell *I'd* set any of them up on a date with Remy. Hell, I wouldn't even leave them alone in a room with him."

Zandra frowned.

At that moment, Remy sent a lazy glance in her direction.

When their eyes met, her breath caught in her throat.

As his hot gaze slid down her body, lust swam into her veins, pooled between her thighs. If she'd been wearing panties, they would have been drenched.

Skylar purred low in her throat. "You lucky bitch."

Zandra smiled.

When Colin suddenly came up beside her and curved an arm around her waist, Remy's face hardened.

Catching his deadly expression, Skylar smiled brightly at Colin. "Having a good time?"

As he turned and responded to her, Zandra hazarded another glance at Remy.

Lips curved mockingly, he lifted his champagne and toasted her before putting the glass to his mouth and drinking.

Zandra dragged in a shaky breath and looked away.

"Hey, there," she said, smiling apologetically at Colin. "Didn't mean to abandon you to Enid. She's a sweetheart, but she can be long-winded."

Colin chuckled good-naturedly. "No problem. She and her husband remind me a little of my parents. Anyway, she says they're gonna be seating for dinner soon, so we should make our way to the gallery."

"All right. I need to use the restroom first, so why don't you and Skylar grab our table and I'll catch up with you."

When Colin hesitated, Skylar slipped her arm through

his and winked at Zandra. "Go on. I'll keep him company for you."

"Thanks." Zandra grinned. "I think."

As Colin and Skylar moved off, Zandra turned and began weaving her way toward the restrooms, demurely fending off advances from flirtatious admirers.

The line inside the ladies' room was ridiculously long, and she really had to pee. So she left, went down the hall and around the corner, and crept to the rear stairwell Enid Roche had shown her during a previous tour of the museum.

Surprised and relieved that no security guard stopped her, Zandra ascended the stairs to the darkened second floor, which would be opened for viewing after dinner.

Moving quickly and quietly, she strode to the door of the ladies' room and slipped inside, breathing a sigh of relief when she saw that the elegantly refurbished room was empty. Her heels clicked smartly on the polished marble floor as she strode past the gleaming row of sinks and ducked into the last stall.

When she'd finished emptying her bladder and freshening up with a feminine wipe, she flushed the toilet and grabbed her satin clutch. Unlatching the stall door, she opened it and stepped out.

And ran smack into the massive wall of a man's chest.

Not just any man.

Remy.

She sucked in a shocked breath, staring up at him. "What are you—"

He lowered his head and kissed her.

Before she could gasp, his tongue invaded her mouth, stealing the breath from her lungs.

Electric fire swept through her, hardening her nipples.

As her arms went around his neck, her clutch fell to the floor.

He backed her into the stall as his hands moved downward to grip her ass, pulling her tight against his scorching erection. She moaned into his mouth.

He worked her dress up her thighs, then lifted her off the floor. She wrapped her legs around his waist as he turned in the small space and pushed her up against the door. His mouth ran down her throat and over her breasts as she reached beneath his tuxedo jacket to stroke his broad chest.

When his fingers delved between her thighs and encountered bare flesh, he made a primal sound and lifted his head to stare at her, his eyes blazing with lust. "No panties?"

"It's Herve Leger," she gasped out, as if the answer should be obvious. "No panties required."

Remy gave a shuddering groan. "Thank you, Herve."

He curled two fingers inside her, sending shivers down her spine and blood to her clitoris. She moaned, her head falling back against the door as he pressed deeper, his thumb slowly circling her engorged clit.

"You're so fucking wet," he growled huskily against her throat. "You've been wet for me all night, haven't you?"

Zandra could only nod and thrust against his hand, aching for more. His fingers tunneled deeper, probing the hot wetness of her pussy until her juices seeped out onto his knuckles. She gasped and bucked her hips as he slid in and out of her, watching her face contort with ecstasy.

And then he curved his fingers right into her G-spot.

As she lost it, he crushed his mouth to hers to muffle the sounds of her orgasm.

Closing her eyes, she rode out the waves of mind-numbing sensation.

She heard the soft hiss of a zipper, then felt the blunt head of Remy's cock nudging between her folds.

"Open your eyes," he whispered.

When she obeyed, he shoved into her.

She almost screamed with pleasure.

As he began fucking her, there was something so erotic about the way he stared into her eyes that hedonistic chills raced down her spine.

She clung to him, her stilettos dangling off her feet as he pounded her against the door, rocking the walls of the stall. Her dress was bunched around her waist and his hands were wrapped around her ass, spreading her cheeks wide as he thrust so deep she felt him in her stomach.

He leaned down, and their mouths came together in a heated frenzy. The kiss was raw, primal, teeth clashing, tongues plunging and retreating.

Moments later Remy groaned and went off like a geyser, coming inside her.

Zandra erupted at the same time, biting her lip hard to keep from screaming his name.

In the minutes that followed, they held each other tight, their harsh breaths echoing in the silence of the empty bathroom.

When Remy lifted his head from her shoulder, Zandra slapped him across the face.

Surprised, he scowled at her. "What was that for?"

"For making me worry about you. I heard about what happened in Abu Dhabi. The details were sketchy, so I had to call a friend at the U.S. Embassy just to make sure there were no American casualties before I got ahold of

Roderick." She poked Remy in the chest. "Why the hell didn't you call me when you got home yesterday?"

He stared at her, his eyes glimmering with mirth.

"You think this is funny?"

"No, ma'am." He sobered. "I didn't mean to worry you, but considering the way we parted on Monday, I didn't think you'd want to hear from me."

"*What?* You didn't think I'd want to know if you were dead or alive?"

He grinned. "Last time I saw you, darling, you looked mad enough to kill me yourself."

"That's besides the point." But her lips were twitching. "The *next* time something like that happens, at least have the courtesy to let me know you're okay. Okay?"

"Aye aye, Miss Kennedy."

"Thank you."

She couldn't help smiling as he tenderly kissed her forehead, her closed eyelids and the tip of her nose before nibbling her lower lip. Running her hands up and down his strong back, she sighed languorously. "This is crazy, Rem. Someone could have walked in on us."

"And they'd have walked right back out," he murmured.

She laughed softly. "You don't know that."

"Don't care either."

Zandra grinned, Skylar's words echoing through her mind. *You need a bad boy.*

Skylar would be so proud—and probably jealous—if she knew what Zandra and Remy were up here doing.

She sighed again. "We'd better get back downstairs before we're late to dinner."

"I'd rather stay right here and have dessert."

"Mmm." She shivered as his warm lips nuzzled the

sensitive skin below her ear. "Stop by my apartment later, and you can have all the dessert you want."

Remy met her gaze, his eyes glinting wickedly. "Is that a promise?"

"Absolutely." Tracing his lips with her tongue, she purred, "You were an officer. Now be a gentleman and put me down before someone catches us."

"I had a wonderful time tonight," Noelani told Remy on the way back to his apartment later that evening.

Reclining against the plush leather seat of the Bentley limo, Remy smiled lazily at her. "I did, too."

Noelani smiled with pleasure.

With a cascade of long dark hair, exotically slanted eyes, dusky skin and curves galore, she was a stunner. When she seductively crossed her legs, Remy couldn't help watching as the slit in her red gown exposed her smooth bare thighs.

Slowly lifting his eyes to hers, he took a deep swallow of the Hennessy and Coke she'd fixed him.

"Is it good?" she purred.

"Yes, ma'am."

"Wonderful."

He smiled at her.

She smiled back.

When he softly began rapping the lyrics to an old eighties tune, Noelani laughed. "Are you singing 'Hawaiian Sophie' to me?"

Remy grinned crookedly. "Sorry. Couldn't resist. You must get that a lot."

"Often enough." Her eyes glinted. "But this is the first time I haven't minded."

Remy chuckled, sipping his drink.

Noelani shifted on the seat, revealing more thigh.

"So," Remy began conversationally, "what made you leave Hawaii?"

"My family moved here when I was fifteen."

"All of, what, five years ago?"

Noelani laughed, batting her dark lashes at him. "You're very sweet, but I assure you that I'm older than twenty."

He knew that, of course. Beneath her flawless makeup, he could see faint lines fanning out from the corners of her eyes. Zandra didn't hire anyone under the age of twenty-four. She preferred her escorts to be older, which translated into more experience, maturity and sophistication.

He smiled at Noelani. "You like working for Zandra?"

"Of course. What's not to like? Being one of her escorts enabled me to put myself through grad school, and now I'm working on my doctorate. Not only that, but I get to meet great guys like you and attend the ritziest parties." She smiled, her expression softening with warmth. "On top of all that, Zandra's pretty damn amazing."

"That she is," Remy softly agreed.

From the moment he saw Zandra tonight, he'd wanted nothing more than to toss her over his shoulder, carry her out of the museum and take her home for a long, hot, raunchy night of sex. Lovemaking. Fucking. Whatever you wanted to call it, as long as he was buried balls-deep inside her.

Every time they'd made eye contact, it had taken every ounce of self-control he possessed not to act on his primal urges. Watching her slink around in that dress had been more torturous than anything he'd suffered during Hell Week at Coronado Island. She'd wafted through the crowd—hair swaying, lips glistening, hips undulating—mesmerizing and seducing every male whose path she crossed.

When he saw her sneak out to use the restroom, he couldn't pass up the opportunity to follow her and let nature take its course.

Just thinking about the smokin' hot sex they'd had made his dick hard.

Which was damn inconvenient at the moment.

Reminding himself of the purpose of his mission, Remy forced Zandra from his mind and refocused his attention on Noelani.

Unless he was imagining things, she'd moved closer to him on the seat.

*Not. Good.*

But he had to see this through to the end.

"So, Noelani," he said casually, setting aside his drink, "how does your boyfriend feel about you working as an escort?"

She gave him an amused look. "What makes you think I have a boyfriend?"

"Come on," Remy gently guffawed. "A beautiful woman like you?"

A coquettish smile curved her lips. "The world is full of beautiful women who are alone," she pointed out.

"And that's why the world is so messed up."

She laughed softly.

Making his move, Remy bent his head and kissed her bare shoulder.

She shivered, gooseflesh teasing his lips.

*Come on,* he silently urged. *Push me away. Tell me to stop.*

"Remington?"

He smiled against her skin. "I thought I told you to call me Remy."

"Right." Her voice quivered. "Remy?"

"That's better," he murmured.

She closed her eyes, letting him kiss his way up the smooth curve of her neck. When she didn't speak, he prompted, "Yes, Noelani?"

He felt her swallow.

"Are you and Zandra sleeping together?"

The question took him by surprise. He went still, then pulled back and stared at her. "What?"

She met his gaze. "I could tell by the way you were watching her this evening that you have feelings for her."

*Shit,* Remy thought. He'd tried like hell not to even look at Zandra. When that failed, he'd tried not to be too obvious. But he just couldn't help himself.

"Did you set up this date to make her jealous?" Noelani asked bluntly.

*If only it were that simple.*

"No," Remy answered. But he acknowledged that the timing of his request had been fueled by Zandra's insistence on going out with that loser.

As Noelani quietly studied him, he felt an unwelcome pang of guilt for deceiving her. For deceiving Zandra.

Turning his head, he glanced out the window. They had reached his downtown apartment building.

The driver got out and came around to open the back door for Remy.

He hesitated for a long moment, then looked at Noelani and winked. "Thanks for a great evening."

She smiled. "My pleasure."

As he moved to climb out of the limo, she said softly, "Remy."

He glanced back at her.

She reached out, gently cupping his cheek in her hand. Her quiet smile was tinged with something like regret.

"I hope Zandra knows what a lucky woman she is. And if she doesn't…you owe it to her to tell her."

# *Chapter Eleven*

As a young woman, Johanna Sturgill-Kennedy had spent her summers working as a hostess at a posh country club. It was there that she met and snagged her first husband, the heir to a waterproof fabric fortune. Gunther Sturgill gave Johanna all the trappings of wealth she'd always coveted—a mansion on Lake Shore Drive, a horse farm in Kentucky, fancy cars and jewelry, lavish furs to keep her warm during brutal Chicago winters. She'd had the best of everything.

When Gunther became sick, he'd entrusted his estate planning to Landis Kennedy, a shrewd, quietly intense attorney who'd piqued Johanna's interest from the moment they met. He'd struck her as an ambitious man who was going places, and something about the way he looked at her brought a forbidden shiver to her skin.

Three days after Gunther's funeral, she and his family had gathered in the library for the reading of the will.

There were no surprises. As expected, Gunther had left his grieving widow and two children a sizable fortune.

After everyone departed, Johanna poured herself and Landis a glass of bourbon. After just two sips, they were fucking like animals on top of the antique desk. It was exhilarating, like nothing she'd ever experienced with Gunther.

Four months later, she and Landis were married. Their wedding set tongues wagging, but Johanna was used to that.

When Landis became involved in politics, she began dreaming of state dinners and gracing the covers of magazines. So she was ecstatic when Landis shared his decision to run for mayor. She had the wealth. Now she desired the prestige of ascending to the top of Chicago's power structure. And there was no reason to stop there. If voters wanted to send another Chicago politician to the White House, let it be her husband.

But for now, she had to do whatever was necessary to help get him elected to mayor.

That meant dealing with his estranged daughter.

Mentally squaring her shoulders, Johanna strode toward the curb where an older black man stood sentry beside a Rolls-Royce Phantom. He nodded to her and opened the back door, and she lowered herself into the car.

Zandra Kennedy sat at the other end of the plush seat. She was gazing out the window, her eyes shaded by designer sunglasses.

Johanna stared at her striking profile. Zandra was even more beautiful than she'd appeared in photographs.

Johanna hated her on sight.

She waited for the girl to turn and acknowledge her.

When that didn't happen, she frowned and said crisply, "Thank you for agreeing to see me."

"I have a luncheon at noon," Zandra said with cool hauteur, "so I don't have much time to waste."

Johanna bristled at the affront. "I'm sorry that you consider taking a drive with your stepmother such a waste of your time."

Zandra slowly removed the sunglasses and lowered them to the lap of her white linen pantsuit. Dark, long-lashed eyes met Johanna's.

"What do you want? Or do I even have to ask?"

"Hello to you, too, Zandra," Johanna parroted mockingly. "It's a pleasure to meet you after all this time."

Zandra just looked at her.

Beneath the veneer of sultry femininity, Johanna sensed an iron will that would not be easily broken.

Mentally reassessing her approach, she settled deeper into the seat and smoothly crossed her legs. "Your father was disappointed that you were unable to attend our wedding."

"Oh, I was able," Zandra countered sardonically. "I was *unwilling.*"

Johanna gave her a look of reproach. "Your father is the only family you have left."

"Oh, I have some distant cousins who come around every now and then when they need money." Zandra smirked. "*They're* more family to me than your husband."

Johanna frowned. "I'm sorry you feel that way, especially since you're Landis's only child. I have two boys, but I always wanted a daughter. I wouldn't have minded getting to know you."

Zandra sighed with exaggerated patience. "I have no quarrel with you, Johanna."

"Maybe not, but your quarrel with your father impacts me." Johanna paused. "I wanted to attend yesterday's fundraiser gala, but your father refused because he knew you'd be there. And it's not the first time."

"Pity. But that's not my problem." Zandra glanced at her gold wristwatch. "Can we get on with this?"

Johanna clenched her jaw. "Very well. As you may know, your father has decided to run for mayor. In the process of vetting his background, his campaign advisors discovered that—"

"I know where this is going," Zandra coldly interrupted, "so let me just cut to the chase. I'm not relocating my escort agency. Period. If I were dealing with anyone else, I would be shocked and appalled by the unmitigated audacity of such a request. But since I'm dealing with Landis Kennedy, nothing he says or does could ever shock me. Apart from that, it's utterly absurd to think that running me out of town will solve his dilemma. If his political opponents want to use me as a pawn, it won't matter *where* my business is located."

Johanna secretly agreed. But Landis was convinced that Zandra would be a liability to his campaign, and Johanna couldn't have that.

"From what I understand," she said coolly, "people in your line of work move around all the time."

"I don't," Zandra said with implacable calm. "I have no reason to run and hide from the authorities."

"Don't you?" Johanna challenged.

"No. I don't."

Johanna pursed her lips with distaste. "I don't even understand why you're involved in that type of business. You're an intelligent, highly educated woman. Your father told me that you have an economics degree from Oxford and a master's from Northwestern. You're influential and well regarded in artistic circles. You could be running your own art gallery instead of a…a…"

"Brothel?" Zandra supplied.

Johanna flushed uncomfortably. "I wasn't going to use that word."

"You didn't have to. Your husband already did." A trace of mockery curved Zandra's lips. "You know, we're not so different, you and I. We both came from nothing, and we both did whatever it took to survive."

Johanna held Zandra's steely gaze for a moment, then swallowed hard and glanced out the window. They were heading south on Michigan Avenue, passing the manicured greenery of Grant Park on one side, and modern skyscrapers and hotels on the other.

Johanna turned back to Zandra. "I don't understand why you and your father can't put the past behind you once and for all. Your father—"

"—has demons." Zandra's lips twisted cynically. "And I happen to be one of them."

Johanna frowned, nervously fingering the cultured pearls around her slender throat. "I know you may find this hard to believe, but I love Landis."

"So did my mother. And loving him destroyed her." Haunted dark eyes met Johanna's. "If I were you, I'd be careful."

A chill ran through Johanna. "I don't know what happened in the past. I've never asked, and I don't plan to. All I can tell you is that your father is a wonderful man, and he's been nothing but good to me and my children."

Zandra smirked. "Then you're lucky. He was never good to me or my mother."

Johanna frowned.

"Everything is going well for him now," Zandra smoothly continued. "After my mother passed away, he was able to attend law school like he'd always wanted. And then he struck gold by meeting you. Now he gets to enjoy your wealth and connections, his political career looks promising, and he doesn't have the burden of raising a child he never planned for or wanted. Life is good for him." Zandra paused. "Let his circumstances change, and you may see an entirely different side of him."

Johanna swallowed with difficulty.

"Does he know you came to see me?" Zandra inquired.

Johanna hesitated for a moment. "No."

"Then you'd better hope he doesn't find out."

Johanna felt another chill of foreboding.

Zandra lowered the privacy glass to speak to her driver. "Norman, would you please turn around and take Mrs. Kennedy back to the restaurant?"

"Yes, ma'am."

Zandra slid her sunglasses back on, all but dismissing Johanna.

It infuriated her. Who the hell did this girl think she was?

"People are very fickle, Zandra. One day you're the toast of the town. The next day you're a pariah." Johanna smiled narrowly. "You'd do well to remember that."

Zandra gave her a smile etched in steel. "And you'd do well to remember what I said about your husband. Perhaps the reason you've never asked about the past is that you don't *want* to know. One can only wonder why."

Long after Johanna returned to the opulence of her mansion, Zandra's warnings haunted her.

Zandra smiled her way through the women's empowerment luncheon.

She kissed rouged cheeks, laughed charmingly, received invitations to more socials.

She posed for photographs, and accepted congratulations for raising the funds needed to renovate a cultural arts center on the South Side.

She pretended that everything was perfectly normal.

On the way home, she asked Norman to stop at her favorite gourmet coffee shop. She ordered a café au lait, sat at a small table in the corner and stared out the window until she was transported back in time to the bustling streets of Paris.

When she arrived home, she peeled off her clothes and put on her robe. Then she padded to the living room and roamed around gazing at her mother's paintings, feeling Autumn's spirit through every delicate but powerful brushstroke.

When she felt strong enough, Zandra made her way to her bedroom closet, unlocked the hidden safe and retrieved the letter that had been delivered to her a week after her mother's funeral. The letter no one but Remy knew about.

Autumn's suicide note.

Zandra ran her eyes over the page, though she'd long ago memorized every word, knew the slanting curve of each letter.

> My dearest Zandra,
>
> I'm sorry. I know those words cannot begin to assuage the pain and confusion you're feeling right now, but I had to say them. I'm sorry. I tried for so long, but I can't run this race anymore. I'm tired, and my spirit needs rest.
>
> Thank you for Paris. Being there made me the

happiest I've been since the day you were born. I don't know how someone like me could have given life to such a ferociously strong daughter, but I thank God for it, and I thank God for you.

Be your own woman, darling, but never be afraid to open your heart. The right man will know how to take care of it.

I hope, in time, you will forgive me for leaving. I had to, and now I'm at peace.

Love forever and always,

Mom

Zandra carefully folded up the letter, but she didn't put it away. Her throat ached, but her eyes were dry. She wouldn't cry.

Not this time.

She sat down on her bed, curled her legs up to her chest.

Night fell, plunging the room into shadows.

She didn't move.

Her cell phone rang.

Calls from Colin, Skylar and Racquel Brand went unanswered.

When Remy called, she reached over and picked up the phone because she knew he'd come over if he couldn't get in touch with her. And if he found her like this, he'd hold her and murmur soothingly to her, and she would cry.

Sounding as normal as she could, she told him she was having dinner with a client, and he told her he was hanging out with his brothers. She smiled, sent them all her love and wished Remy a good time.

Then she calmly hung up the phone.

Still holding her mother's letter, she closed her eyes to the darkness blanketing her bedroom, wishing it were as easy to banish the darkness in her soul.

# *Chapter Twelve*

That evening Remy met his brothers for drinks at their favorite sports bar and grill on the South Side, just minutes from the rough neighborhood they'd once called home.

Even though they'd moved on to greener pastures and become successful in their own right, they'd never forgotten the hardscrabble days of their childhood, when crime and violence had plagued their block, and their parents had scraped and struggled to feed and clothe six children. They'd never forgotten who they were and where they came from.

So when Remy walked into the South Side pub and was greeted boisterously by the owner, he felt right at home.

He sidled up to the bar, and without being asked, Donnie poured him a tap beer. Sipping from the foamy glass, Remy spent a few minutes shooting the shit with the burly, bald-headed owner while ESPN highlights blared from a plasma television mounted in the corner, and the mouthwatering aroma of baking pizza wafted through the air. When it came to deep-dish, Donnie served up some of the best in town.

The bar's dark wood walls were covered with newspaper clippings and Chicago sports memorabilia. There were old baseball tickets, vintage photos of Comiskey Park, autographed jerseys from various Sox, Bears and Bulls players—most notably Frank Thomas, Walter Payton and Michael Jordan.

After Donnie topped off Remy's beer, he got up and sauntered toward the back, where his brothers sat around their regular table swigging beers and cracking jokes. They were in shirtsleeves, sporting five o'clock shadows and the broad, wicked grins that left no doubt they were all related.

They'd saved Remy an empty chair facing the door, because they knew he never sat with his back to the entrance of any establishment. Even though he'd been out of the navy for three years, he still did a mental headcount of other diners upon entering a restaurant. He still noted the number and location of windows, still checked for things like thick tables for absorbing shrapnel or bullets. He always had to know where the rear exits were, and he never left home without packing heat. But if he was going to see Zandra, he'd usually leave his weapon in the car, because even though he'd taught her how to shoot, the sight of guns still made her uneasy.

"Fellas." Remy grabbed the vacant chair, turned it around and nimbly straddled it. "What're we talking about?"

Royce drawled humorously, "I was just telling Rod to

enjoy having all the sex he can with Lena, because once the baby gets here—"

"—he's in for a serious drought," River cracked.

As the two brothers laughed, Remy grinned at Roderick, remembering how excited he'd been when Rod called a few days ago to tell him that Lena was pregnant. He wasn't ashamed to admit that hearing the emotion in his twin brother's voice had gotten him choked up.

Roderick chuckled, shaking his head at Royce and River. "Why do you clowns assume that having a baby will put an end to my sex life? It sure as hell didn't hurt Mom and Dad's, unless you think they got six kids by osmosis."

At the mere thought of their parents having sex, the brothers groaned in laughing disgust, which made Roderick grin with satisfaction.

"Point taken," Royce conceded.

"Definitely," Remy agreed.

River grinned, swigging his beer. "We were just teasing you anyway. As hot as Lena is, you'd be crazy to let anything keep you from hitting that every night. I know *I* wouldn't."

Roderick chuckled. "Watch it now. That's my wife you're talking about."

"Only because you met her first."

"Please," Roderick snorted. "Lena wouldn't have given you the time of day."

But she would have been in the minority. With his dark good looks and cocky swagger, River Brand had women eating out of the palm of his hand. He was the youngest of his siblings, and the one least likely to ever settle down.

Leaning back in his chair, Royce hitched his chin toward River. "I've been meaning to ask what's going on between you and Lena's sister."

River frowned. "What do you mean?"

"Well, the way you were putting the moves on her in St. Lucia, I just figured you two would be dating by now."

"Nah," River said dismissively. "We were just having fun, passing time. Besides, Morgan's not really my type." At Royce's raised brow, he elaborated, "I mean, don't get me wrong. She has a great personality and a pretty face. But she's, like, a size zero. And you guys know I prefer my women with more meat on their bones. We all do."

Royce, Roderick and Remy looked at one another, then broke into wide, knowing grins and chorused, "She turned him down."

River scowled. "She didn't turn me down."

"Uh-huh," the others laughingly mocked. "Yeah, sure."

River's scowl darkened. "Only because she's already seeing someone. Some dude named Isaac."

"Isaiah," Roderick corrected. "His name's Isaiah. He and Morgan have been dating off and on for the past few months. You would have met him at the wedding, but he had to go out of town on business."

River shot him a dark look. "It would have been nice if you'd told me that *before* we went to St. Lucia."

Royce snorted a laugh. "As if that would have stopped you from hitting on her."

"It might have." River gulped down more beer, smacked his lips and shrugged a broad shoulder. "Anyway, it doesn't matter. Like I said, she's not my type."

Trading amused glances with Royce and Roderick, Remy drawled, "Methinks the boy doth protest too much."

As they laughed, River smirked and gave them the finger.

When the humorous moment passed, Roderick said casually to Royce, "Yesterday when I spoke to Robyn, she mentioned that Daphne was upset because she wasn't invited to St. Lucia. Is that true?"

Royce grimaced, a muscle tightening in his jaw. "Unfortunately, it is."

"Are you serious?" River demanded incredulously. "Why the hell should she have been invited? Ever since the divorce, she's barely wanted anything to do with our family."

"Except, apparently, when it comes to taking all-expenses-paid trips to the Caribbean," Remy said sardonically.

Roderick sipped his beer, then calmly set the glass down on the table. "As Lena and I explained to everyone, the trip to St. Lucia was our way of thanking all of you for your love and support. Now, Royce, I know you were married to Daphne and she's the mother of your two children, whom I adore. But I don't consider her a member of this family anymore, and I make no apologies for that."

"Nor should you have to," Royce grimly agreed. "Daphne had no right to complain to Robyn, and I'm sorry you had to hear about it. I'll talk to her."

"Nah, don't worry about it. You're not responsible for Daphne's petty behavior." Roderick grinned. "Besides, she already got an earful from Robyn."

The four brothers chuckled at the thought of their big sister reading Daphne the riot act. Robyn had always been fiercely protective of her family. It was well-known that anyone who harmed a member of the Brand clan would invariably incur the wrath of Mama Bear Robyn.

"Speaking of getting an earful," River drawled, grinning lasciviously at Remy, "when are we gonna talk about all that moaning and groaning I heard coming from Zandra's hotel room in St. Lucia? Either she hooked up with one of those cabana boys who were checking her out—or you finally got your prayers answered."

Heat crawled up Remy's neck as his brothers stared expectantly at him, their eyes gleaming with salacious curiosity. He hadn't told any of them—not even Roderick—that he and Zandra had become lovers, because she'd asked him not to.

So he looked River in the eye and said with a straight face, "I don't know what you're talking about."

As a roar of incredulous groans went around the table, he grinned.

"C'mon, Rem," River complained. "How're you gonna hold out on us like that? Haven't we been nothing but supportive of your secret crush on Zandra?"

*"Secret crush?"* Remy scoffed. "Fug outta here. How old do you think I am?"

Royce chuckled. "You've spent the past two years secretly pining away for your childhood friend. What would *you* call it? A discreet longing?"

Remy scowled as his brothers hooted with laughter. When he leveled a glare at his twin, Roderick only laughed harder.

Shaking his head in amused defeat, Remy drank his beer.

"You know," Royce said, eyes glinting as he stroked his trim goatee, "I've been giving this some more thought."

"What's that?" Roderick asked.

"Well, I think our dear brother here has been in love

with Za-Za a *helluva* lot longer than a couple years. Hold on," he added when Remy opened his mouth to protest. "Hear me out."

Roderick grinned. "*I'm* all ears."

Royce sat forward. "Do you remember Zandra's prom night? Remember you and Remy were home from college, and Robyn and Mom had gone to Zandra's grandmother's house to help her get ready? So we decided to head over there to meet her prom date, give him the talk, etcetera, etcetera."

A slow grin spread across Roderick's face. "And Remy went overboard, started lecturing the guy about Zandra being a virgin and a nice girl, not one of those skeezers at school. He told him he expected Zandra to be returned home in the same condition she'd left—or else." Roderick laughed at the memory, wagging his head at Remy. "You scared the shit out of that poor kid."

Remy scowled. "That 'poor kid' was the captain of the football team. He knew *exactly* where I was coming from."

Royce laughed. "Remember how Remy wanted to follow them to make sure they didn't take any detours?"

"Yeah, and when we talked him out of that idea, he actually suggested hanging out at Zandra's grandmother's house to wait for her to come home."

Remy's face heated as his brothers burst into another round of laughter. Damn, he should have kept his ass at home tonight.

Roderick looked at him, his eyes dancing with mirth. "All of us were protective of Zandra, so at the time we just figured you were acting out of brotherly concern for her. But now..." He trailed off, a broad grin stretching across his face. "Knowing what we know now, it puts the past in a whole new light."

Remy frowned, dropping his gaze to the frothy dregs of his beer. He didn't want to consider the implications of what his brothers were saying. He didn't want to believe that he'd been carrying a damn torch for Zandra all these years, and he'd done nothing about it.

Grinning mischievously, River slung an arm around Remy's neck and offered consolingly, "Look on the bright side. Unless that was a cabana boy in Zandra's hotel room that night, you're—as they say—in like Flynn."

## *Chapter Thirteen*

On Wednesday afternoon, Remy was in his office reviewing holographic schematics of a secret military compound located off the coast of Norway.

That morning he and Roderick had met with a defense contractor, who'd given Remy the classified diagram in exchange for information about the new technology under development by Roderick's team of engineers at Brand International Corp. The project, spearheaded by Remy, featured a high-tech military uniform outfitted with a computer system to provide situational awareness displays, which would give soldiers a tactical advantage in combat. The technology was expected to be fully developed well ahead of the Department of Defense's own version of the futuristic uniform.

By the end of the meeting, Remy and Roderick had a new multimillion-dollar contract, which they celebrated with cigars and a back-slapping hug before Roderick left to accompany Lena to her first prenatal appointment.

Remy was watching holographic soldiers march through the diagrammed compound when a knock sounded at his door.

"You wanted to see me?"

Remy glanced over his shoulder, meeting the glacier-blue eyes of a tall, muscular man leaning negligently against the doorjamb.

"Yeah." Remy pressed a button on the remote control, and the hologram vanished.

Duke grinned, shaking his head. "That is the coolest thing I've ever seen. It's like something out of *Star Wars*."

Remy chuckled. "Pull up a seat, Gannon."

Duke sauntered to the visitor chair and flopped down, thick black hair falling over his eyes. When he reached up to push the unruly mass off his forehead, his short sleeve rose over his biceps to reveal the same trident tattoo worn by Remy.

Duke Gannon was the newest addition to Brand Security Solutions. After suffering a near-fatal injury during a reconnaissance operation gone awry, he'd been relieved of duty and sent home to Chicago to undergo months of therapy and rehab. He'd been doing well until he received his discharge papers, spelling out in black and white that his days as a Navy SEAL were over. He'd sunk into a deep depression until a friend of a friend referred him to Remy's company.

As Remy walked to his desk and sat down, Duke drawled lazily, "What's up, Chief?"

"I have an assignment for you." Remy slid a folder across the desk to Duke, who picked it up and opened it. "I need you to go undercover as Jonah Spanier, a wealthy financier from California. You just relocated to Chicago, so you gotta lose the accent."

Duke frowned. "What accent?"

Remy snorted out a laugh. He was a native Chicagoan, and even *he* thought Duke had the thickest damn accent he'd ever heard. He dropped consonants and flattened vowels so hard that words like "hockey" and "socks" became "hackey" and "sacks."

Remy shook his head at him. "Just lose it, all right?"

"If you insist." Duke perused the contents of the folder. "So let me get this straight. You want me to investigate an *escort agency?*"

Remy nodded, guilt gnawing his insides.

Duke frowned. "With all due respect, I didn't realize this is the kind of undercover work we're doing here."

"It's not," Remy grimly admitted. "This is more of a...personal favor."

Duke studied him, blue eyes narrowed with speculation.

Remy offered no more.

"There's a lot of information here," Duke noted, holding up the folder. "Can't I just call up the agency and ask for a girl?"

Remy grimaced. "It's not that simple. The owner runs background checks on all prospective clients."

Duke raised a brow. "Suspicious much?"

"Smart. Very smart. That's why she's the best in the business, and her escorts are first-rate."

"Yeah?" Duke suddenly looked interested. "How first-rate?"

Remy sketched an hourglass with his hands, kissed his fingertips. *"Bellissima."*

Duke grinned. "This is sounding better and better. How many girls are there?"

"Nine." Zandra hadn't found a replacement for Lena yet.

Duke's eyes widened. "You want me to go out with *nine* different women?"

Remy cocked an amused brow. "Is that a problem?"

"Not at all," Duke drawled, grinning wickedly. "I'm sure I can handle it."

Remy chuckled. He knew that Duke, like any Navy SEAL, had enjoyed his fair share of attention from groupies—aka frog hogs—who hung around military bases and bars hoping to pick up a SEAL. Remy wasn't particularly proud of the fact that he'd woken up many mornings neck-deep in tits and asses after a wild threesome or, on occasion, foursome.

"How am I gonna explain wanting to go out with *all* of the escorts?" Duke asked.

"When you set up the date," Remy explained, "you're going to be asked some interview questions. Just explain that you're new in town, looking to meet new people and make new friends. And hint that you're tired of being a bachelor, and you're thinking about settling down."

Duke raised a brow. "You're telling me to make them think that I'm auditioning for a wife?"

"Basically." Remy smiled wryly. "Believe me, they've heard everything under the sun. And when you've got moronic reality shows on television, it's not a stretch for anyone to believe that a rich, good-looking guy would want to test-drive a bunch of women to find his soul mate."

Duke chuckled, rubbing his stubble-roughened jaw. "But what if the girls talk and compare notes?"

Remy grinned. "Then I guess you'd better give them something good to talk about. But not *too* good," he added warningly. "You're not supposed to get laid, Gannon. You're going undercover to see if any of the escorts will try to have sex with you."

Duke made a face, shaking his head. "It's really gonna fuck up my ego if none of them do."

"I'm hoping they won't," Remy said grimly.

His date with Noelani had produced mixed results. It was clear that she'd been attracted to him. What *wasn't* clear was whether she'd have allowed things to go further if he didn't have feelings for Zandra.

Duke frowned at him. "Why me? Why did *I* get stuck with this job?"

Remy grinned. "Have you seen some of the other men who work for me? Rough-looking motherfuckers who'd probably scare the bejesus out of those poor girls. Sorry, but you're the only pretty face I've got around here."

Duke scowled. "Gee, thanks."

"Hey, don't blame me. Blame genetics."

Duke glowered another moment, then heaved a resigned breath and muttered, "Fuck it. You wanna pay me to go out on dates with a bunch of hot chicks? Suit yourself."

"Your gratitude is overwhelming," Remy said dryly.

Duke gave him the finger, and Remy laughed. Working with these men was almost like being part of a platoon again.

As Duke rose to leave, Remy told him, "Do a good job on this one, and I'll put you on the Norwegian op."

Duke's eyes sparked with interest. "Norwegian?"

Remy nodded. "Hot extract. Off the grid. We'll take a submarine to get there."

Duke's face lit up, as Remy had expected. Uncle Sam may have declared him unfit for duty, but Duke was a warrior. Once a warrior, always a warrior.

*"Hooyah!"*

Remy grinned. "Hell, yeah."

After Duke left, Remy decided to tackle some of the paperwork on his desk.

Moments later, Mona announced cheerfully from the open doorway, "You have a visitor."

He glanced up.

At the sight of Zandra standing behind his assistant, he felt a surge of pleasure, followed by a jolt of alarm.

Duke had just left his office. Had Zandra passed him in the hallway?

"Hi." She smiled hesitantly. "Is this a bad time?"

"For you? Never." Remy stood, came around the desk and crossed the room to greet her. As Mona stepped aside, he wrapped his arms around Zandra and hauled her close, savoring the honeysuckle scent of her hair and the luscious warmth of her body. She clung to him, pressing her face into his chest, and he wondered if she was as happy to see him as he was to see her.

Drawing back reluctantly, he kissed her forehead and smiled into her eyes. "Hey, you."

"Hey, yourself."

Her hair was scooped back into a high ponytail. She wore a pink T-shirt, a fitted denim skirt and flat sandals. She looked fresh and wholesome. She looked like the Zandra of his youth.

His chest swelled as they stood there staring and smiling at each other.

"I'll just leave you two alone," Mona said, her voice laced with knowing amusement. She'd always liked Zandra, so she never gave her a hard time about showing up unannounced—which Zandra didn't do often enough, as far as Remy was concerned.

As Mona closed the door behind her, Zandra asked, "Are you sure I'm not disturbing you?"

She really had no idea, did she? "Positive."

She smiled. "Good."

He watched as she brushed past him and strolled across the room, ponytail swinging from side to side. She walked around his desk, sat down in the chair and propped her feet up on the corner, her skirt riding up her thighs just enough to make him salivate. As she crossed her silky legs at the ankles, Remy cocked his head to one side, angling for a better view.

She narrowed her eyes at him. "Are you trying to look up my skirt?"

He gave her a look of sham innocence. "Of course not."

"Better not be."

He grinned. He loved seeing her like this, all sparkling eyes and flushed cheeks. He knew, even without asking, that she'd just come from the cultural center where she volunteered several hours a week, working with disadvantaged youth through a community arts program.

Remy sauntered over, rounded the desk and perched a hip on the corner. "How'd everything go today?"

"Wonderful." She beamed. "Those kids are *amazing,* Remy. So gifted. So much raw potential."

"Yeah?"

"Oh, yeah. You should see some of their work. One boy drew a picture of the Buckingham Fountain that was so good, it ought to be a postcard."

Remy smiled. "Impressive."

"*Very* impressive." Her soft smile held a trace of sorrow. "My mother would have loved working with these kids."

"I bet," Remy murmured.

Autumn Kennedy had been an elementary school art teacher and a tremendously talented artist. Her death had devastated Zandra. She hadn't been the same since, and sometimes Remy worried that she never would be.

As he watched, she leaned her head back against the chair and sighed.

"What's up, baby girl?"

She hesitated. "I'm thinking about changing my last name."

Remy was surprised. "Really?"

She nodded.

"Why?"

A shadow crossed her face before she shrugged. "No particular reason."

Remy didn't believe her.

After another moment, she said almost defensively, "It'd be one thing if I were close to my father. But I'm not, so there's no reason for me to keep his name. Honestly, I don't know why I never changed it before."

Remy swallowed at the sudden tightness in his throat. "Well," he said carefully, "why don't you just wait until you…you know, get married."

Zandra snorted. "*That* won't be happening anytime soon."

Remy winced, her words plunging a dagger through his heart.

Oblivious to his reaction, she reached across his desk and picked up the small rubber frog she'd sent to him when he became a SEAL. She'd enclosed a card with the message, *A frog for the new frogman. May you keep each other safe.*

The simple gift had meant more to him than anything he'd ever received before. His teammates had joked that it was his good luck charm, because he'd carried it in the left breast pocket of his uniform, close to his heart.

He watched as Zandra absently toyed with the rubber frog, lost in thought.

"What's on your mind?" he gently probed.

Her eyes lifted to his. "I've been thinking about going somewhere."

"Where?"

"I don't know. I haven't really decided." She sighed, setting down the frog. "I know we just returned from St. Lucia, and it was wonderful. But I guess I wouldn't mind taking another trip, just to get a change of scenery."

"Funny you should say that."

"Why?"

"Because I have to travel to London next week. I've been invited to speak and serve as a panelist at an international conference for private security service providers."

"Really? That's wonderful, Remy."

He made a face. "You know I'm not big on public speaking, but I figure my attendance will be good for business." He paused. "I was going to ask you to go with me."

"To London?"

"No. The moon." He chuckled. "Of course London. Go with me."

Her expression turned wary. "I don't know."

"Come on. You haven't been back to London in years, and I know how much you loved living there when you were at Oxford."

A soft, reminiscent smile touched her mouth. "I did. And I always enjoy visiting whenever I can."

"So come with me," Remy cajoled. "We'll have fun, and you can show me some of your old hangouts."

He could tell the idea appealed to her. But she wavered, tugging her lush lower lip between her teeth.

"Let me think about it and get back to you."

Remy swallowed his disappointment. "Fair enough. In the meantime—"

She let out a squeak of surprise as he suddenly scooped her out of the chair and into his arms, then sat down and pulled her onto his lap. The lush curve of her ass sent an instant rush of heat to his groin.

"What do you think you're doing?" she demanded teasingly.

He nipped her ear. "Reclaiming my chair, woman."

She giggled, reaching across the desk and picking up the remote control to the hologram schematics. "What's this?" she asked curiously.

"Nothing for you to worry about," Remy murmured, smoothly plucking the device out of her hand.

"Ooh. Sounds top secret."

"It is. If you saw it, I'd have to kill you."

She looked over her shoulder at his face. "That's not funny."

"Sorry. It was a joke…sort of." Nuzzling the nape of her neck, he savored the scent of her skin, an elusive fragrance he'd never smelled on any other woman. He wished he could bottle it.

"So," she began casually, "I spoke to Noelani this morning."

He instinctively tensed. "Yeah?"

"Umm-hmm."

"What'd she say?" Remy asked, matching her casual tone.

Zandra hesitated. "She said she had a wonderful time with you."

"Yeah?"

"Yeah." Another pregnant pause. "She thought you were very handsome and charming, and she said she wouldn't mind going out with you again if you're ever interested."

Remy smiled. "Good to know," he murmured, loosening Zandra's ponytail and sifting his fingers through her soft, thick hair.

She purred in her throat, arching against him like a contented feline. Lust heated his blood.

"So are you?" she whispered.

Remy buried his face in her fragrant hair, closing his eyes. "Am I what?"

"Are you interested in seeing her again?"

"Who?"

"Remy," Zandra warned.

He chuckled softly. "I had a great time with Noelani. She's a beautiful woman, like you promised."

"So is that a yes?"

Some perverse impulse made him respond, "I wouldn't mind going out with her again."

"I see." There was an edge to Zandra's voice. "Are you going to set up another date with her then?"

He swept her hair over one shoulder. "Maybe."

"That's not an answer."

He pressed an openmouthed kiss to her nape, making her shiver. "Why are you so concerned?" he murmured, sliding her shirt aside as he nibbled his way across her bare shoulder. "Aren't you dating what's-his-name?"

"Don't change the subject."

"Answer my question."

She let out a deep, shuddering breath. "I'm not dating Colin. I told him we should just be friends."

If she'd been facing Remy, she would have seen the slow, satisfied smile that curved his mouth.

"Just friends, huh?"

"Yes. Are you satisfied?"

"Very. Speaking of satisfaction…"

Zandra gave him a sultry look over her shoulder, her hips provocatively undulating against his crotch. His dick hardened even more, straining against the seam of his pants.

"Oh, my…" Zandra purred wickedly.

He leaned forward and kissed her, running his tongue over the plump bottom lip that had been tormenting him. She let out a soft moan, sending another jolt of lust to his groin.

He opened her mouth with his tongue and slid inside. She tasted so damn good. Sweeter than the sweetest honey.

"Should we be doing this right now?" she murmured.

"Doesn't matter. We're going to."

She didn't protest as he hiked her denim skirt up around her waist and reached between her thighs. She gasped at the brush of his fingertips as he pushed aside the damp strip of her thong. He eased his middle finger inside her creamy wetness, and almost lost his mind.

She was soaked. So soaked he had to have her. Not later. *Now.*

He fumbled down his zipper, gripped his throbbing cock and slid inside her, groaning as her soft flesh expanded around him.

She moaned, her head falling back as she slowly spread her thighs, taking him deeper.

He shuddered. The hot clasp of her pussy, coupled with the lush roundness of her ass, was almost too much for him.

Bracing her hands on the arms of the chair, Zandra began riding his dick with long, deep strokes that made his toes curl inside his boots. Reaching beneath her shirt, he slid his hands up her stomach and cupped her luscious breasts. She shivered as he rubbed her hard nipples through her satin bra.

"Remy… Oh…"

There was a sudden knock on the door.

*Shit!*

Before he could tell the intruder to come back later, Zandra shocked him by calling out shakily, "Come in!"

He'd barely snatched his hands from her tits before the door opened, and Mona poked her head inside the room.

"Sorry to interrupt—"

"Oh, you're not interrupting," Zandra said sweetly.

Mona paused, one brow lifting at the sight of Zandra seated on Remy's lap. He knew that the humongous desk concealed what they were doing—as long as Mona didn't come any closer.

She cleared her throat. "I'm taking lunch orders, so I just wanted to see what you two wanted."

Zandra smiled. "Oh, that's very thoughtful of you, Mona, but I'm not staying for lunch."

"No? You can't?"

"Afraid not. Actually," Zandra elaborated, subtly rolling her hips against Remy's groin, "I'm supposed to be having lunch and going shopping with Remy's sister, Racquel."

"Oh, okay. Sounds like fun." Mona flashed one of those rare smiles, then looked at Remy. "What about you, boss? What do you want?"

*To bust a fucking nut!*

"Uh…I don't care. Whatever you, uh, decide is fine."

Her eyes narrowed. "Are you sure?"

As Zandra tightened her pussy muscles around his dick, he smothered an agonized groan and nodded quickly. "I'm sure."

"Okay," Mona said dubiously. "Just don't blame me if I get something you don't like."

"I won't. I promise." *Now just go!*

"On second thought, Mona," Zandra interjected. "Maybe I *will* stay for lunch."

"Great," Mona said cheerfully. "What do you want?"

"Umm. I think I'm in the mood for something hot—" *squeeze* "—and spicy. Maybe curry pork from our favorite Thai restaurant."

Remy shuddered, his fingers digging into her thighs. "Works for me," he said quickly.

Mona smiled. "Okay."

As she moved to leave, Zandra called out, "No, wait."

*Fuuuccckkk!*

Mona turned back expectantly. "Yes, Zandra?"

"I changed my mind." There was a husky rasp to her voice. "I'd prefer a…spicy chicken sandwich…from that Vietnamese place…a few blocks away."

"Mmm, I could go for that," Mona agreed. "But they have funny hours, so let me check to see if they're open for lunch yet."

"Good idea," Zandra breathed.

As Mona placed the call through her Bluetooth earpiece, Remy could feel the slow, hot trickle of Zandra's juices sliding down his shaft, bathing him in erotic lava. He closed his eyes and buried his face in the back of her neck, biting the tender flesh there.

She shivered.

When she retaliated with another squeeze of her pussy, he almost nutted in her.

Deciding two could play that game, he reached between her thighs and stroked her hard clit.

She hissed.

Mona frowned at her. “What’d you say, Zandra?”

“I…ah…nothing.” Remy could hear the shallowness of her breath, could feel her thighs shaking on his lap. She was as close to losing it as he was.

Hiding a smile against her hair, Remy rubbed her swollen slit where it was stretched around his cock. More honey coated his fingers.

“Okay, they’re open,” Mona announced, ending the call. “Let me go see what the others want, then I’ll place the order.”

“Th-thanks, Mona,” Zandra stammered.

“Yeah, thanks,” Remy grunted.

The second the door closed, he growled in Zandra’s ear, “Now you’re gonna get it.”

She gave a throaty laugh as he lunged from the chair and bent her over the desk. She braced her hands on the surface and spread her legs apart. Remy grabbed her by the hair and began pumping, fast and furious, slamming into her wet pussy.

Within moments they exploded violently together, Remy clamping his hand over Zandra’s mouth to smother her scream.

Gasping and shaking, they collapsed upon the desk, scattering papers.

Sucking Zandra's earlobe, Remy demanded hoarsely, "Mind telling me what that little stunt was about?"

She laughed, breathless and sexy. "*That* was for not answering my question about Noelani."

"I did answer you. Apparently—" he slapped her butt cheek "—you didn't like what I had to say."

"Do that again."

He smacked her other cheek hard, and she gave a lusty moan that shot straight to his balls.

"Little freak," he growled, nipping her ear.

She chuckled softly. "Get off me."

He rubbed against her round ass. "Not yet."

"C'mon, Rem. I have to go."

"Go where?"

"To lunch with your sister. Weren't you paying attention?"

He frowned. "You told Mona you were staying for lunch."

"Only to prolong the conversation." She grinned, blowing her hair out of her eyes. "Now let me up. You're heavy."

He reluctantly lifted off her and stepped back, then pulled her upright.

As he zipped up his pants, she tugged down her skirt and straightened her shirt. With her hair tousled and her face flushed, she looked every bit like a woman who'd just been fucked.

He wanted to strip her naked, spread her out on the desk and do unspeakable things to her with his mouth and his still-throbbing cock.

He settled for kissing her deep and hard, as deep and hard as he'd just been inside her body.

As he drew away, she opened dazed eyes and stared up at him.

He smoothed down her hair. "You're going to London with me."

She blinked slowly, then frowned. "I thought I told you I'd think about it."

"You have," he said implacably. "You haven't *stopped* thinking about it since I asked you. So I'll make it easy for you. You're going."

Her frown deepened into a mutinous scowl. "You know I don't like being told what to do."

"Then do without being told."

Her eyes narrowed dangerously.

He stared her down.

She smirked, giving him a mock salute. "Thanks for the quickie, sailor. Bon voyage."

As she pivoted on her heel and stalked off, Remy lowered himself into his chair.

When she'd nearly reached the door, he drawled casually, "Do you know if Noelani has ever been to London?"

Zandra froze, her back going rigid.

Remy waited.

As he watched, she spun around and stalked back across the room, those magnificent eyes flashing with fury. Slapping her palms down on his desk, she leaned over and snarled, "Sometimes you can be a real asshole."

"I know." Remy leaned forward, bringing his face so close to hers that their breath mingled and he could see her pupils dilate. "And this asshole wants to spend every damn moment he can with you."

That disarmed her.

Her face softened, her eyes flickering with something

warm and tender. She stared at him for several moments, then swallowed hard and stepped back.

"Fine."

"Fine what?"

"I'll go to London with you."

His chest expanded with joy and relief. "Thank you."

She shrugged a shoulder, feigning nonchalance. "I was planning to go someplace anyway. Might as well be someplace I love."

*With someone I love,* Remy wanted her to add. But he'd take what he could get for now. "We leave on Tuesday morning."

"All right."

They stared at each other, then she glanced at her watch. "I'd better not keep Rocky waiting. You know how she hates that."

"I know." Remy smiled. "Have a good lunch."

"You, too." Her lips twitched. "Give my apologies to Mona."

"Will do."

Zandra held his gaze another moment, then turned and strolled from the room, swinging her perfect ass as she went.

Only when she was gone did Remy allow a broad, delighted grin to sweep across his face.

Leaning back in his chair, he folded his hands behind his head and swiveled toward the window. As he gazed outside, he saw nothing but blue skies and sunshine.

He could only hope it would stay that way.

## *Chapter Fourteen*

On Saturday Remy and Zandra braved the heat and crowds to attend the Taste of Chicago, the city's annual outdoor food festival held in Grant Park. They strolled leisurely through a procession of vibrantly colored tents set up by more than seventy local restaurants. Musicians performed from various stages throughout the park, serenading festivalgoers with a medley of pop, country, blues and Latin music.

Mouthwatering aromas wafted thickly through the air, luring Remy and Zandra to sample an exotic array of cuisine ranging from goat with saffron rice to pork-stuffed banana dumplings. They fed each other, laughing as they licked fingers and lips, sharing a delicious kaleidoscope of flavors.

Too absorbed in each other to mind the throng of people or sweltering humidity, they wandered to the gourmet pavilion to watch cooking demonstrations by some of Chicago's best chefs and sommeliers.

Afterward they met up with Roderick and Lena at the Petrillo Music Shell, where they all stretched out on a huge blanket to enjoy a concert. As the band performed, Zandra lay between Remy's long legs while Lena lay between her husband's. Lena wore a soft, blissful smile as Roderick gently rubbed her stomach, marveling at their unborn child growing inside her.

As Remy ran his fingers through Zandra's hair and massaged her scalp, a delicious languor spread through her veins and melted her bones.

It was one of those perfect summer days that made it impossible to have a care in the world.

When the band took a break, Zandra smiled at Roderick and Lena. "Have you guys decided on any baby names yet?"

A warm look passed between them.

"We're still tossing around ideas for a girl," Roderick answered.

"But if it's a boy," Lena said, "he'll be named after his daddy."

"Roderick Junior." Remy nodded approvingly. "Has a nice ring to it."

"It does," Zandra agreed.

Lena smiled. "Of course, if we have a boy, we already know he's going to come out looking just like Roderick and Remy and the rest of them. The Brand men have the strongest genes I've ever seen."

"Don't they?" Zandra chuckled. "It's crazy."

"I think it's good." Roderick grinned, turning his head this way and that to show off his handsome profile. "Why should all *this* go to waste?"

"Oh, please," Zandra snorted, and they all laughed.

"Oh, my God." An excited feminine squeal cut through the crowd. "Is that Roderick and Remy Brand?"

The foursome glanced around to see a honey-toned, heavyset woman bearing down on them. If it hadn't been for the gratingly perky voice, Zandra wouldn't have recognized the approaching newcomer. But as she peered closer, she realized, with a surprised jolt, that she was about to come face-to-face with her former high school nemesis.

Tawny "The Tiara" Forrester, so dubbed because she'd been crowned homecoming royalty four years in a row. By the time she was named homecoming queen during senior year, it had been so anticlimactic that the crowd had only reacted with halfhearted applause. Though many students had privately bemoaned the unfairness of Tawny's long reign, no one had been bold enough to publicly vent their displeasure for fear of antagonizing her. Not only was she one of the most popular students, cheerleading captain and president of the drama club, she'd also been the most vicious.

She and Zandra had been bitter rivals, but not because they'd wanted the same things. Zandra was an honors student, the first female president of the math club and a student ambassador. She was a brainiac who'd had the misfortune of being just pretty enough to make Tawny feel threatened. Her jealousy had been cemented when Zandra began tutoring her boyfriend, Kevin, in math. When the couple broke up a month before prom and he asked Zandra to be his date, Tawny had been livid. She'd glared at them the whole night, and threw a hissy fit when Kevin and Zandra were crowned prom king and queen.

But she'd gotten her revenge. After the prom, Kevin

had dropped Zandra off at home and headed straight to Tawny's house to spend the night. Two days later at school, she'd taken great satisfaction in bragging to everyone that Kevin had come crawling back to her after ditching lame Zandra on prom night.

As Zandra watched her old nemesis approach, she realized that she hadn't seen Tawny since graduation, when she'd sneered her way through Zandra's valedictorian speech.

"Help me out here," Remy murmured in Zandra's ear. "Who is that?"

Zandra smiled thinly. "Tawny Forrester."

Recognizing the name—but not the woman coming toward them—Remy chuckled under his breath. "Damn. This ought to be interesting."

By the time Tawny reached them, she was slightly out of breath from her trek across the crowded concert grounds. "The twins. Oh, my goodness, I can't believe it. It really *is*—" As her gaze belatedly landed on Zandra nestled between Remy's legs, her eyes widened in surprised recognition.

*"Zandra?"*

Zandra sat up slowly, but made no move to stand and greet Tawny. They'd hated each other in high school, so she saw no reason to be phony. "Hello, Tawny."

She watched, quietly amused, as the other woman's mouth flapped open and closed like a guppy out of water.

Taking pity on her, Zandra said smoothly, "It's nice to see you again. You obviously remember Roderick and Remy."

"Hey, Tawny," they greeted her. "How's it going?"

Recovering from her shock, Tawny beamed at them. "Hey, fellas. This is such a crazy coincidence. I was just asking one of my neighbors about you guys. She went to our high school and was in your grade, but you two were so popular you might not remember her. Anyway, you both look *great.* But that's nothing new." Spying the diamond wedding and engagement rings twinkling on Lena's hand, Tawny tacked on a smile that was just as bright, but not an ounce genuine. "Lisa told me that you'd gotten married, Roderick. She said your wedding was splashed all over the papers. Aren't you going to introduce me?"

Roderick smiled indulgently. "Tawny, I'd like you to meet my wife, Lena."

As the two women smiled politely and shook hands, Tawny openly assessed Lena, always sizing up the competition—even when they weren't.

"Congratulations on snagging one of the twins," she told Lena. "Every girl at school had a crush on these two. Roderick was voted Most Likely to Succeed, and Remy was voted Most Likely to Save the World."

Lena chuckled. "I can believe that."

As Tawny's eyes returned to Zandra and looked her over, her lips tightened with envious displeasure. Though she'd gained a lot of weight since high school, Zandra thought she was still very pretty. She might even have told her so if there hadn't been such bad blood between them.

Tawny eyed Zandra and Remy speculatively. "You two look pretty cozy. Are you…?"

Before Zandra could respond, Remy drawled, "I'm working on it."

Tawny's eyes narrowed before she stretched her lips into another one of those fake smiles. "Oh, how nice for both of you. I must say I'm a little surprised though. You two were always more like brother and sister. It'd seem almost, well, incestuous if you wound up together."

Remy chuckled, nuzzling behind Zandra's ear. "Nothing incestuous about this good thing right here."

"Mmm." Purring contentedly as his lips caressed her sweet spot, Zandra smiled at Tawny, whose face looked pinched. "So how have you been?"

Tawny's expression brightened. "Oh, I've been wonderful," she preened with a toss of her long dark hair. "Kevin and I stayed together after high school and went away to the same college. After he was drafted by the Browns, we got married—" she paused deliberately, letting Zandra absorb this news "—and moved to Cleveland. We had a *huge,* beautiful house with a swimming pool."

"Hey, I didn't know Kevin played for the Browns," Roderick interjected. "That's great. What was his number?"

Tawny faltered. "Oh, goodness, can you believe I'm actually drawing a blank? Unfortunately he, um, got injured and had to retire a few years early. But we liked Cleveland so much that we decided to stay there. We just moved back to Chicago this summer, so I've been trying to get caught up on everyone's lives."

"Welcome home," Zandra murmured. "And congratulations to you and Kevin."

"Thank you. We're very blessed." Tawny smiled sweetly. "How are your parents?"

Zandra stiffened, having an instant flashback to the day Tawny had eavesdropped on her conversation with their homeroom teacher. Noticing the bruise on Zandra's cheek, the concerned woman had detained her in the hallway before class, listening compassionately as Zandra tearfully explained that she had to go live with her grandmother because her father had beaten her the night before. It was the first time Landis had struck her, but it was enough to convince Autumn to get Zandra out of harm's way. If only she'd done the same for herself.

Before Zandra could answer Tawny's question—which had clearly been intended to draw blood—Roderick murmured thoughtfully, "Hmm. That's odd."

Tawny's gaze shifted to him. "What?"

Roderick glanced up from his smartphone. "I'm on the Browns' website looking through their old team rosters, and I don't see Kevin's name anywhere."

"Really?" Tawny's face flamed. "They, ah, probably just haven't had a chance to, um, update the rosters."

"Right." Roderick smiled, eyes glinting. "I'm sure that's what it is."

Tawny looked like she wanted the ground to open up and swallow her whole.

Zandra didn't miss the amused glances that passed between Roderick and Remy. While Remy could strike fear with a look, Roderick could cut you down to size with just the keen edge of his smile. Both were equally formidable.

"Oh, look," Roderick drawled. "Here comes Kevin right now."

Everyone followed the direction of his gaze.

Zandra did a double take when she saw the rotund man lumbering toward them, munching on a giant turkey leg. His rumpled gray T-shirt was ringed with sweat, and he'd spilled some food down the front. He looked nothing like the cute, popular jock she'd once tutored and gone to the prom with.

"There you are," he groused to Tawny. "I thought you were gonna find a spot closer to the stage."

Tawny glanced at Remy and Roderick, then at her husband, and Zandra knew by her embarrassed flush that Kevin had been found woefully lacking.

"Look at you," she sniped at him. "You look a hot mess."

"Gee, thanks, baby. Love you, too." Kevin rolled his eyes, then grinned at Remy and Roderick. "Wassup, fellas. Been a long time. I—" He broke off, his jaw going slack as he stared at Zandra.

"Close your mouth," Tawny hissed in disgust. "Nobody wants to see your food."

Kevin did, slowly looking Zandra over with frank male appreciation. As his eyes lingered on her bare legs revealed by her cutoff shorts, he licked his greasy lips. "Damn. You look good, Zandra."

Her smile was cool. "Hello, Kevin. Nice to see you again."

"You have no idea." He looked from Zandra to Remy, then shook his head and snorted out the disbelieving laugh of someone who just realized he'd been duped. "That talk on prom night. It all makes sense now."

Remy smiled narrowly.

Zandra threw him a curious glance and mouthed, *What talk?*

He ignored her.

"Well, it was nice running into all of you again," Tawny said with a strained smile that suggested otherwise, "but we need to get home to our kids."

Kevin looked disappointed. "I thought we could all hang out together and catch up."

"I don't think so." Gripping his fleshy arm until he winced, Tawny nodded tightly to Zandra, Remy, Roderick and Lena. "Enjoy the rest of the concert."

As the bickering couple moved off, Lena raised amused brows at Zandra. "Well. That was interesting."

"Very." Zandra narrowed her eyes at Remy. "Did you say something to Kevin on my prom night?"

When he just looked at her, she shot a glance at Roderick. "Did he?"

Roderick laughed, holding up his hands in surrender. "I'm not getting in the middle of this."

"Oh, my God," Zandra shrieked staring accusingly at Remy. "No wonder Kevin looked so nervous when I came downstairs that night. I kept asking him what was wrong, but he wouldn't tell me. And after the prom, he couldn't get rid of me fast enough. All this time, I just thought he was bored with me, and I knew Tawny had promised to sleep with him if he went over to her house. But I never once suspected that you...you had *threatened* him!" Sputtering with indignation, she punched Remy on the arm. "You *jerk!*"

He laughed. "Come on, Z. Don't be mad. I was just looking out for you. Kevin had a reputation at school. I didn't want him taking advantage of you."

"*So what!* You had no right to interfere!"

"Did, too."

"Did not."

Remy heaved a sigh. "Come on, baby girl."

Not wanting to cause a scene, Zandra didn't resist as he pulled her back against his chest, curved an arm around her waist and leaned down to nuzzle the side of her neck. "Tell the truth. You didn't even like that meathead. The only reason you went to the prom with him was to piss Tawny off."

"That's not the point."

"See, look at you," Remy chuckled. "You didn't even bother to deny it."

Zandra sighed, lips quirking as she fought the tug of a grin. "I didn't exactly have boys beating a path to my door to take me to the prom."

"Which goes to show how stupid those boys were." Remy kissed her cheek. "I'd have taken you."

She went still. "You would have?"

"Yeah. But you never asked."

"It didn't occur to me." She hesitated, then shyly admitted, "You were a college sophomore. You barely wanted to go to your own prom, so I didn't think you'd want to go to mine."

"You thought wrong."

Zandra smiled, a warm glow spreading through her.

"Look what I saved you from," Remy murmured, his tongue tracing the shell of her ear.

She shivered. "What?"

"If you'd lost your virginity to Kevin that night, for the rest of your life, you'd have had to live with knowing that your first was that sloppy motherfucker whose wife is so miserable with him, she has to resort to lying about him playing for the Browns, of all teams."

Zandra fought not to laugh, but it escaped anyway. She'd never been one to bask in the misfortunes of others, but seeing Tawny and Kevin today made her grateful that she *had* been ditched on prom night.

As the band returned to the stage, Zandra settled more comfortably against Remy's chest. When he leaned over her, she raised her face to his. They shared a slow, steamy upside-down kiss that had her insides clenching with pleasure.

When Roderick and Lena whistled encouragingly,

Remy and Zandra pulled apart and smiled softly at each other.

After the concert, they left the park and headed to Royce and Bernadette Brand's home in Hyde Park, where the rest of the family had gathered for a summer cookout. Holding hands, the two couples made their way through the beautifully furnished house to reach the French doors leading out to the lushly landscaped backyard.

The scene that greeted them sent a wave of nostalgia through Zandra.

Remy's parents and grandparents lounged companionably on the wraparound brick patio, sipping lemonade and laughing quietly. Flame and smoke billowed from the grill, where Royce flipped thick steaks and burgers while joking raucously with River and Racquel. Dozing on the ground near the outdoor fireplace was the family's presciently named cocker spaniel, Zeus, who'd long surpassed his breed's life expectancy.

Robyn and her husband, Harper, chased their four young children around the sprawling yard, while Royce's handsome sons tossed a football back and forth.

Observing the idyllic scene filled Zandra with a poignant sense of homecoming.

The Brands' summer barbecues had been one of the few highlights of her childhood. She'd looked forward to them the way most kids looked forward to Christmas. They were always held on a Saturday afternoon, the day after Royce Senior received his bonus from the steel mill where he worked. Though money had been tight, he'd always set aside funds to buy plenty of meat for grilling.

On the day of the cookouts, Zandra would rush through her chores, then race down the street to Remy's house. The outside may have appeared as old and rickety as her own, but unlike her home, the Brand residence was filled with love, laughter and warmth. It had truly been a *home*.

Sometimes Zandra's mother had accompanied her to the cookouts. Her father rarely came, and for that she'd been grateful. His surly presence would have ruined her enjoyment of the festivities, and he'd always seemed intimidated by Royce and Desmond Brand, a sense of inadequacy he would later take out on Zandra's mother.

Whenever she'd gone on vacation with the Brands, she'd liked to pretend that she was a member of their family, that Remy and his siblings were her brothers and sisters. And as much as she'd loved and adored her mother, she'd often wished—secretly—that Royce and Bernadette were her parents. She knew Royce would never lay a hand on his wife or children, would never cause them to dread the very sound of his voice.

The Brands had always been there for Zandra, cheering her on at every important event, giving her the strength and courage to believe that she could transcend the horrors of her home life. If Racquel's high school graduation hadn't coincided with Zandra's college commencement ceremony, the Brands would have found a way to make it to England to show their support.

Zandra's mother and grandmother were gone, but they hadn't left her without a family.

The Brands were her family. Always had been. Always would be.

When she appeared on the patio, they greeted her with such affectionate enthusiasm, she almost forgot that they'd recently vacationed together in the Caribbean. After she kissed Remy's parents and grandparents, she sauntered over to the grill and laughed as Royce caught her, lifted her off the ground and swung her around before setting her back on her feet.

"Hey, baby girl." He playfully tweaked her nose. "You're just in time to be served the first burger, hot off the grill."

"Oh, no," Zandra protested, patting her stomach. "After the way I stuffed myself at the Taste, I couldn't possibly eat another thing."

Royce guffawed. "When has Za-Za ever turned down food?"

She grinned sheepishly as everyone laughed. Her huge appetite had been a running joke in the family for as long as she could remember. She loved to eat, and even now she couldn't deny that her mouth was watering at the aroma of steaks, burgers and hot dogs sizzling on the grill.

Royce grabbed a paper plate. "Let me hook you up with a burger."

She surrendered with a sigh. "Okay. If you insist." She paused. "While you're at it, add two of those beef kabobs."

Royce laughed uproariously. "That's my girl."

Edging closer, River hummed appreciatively. "I don't know where you're putting all that food, Za," he drawled, slowly looking her over, "but it sure ends up in all the right places."

Remy scowled and slapped the back of his brother's head, drawing another round of laughter from everyone.

Gathered on the large brick patio, they spent the rest of the afternoon feasting on Royce's mouthwatering barbecue, grilled corn on the cob, and Robyn's scrumptious pasta and potato salads. They teased one another, howled with laughter and chattered animatedly, several conversations often running at once. When Zeus roused himself from his nap and sidled up to the table, Mackenzie snuck scraps of food into his mouth, and was gently scolded by her mother.

"Aw, leave the child alone, Robyn," Royce Senior interjected. "You and your siblings used to feed Zeus human food all the time, and it certainly never hurt him. Heck, that ol' hound might outlive us all."

Everyone laughed in agreement.

Throughout the boisterous meal, even when Zandra wasn't looking at Remy, she knew that he watched her. She felt the naked heat of his gaze as palpably as she felt the sun on her skin, and it made her shiver every time.

She didn't appreciate the way he'd manipulated her into accompanying him to London. But she hadn't wanted to call his bluff by daring him to take Noelani instead. She knew he would have gone through with it, if for no other reason than to torment her. And she definitely would have been tormented as she imagined him wining and dining Noelani and making love to her with the same passion and intensity he'd unleashed upon Zandra.

But she knew jealousy hadn't been the only motivating factor in her decision to go away with Remy. The truth was that she wanted to be with him. Wanted it more than she should have.

She didn't know where their relationship was headed. She'd been telling herself that they were just two old friends enjoying a casual summer fling, one that allowed them to satisfy each other's sexual needs without expecting or demanding more.

But as she held Remy's gaze across the table, she knew that their summer fling was becoming so much more than that.

•

And it terrified her like nothing ever had before.

Because this was Remy, the man who knew her better than any other man she'd ever known. If anyone could hurt her, if anyone could deal a mortal blow to her fractured soul, it was Remy.

As day drifted into evening, Zandra found herself curled up on the cushioned wicker sofa between Bernadette and Grandma Eleanor.

After dinner, Racquel had left to meet a date for drinks, while Robyn had escorted her brood inside the house to watch a movie. Lena had followed, yawning hugely as she rubbed her full belly and joked about needing a nap. At the other end of the patio, Royce Senior and Papa Desmond were huddled intently over a chessboard, oblivious to the rowdy shouts and laughter coming from the yard where the rest of the men were playing football.

Zandra watched as Royce's son, Parker, hiked the ball to Remy, who dropped back, scanned the yard for his receiver and lobbed a deep spiral that River caught for a touchdown. Remy laughed and pumped his fist as River swaggered over, and the two brothers celebrated with macho chest bumps and high fives. Then Remy walked over to their other nephew, Rocco, the defender who'd gotten burned. He consoled the sulking boy, affectionately rubbing the back of his head until Rocco relented with a surly grin.

The scene had Zandra's lips curving with amused pleasure.

Bernadette sighed contentedly. "It's wonderful to see Remy looking so happy and relaxed again."

"Umm-hmm," Grandma Eleanor agreed. "Does my heart good."

Bernadette affectionately patted Zandra's arm. "And we have this young lady *right* here to thank."

Eleanor beamed. "We sure do."

Zandra's face heated. "But I, um, haven't done anything."

The two women shared a knowing chuckle. "Sure you haven't."

Zandra blushed harder, suddenly wishing she'd gone inside with Robyn and Lena when she had the chance.

Bernadette continued warmly, "Ever since we came back from St. Lucia, Remy's been like a new man. I'm not going to pry," she glided on when Zandra opened her mouth. "You and Remy are grown, so it's none of my business what goes on behind your closed doors. But whatever happened must have been good, because he hasn't stopped smiling since."

Just when Zandra thought her face couldn't get any hotter, Eleanor waggled a warning finger at her. "Just make sure I get my wedding before you start popping out pretty babies."

Zandra groaned and covered her face with her hands as the two women dissolved into laughter.

"No one's popping out any babies, Grandma," she mumbled.

"I don't know," Eleanor intoned slyly. "Roderick told me you two looked *mighty* cozy at the festival. Like bona fide lovebirds."

Zandra uncovered her face to glower across the yard at Roderick, who was grinning and pointing at Remy as they lined up opposite each other at the line of scrimmage.

Bernadette laughed, squeezing her hand. "Don't be

mad at Roderick. He's just glad to see his twin acting like his old self again."

Eleanor nodded. "We all are."

Zandra couldn't help smiling as she watched the two brothers taunting and roughly shoving at each other, sweat glistening on their faces and muscled biceps.

"We all remember how Remy was after he got discharged," Bernadette reflected with a mother's quiet pain. "Came home like a wounded bear. Hurt my heart to see him like that."

Eleanor sighed. "Me, too. He was so lost and depressed. And he wouldn't talk to anyone, barely even Roderick."

"He shut me out, too," Zandra murmured, still feeling the sting of Remy's rejection three years later. She'd wanted to be there for him the way he'd been there for her after her mother's death. But he'd rarely returned her phone calls or emails, and if she ventured to his apartment to see how he was doing, he'd come to the door wearing a fearsome scowl and several days' worth of dark stubble on his jaw. He was brusque with her. A cold, distant stranger she hadn't recognized. Unable to get through to him, and afraid to push him too far, she'd eventually backed off to give him space to work through his demons, because that was something she knew all about.

"He was devastated," Bernadette said gently, as if to console Zandra. "You remember how much he'd always wanted to be a SEAL."

"I remember." Zandra smiled quietly at the memory of walking home from school one day with Remy and Roderick.

*"I'm gonna be a Navy SEAL when I grow up," Remy boasted.*

*She wrinkled her nose, puzzled. "What's a seal?"*

*"The baddest soldiers in the world!"*

Eleanor remarked softly, "Starting his own company definitely helped pull him through."

"It did," Zandra agreed.

When Remy landed his first client, he'd showed up at her office bearing two dozen pink roses—her favorite color—and the sweetest smile she'd ever seen. He'd humbly apologized for his boorish behavior and told her that he missed her friendship.

She'd melted, of course. But he'd always known how to melt her.

Bernadette smiled at Zandra, as if she'd intercepted her thoughts. "Not even running his own company has made him as happy as we've seen him these past few weeks."

"Umm-hmm," Eleanor agreed. "That's true."

Zandra didn't want to get their hopes up any higher than they already were. So she smiled and offered diplomatically, "Remy and I are enjoying a new…chapter of our friendship. Operative word being *friendship.*"

As if he'd picked up on her comment, Remy suddenly glanced toward the patio.

When their eyes met, the possessive heat of his gaze sent shivers racing down her spine.

After a breathless moment, he winked at her before jogging off to huddle with his teammates.

Zandra pretended not to notice the knowing, conspiratorial smiles that passed between Bernadette and Grandma Eleanor.

## *Chapter Fifteen*

"You're not going to believe what I just did."

"Uh-oh," Zandra intoned, cell phone pressed to her ear as she sat on the table in one of her gynecologist's examination rooms. She was waiting for Dr. Gill, who had just begun Zandra's exam when she was paged and had to step out to take the call. Shortly afterward, Zandra's cell had rung.

"What did you do, Skylar?"

Her friend sighed. "Well, I stopped by your office this afternoon to take you out to lunch, but I forgot that you had a gyno appointment today. So just as I was about to leave, the door opened and in walked this *god.* Piercing blue eyes, black hair, granite jaw. Stop-your-heart, drop-your-panties gorgeous."

Zandra's eyes narrowed. "Was he a client?"

"A new one. Christine had gone to the restroom, so he asked me whether I could help him. Oh, my God, why did he do that? I opened my mouth to tell him that I didn't work there, and the next thing I knew, I was setting up a date with him."

Zandra groaned. "Damn it, Sky."

"I know, I know. I'm so sorry, Zandra, but I just couldn't help myself. He's *sooo* damn hot. And, honestly, I didn't think he'd believe that I was one of your escorts."

Zandra frowned. "Why not?"

"Well," Skylar said wistfully, "I know I'm not tall and leggy like your other girls—"

"Oh, stop it. You know you're gorgeous. You've got the face of Jessica Biel and the body of Salma Hayek. Besides, not all of my escorts are tall and leggy. Claudia is petite and a voluptuous size twelve, and clients love her. Anyway, *what* am I gonna do with you?"

Skylar gave a lascivious chuckle. "I don't know, but I can tell you what I want that hottie to do with me. Over and over and over again."

"Skylar!"

"What?"

"You can't go out with him."

"Why not?"

*"Why not?"* Zandra echoed incredulously. "Because he obviously went to the office looking to book an escort, and unless I missed something, *you're* not one of my escorts."

"Oh, please let me have him, Zandra," Skylar begged. "Please, oh, please, oh, *pleeeaaase.*"

Zandra couldn't help laughing. "Listen to you. You sound like a child begging for a new toy."

"If you'd seen this particular toy," Skylar purred, "you'd be begging, too."

Zandra frowned. "Sky—"

"Please, Zandra? Pretty please?"

She heaved an exasperated breath, shaking her head at an anatomical diagram of a vagina. Damn Skylar and her raging libido.

"You can't sleep with him, Sky," she warned sternly. "You're only supposed to provide companionship, not sex."

"Aw, man," her friend pouted.

"I mean it. If you want to pose as one of my girls, you have to play by my rules."

She heard grumbling on the other end.

"By the way," Zandra demanded, "where was Christine when all this deception was taking place?"

"I told you, she went to the bathroom. She was in there for a long time—must have had the runs or something. Anyway, by the time she came out, Jonah was already gone."

"That's the client's name? Jonah?"

"Yes. Jonah Spanier." Skylar gave a dreamy sigh.

"I'll need to run his background check just to make this transaction legit."

"Oh, he left all his information. I figured I should, ah, keep it from Christine until you gave the all-clear. Oh, and I told him my name was Brigitte, just in case he calls to follow up."

"Brigitte?"

"Yeah. Like Brigitte Bardot. You know that's always been my dream name."

Zandra frowned, shaking her head. "I can't believe I'm even considering this," she muttered.

"Oh, come on, Zandra. I can impersonate one of your escorts. I'm well educated, I speak French and I'm up on world events. I'm demure and ladylike—"

Zandra snorted.

"—and you just said I'm gorgeous."

"You are," Zandra grumbled. "Crazy as hell, but yeah, gorgeous."

"See? I'm qualified for the job. So what do you say?"

Zandra wavered.

"Please, Zandra? I'll never ask another favor again. Well, not for a while at least."

"Fine," Zandra relented. "You can go out with him. But just remember my rule, Sky. No sex—no exceptions. Got that?"

"Yes, ma'am," Skylar said in a singsong voice.

"Let me know how everything goes."

"Oh, you *know* I will," Skylar purred.

Zandra ended the call and shook her head in exasperated disbelief.

*What the hell have I just gotten myself into?*

Hearing voices outside the room, she returned her phone to her handbag on the chair and climbed back onto the table just as the door opened and her gynecologist walked back in.

"Sorry about that, Zandra. One of my patients just went into labor."

"Oh, wow," Zandra remarked. "That's wonderful. Do you need to leave?"

"Not right away. Let me finish your exam first."

Dr. Gill was an attractive fortysomething woman with a short natural and smooth brown skin. Zandra had always liked and respected her. She was a wife, a mother of three, and very active in her church and community. Though she knew all about Zandra's escort agency, she'd never expressed disapproval or passed judgment on Zandra. That was rare.

As one of Dr. Gill's nurses slipped quietly into the room and closed the door, Zandra lay back on the table and tucked her feet into the stirrups.

Dr. Gill spoke to her as she gently eased the plastic speculum inside her, her voice warm and soothing. "So how's everything going? Are you enjoying your summer?"

"Very much," Zandra murmured, staring up at the ceiling.

"That's good. Got any exciting travel plans?"

"Well, I recently returned from St. Lucia—"

"Oooh, you lucky girl. I've never been there, but I've heard it's beautiful."

"It is. Really breathtaking." The island would always hold a special place in Zandra's heart because of Remy. "You have to visit sometime."

"I know. That's what my husband's been telling me." Dr. Gill sighed. "I just need to clear my schedule and do it, right?"

Zandra grinned. "Absolutely. You won't regret it."

"I'm sure I won't." Dr. Gill used her spatula and brush to gently scrape cells from Zandra's cervix. "Got any other trips planned this summer?"

"Actually," Zandra answered, "I'm leaving for London tomorrow."

"Oh, how nice. I love London."

Zandra smiled softly. "Me, too. It's one of my favorite places in the world." And being able to share it with Remy would make it more special than ever.

When Dr. Gill finished the exam, she passed the Pap smear sample to her nurse and disposed of her gloves, then rose from the rolling stool and walked to the sink to wash her hands.

As Zandra sat up on the table, Dr. Gill asked her, "Are you still happy with the Pill?"

Zandra hesitated for a moment, surprising herself.

"Zandra?" Dr. Gill prompted.

She looked at her. "How long does it take to get birth control pills out of your system?"

"Well, once you stop taking the Pill, the hormones are out of your body quickly, usually within a couple of days. That means your body will start to produce follicles again, which will eventually lead you to ovulate. But every woman is different. Some may take a few weeks to ovulate. Others may take several months. It just depends."

Zandra nodded slowly, absorbing this information with a carefully neutral expression.

Dr. Gill eyed her speculatively. "Are you thinking about coming off the Pill, Zandra?"

She bit her lip, then shook her head. "No."

"Are you sure?"

She wasn't, but she nodded anyway.

"Well, you just let me know whenever you're ready to stop taking the Pill, or if you'd like to explore other options for birth control." Dr. Gill paused, eyes glinting. "Or if you're ready to start planning a family."

Zandra blushed. "I'm not. But…thanks."

Dr. Gill gave her a warm smile. "See you next time."

After the doctor and her nurse left, Zandra got dressed, then walked out of the examination room. She was heading down the bright corridor toward the reception area when she passed a corkboard covered with snapshots of patients' newborn babies.

She'd walked by that corkboard countless times before without giving it more than a passing glance. But today for some reason, she felt compelled to stop.

As she stood there staring at the collection of photos, a deep ache of longing spread through her.

She put a hand to her stomach.

For the first time ever, she allowed herself to entertain the thought of bringing a child into the world.

Not just any man's child.

Remy's.

Remy sat across from Sam Keegan in a leather booth located at the back of a coffee shop on West Jackson Boulevard. Keegan had called him that morning and asked to meet in person. In case the mayor was having him followed, he wanted to look like he was following orders, doing what he'd been told.

Remy waited until the waitress had poured their coffee, winked and sashayed away before he spoke. "It's done."

Keegan met his gaze across the table. "You've started investigating the escorts?"

Remy nodded, his gut churning with guilt.

"You're doing the right thing."

A grim smile twisted Remy's mouth. "Maybe if I keep telling myself that, I'll start to believe it."

Keegan was silent, lifting his coffee cup to his mouth and sipping the black brew.

"Does the mayor know that Zandra is an old friend of mine?"

"No," Keegan said flatly. "And I didn't volunteer that detail. If he finds out on his own, I'll just explain that you're the best person for the job because she'd never suspect your involvement."

"Jesus." Remy closed his eyes, rubbed a hand over

his face and swallowed hard as guilt and self-loathing burned like bile in his throat.

"Kennedy's holding a press conference tomorrow to announce his run for mayor," Keegan informed him. "It might be a difficult day for Zandra."

"She won't be here," Remy muttered.

"Oh? Where's she going?"

"I'm taking her to London. We leave early tomorrow."

"That's probably a good idea." Keegan sipped more coffee. "Her father's a strong candidate, like I told you before. The knives will be out for him soon."

Remy smiled darkly. "Should one of those knives happen to get rammed into his aorta, I'd be ever so grateful."

Keegan chuckled into his cup. "Guess you're still not gonna tell me why you hate the old man so much, huh?"

Remy didn't respond.

When Keegan first came to him, he'd been tempted to tell him about Landis Kennedy's violent past. The revelation would torpedo the man's campaign before it even began. But giving Keegan that kind of ammunition would also thrust Zandra into the harsh glare of the media spotlight, forcing her to relive the nightmare of her childhood. He couldn't do that to her. He *wouldn't.*

Gripping his coffee cup, he brought it to his mouth and drank, grimacing as the strong brew hit his queasy stomach.

"By the way," Keegan said casually, "I recently spoke to someone over at BCNR."

Remy showed no reaction to the mention of the Board for Correction of Naval Records.

"There's been some talk of reinstating you."

Remy went still, but didn't lift his gaze from his coffee.

Three years ago, he would have jumped at the chance to be reinstated into the navy. But no longer. He couldn't go back. Too much had happened. Too much damage had been done.

Keegan watched him. "You have nothing to say?"

"No." Remy drank more coffee.

Keegan sighed heavily. "Well, that brings me to the other reason I wanted to see you today." He paused, waiting for Remy to set down his cup and meet his somber gaze. "Lieutenant Shaughnessy was found dead last night."

The news jolted Remy like a live wire pressed to wet skin. Stunned, he fell back against the booth and stared at Keegan. "Where?"

"In his apartment." Keegan grimaced. "Self-inflicted gunshot wound."

Remy tried to swallow, but his throat was too dry. Turning his head, he stared blindly out the window as dark images flashed through his mind like explosives detonating on a battlefield.

"He was a ticking time bomb," he whispered hoarsely. "He needed help."

"I know," Keegan said grimly. "You tried to warn them."

Remy hardened his jaw, turning from the window.

Keegan's shrewd eyes probed his, seeing through Remy's battle-scarred armor to the anger and grief that had haunted him for the past three years.

Keegan said quietly, "Everyone who matters knows you did the right thing that night in Fallujah."

Remy's mouth twisted bitterly. "For all the good it did me."

Keegan, to his credit, offered no empty platitudes.

A heavy silence lapsed between them. A silence weighted with memories and raw emotion.

Remy drank the rest of his coffee and set down the empty cup, then retrieved two fives from his wallet and slapped them down on the table.

"Thanks for the coffee."

Keegan smiled wryly. "Not if you're the one paying." He watched as Remy slid out of the booth and stood. "Lieutenant Brand."

Remy met the older man's concerned gaze.

"Have faith," Keegan said quietly. "Everything will work out in the end."

Remy's response was a brief, humorless smile.

As he left the coffee shop and slid on his sunglasses, he wished he could share the commander's optimism.

But he knew better.

And Keegan should have, too.

# *Chapter Sixteen*

"So who are you leaving in charge of the agency while you and Remy are off on your love trip?"

Zandra sent an amused glance at Morgan Morrison, who was lounging in the visitor chair in her office. Morgan's feet were propped up on the corner of the desk, showing off the red bottoms of her Louboutins. The razor-edge bangs of her sleek bob accentuated her doe eyes, and she wore a retro-print romper that was so haute couture, she could have been strutting down a runway in Milan.

"I'm leaving Christine in charge." Zandra paused. "And it's not a love trip."

Morgan gave her a knowing look. *"Riiight."*

Zandra deliberately ignored her, returning her attention to her computer screen. "I can't get over what a fabulous job you did with my website," she raved, admiring the ultramodern design that beautifully incorporated shades of pink, brown, silver and black. "It's sleek and stylish and stunningly sexy."

Morgan grinned, flashing exquisite dimples. "I'm glad you're pleased."

"Are you kidding?" Zandra exclaimed, clicking through the pages once again. "I absolutely *love* the new look."

"There was nothing wrong with the previous design—*technically.* But I just thought you needed something fresher. Fun and edgy, but still sophisticated."

Zandra nodded. "You definitely achieved that. And I love the teaser photos of the girls with just their eyes showing. Gives them even more of an aura of mystique."

"Exactly. It'll have users salivating by the time they click on the image to see the full photo and bio."

Zandra grinned. "Brilliant, woman."

Morgan preened at the accolades, folding her hands behind her head and crossing her legs on the desk.

Zandra chuckled. "You really ought to consider starting your own business, Morgan. You could offer graphic design services as part of your public relations consultancy."

"I know." Morgan sighed. "It's very tempting, considering how miserable I am at Adventura."

Morgan worked as a public relations specialist for a nonprofit association, a job she'd loathed for as long as Zandra had known her.

"Life's too short to be miserable, Morg. Especially at twenty-six."

Morgan made a face. "You sound like Lena. She keeps telling me the same thing."

"She's right. You should listen to her. You're way too talented to be slaving away for an employer that doesn't appreciate you. And after this amazing web redesign you've done for me, I'd be more than happy to send business your way."

"Really?"

"Of course."

Morgan pursed her lips, looking thoughtful.

Zandra grinned knowingly. "I see those wheels turning."

Morgan smiled. "The idea definitely has some appeal. I'd just have to do a lot of research."

"Of course. And I can—" Zandra broke off, her gaze skipping past Morgan to the open doorway. She was surprised to see River Brand standing there, his hands tucked casually into the pockets of his charcoal suit pants.

She smiled at him. "Hey, there."

"Hey," he said. "Hope I'm not interrupting."

At the sound of his deep voice, Morgan whipped her head around so fast her bobbed hair slapped her face.

She and River stared at each other for a suspended moment, then Morgan muttered, "Oh. It's you."

River frowned as she turned away, dismissing him. Only Zandra saw the deep flush spreading over Morgan's cheeks.

Amused and intrigued, she waved River inside the office, smiling warmly as he sauntered toward her desk. "To what do I owe the pleasure of this visit?"

"I'm in need of your services," he drawled.

"Oh?"

"Yeah." He stopped at the windows, sweeping a glance over the bright skyline before turning back to Zandra. "I want to book one of your escorts."

She narrowed her eyes at him. "What is it with you and your brother's sudden interest in my girls?"

River chuckled. “C’mon, Za. Don’t give me a hard time. I have to attend an important function, and I need to impress a prospective client. Your escorts are good in those situations. They’ve got class and sophistication.”

Morgan snorted. “Unlike your bimbos.”

River scowled at her. “Who asked you?”

“Oh, please. You walked right into that one. Didn’t he, Zandra?”

“Oh, no,” Zandra said with a laugh. “I’m not getting in the middle of this—whatever *this* is.”

As the two combatants glared at each other, Zandra couldn’t resist adding curiously, “I just have to ask though. What exactly happened between you two in St. Lucia?”

“Nothing,” they both snapped.

“Okay,” Zandra relented, holding up her hands. “Sorry I asked.”

River glowered at Morgan another moment, then shifted his gaze back to Zandra. “As I was saying before I was so rudely interrupted—”

Morgan smirked.

“—I’d like to take one of your escorts to the party.”

Zandra nodded. “When is it?”

“Next Saturday.”

“Hmm.” She swiveled back to her computer, pulled up a new screen. “Let me just check the schedule to see who’s available. I think Laurel would be—”

“I’ll go with him.”

Zandra and River whipped their heads around to stare at Morgan.

“What did you say?” they chorused.

She looked calmly at River. “I said I’ll go with you.”

His eyes narrowed challengingly. "Who says I want you to?"

She shrugged a shoulder. "I work in public relations. I know how to schmooze and work a room. But, hey, you're not interested. No skin off my teeth."

River watched as she uncrossed her long, slender legs and swung them from the desk, then glided to her feet with sylphlike grace.

He gave her a mocking look. "Don't you have a boyfriend?"

"Look, you already said you don't want to take me. So let's just leave it at that."

But it was clear that she'd piqued River's interest—especially when she bent over to pick up her quilted Chanel handbag, and the fabric of her romper pulled snug across the round curve of her butt.

River swallowed visibly.

As Morgan straightened and slung the purse strap over her shoulder, he asked suspiciously, "What's in it for you?"

"Nothing."

"Bullshit."

Morgan wavered for a moment, then sniffed and gave a careless toss of her head. "If you must know, Isaiah has been working a lot of hours and breaking dates. He, ah, needs a gentle reminder not to take me for granted."

One corner of River's mouth quirked upward, such an innately Brand gesture that Zandra couldn't help smiling. "So you wanna use me to make him jealous. Is that it?"

Morgan blushed, biting her lip. "Oh, just forget it."

"Nah. Too late to back out now. I'm taking you."

"Fine. Start by taking me out to lunch, and we can discuss our arrangement."

"Lunch, huh?" He gave her a slow, deliberate perusal and drawled, "Yeah. You could use a good steak."

*"Excuse me?"* Morgan sputtered indignantly. "Is that a crack about my weight?"

"No crack. Just an observation." He gestured to indicate that she should precede him from the room. "After you."

Morgan glanced back at Zandra, her dark eyes twinkling. "Sorry for costing you a client."

Zandra laughed. "Oh, I think I can forgive you."

Morgan grinned. "You and Remy enjoy your love trip."

"Yeah," River added, winking at Zandra. "Have fun."

"Thanks, guys. You, too."

They left, River staring appreciatively at Morgan's backside.

Zandra grinned after them.

It appeared that Morgan was about to fall victim to the same Brand magnetism that had not only ensnared her sister, but Zandra, as well.

She sighed, shaking her head.

*God help us, Morgan. God help us both.*

# *Chapter Seventeen*

Zandra hummed Adele's "Chasing Pavements" as she strolled along London's Regent Street, passing upscale shops and outlet stores housed in elegant buildings. It was the second full day of her trip to England, and she was on her own.

After the way she'd behaved during Remy's speech yesterday, he'd forbade her from attending his panel session that morning.

The memory of what led to her banishment brought a wicked grin to Zandra's face.

After arriving in London late Tuesday evening, she and Remy had been too weary from their travels to do much more than check into their luxurious hotel suite, order dinner and fall asleep in each other's arms. They'd awakened early the next morning and shared a steamy, decadent shower before breakfast was delivered—hot porridge, fresh fruit and coffee. After they ate, they'd quickly dressed and taken a chauffeured car to the conference hotel for Remy's scheduled presentation.

The ballroom had been filled to capacity, but Remy had already reserved a front-row seat for Zandra. She'd sat down, crossed her legs and focused intently on his handsome face as he began speaking authoritatively about the global landscape of terrorism. The audience was riveted, hanging on to his every word. And Zandra had been fascinated, too—until the deep, masculine timbre of his voice started doing things to her.

Wicked, dirty things.

Before she knew it she was imagining the rough stroke of his hands on her body…his mouth between her thighs…his tongue licking the moist flesh of her pussy.

As a hungry ache spread from her pelvis to her breasts, she'd uncrossed and crossed her legs, inadvertently drawing Remy's attention.

Their eyes had met and held.

She'd bit her lower lip, taken a shallow breath. The inhalation sent his gaze lower, to her breasts. Without glancing down, she'd known that her nipples were thrusting brazenly against her blouse.

Remy's nostrils had flared, his hands curling around the edges of the wooden lectern. Just a brief clenching of fingers, but it was enough to send a naughty thrill of excitement through her.

He'd faltered for a moment, losing his train of thought. His black lashes swept downward as he glanced at his notes. Before members of the audience could begin to stir and glance around curiously, he'd recovered his composure and smoothly soldiered on.

Though he hadn't looked at Zandra again, she'd known

that he was hyperaware of her presence. She'd sensed his agitation as he fought to remain focused on his lecture.

When it was over, he'd been mobbed by people who were eager to comment on his presentation and pick the brain of a former Navy SEAL. He'd patiently answered their questions, flashed that killer smile, collected business cards and posed for photos—all the while tracking Zandra around the room as she smiled and chatted with other attendees.

Once the crowd began to thin, Remy had made his way over to her. Without a word, he'd gently cupped her elbow and guided her from the ballroom.

She didn't have to ask where they were going. She knew.

Back to their hotel.

But Remy apparently couldn't wait that long. Instead of ushering her outside to their chauffeured car, he'd led her down an empty corridor toward the rear stairwell. He'd moved with unerring purpose, making her wonder when he'd had the opportunity to learn the layout of the hotel.

The thought fled her mind the moment he shoved open the stairwell door and pulled her after him. Once the heavy door swung shut, she didn't have time to worry that someone might wander upon them. Frankly she didn't care.

Remy hiked her skirt up her thighs, ripped her silk panties off her legs, then stood and pushed her up against the wall. She was already soaked, her juices smearing the tops of her thighs. As he touched the glistening wetness, his eyes blazed with lust.

He'd licked his coated fingers, nostrils flaring with carnal pleasure. Then he'd grabbed her wrists in one hand

and pinned them above her head as he reached down with his other hand to unzip his pants. She'd wrapped her shaky legs around his waist. Then he'd thrust into her, driving his dick so deep her spine contracted.

They'd both gasped and shuddered violently.

His hand gripped her buttocks as he began pumping into her, one long stroke after another. She'd wanted to touch him, to rake her manicured nails across his Armani-clad back. But his hard, strong fingers kept her wrists shackled to the wall.

It was thrilling. Intoxicating. Wildly erotic.

He hadn't spoken a word since they'd left the ballroom, and neither had she. Even if she'd wanted to speak, the maelstrom of sensation pounding through her body made coherent speech impossible.

They'd kissed frantically, panting hotly into each other's mouths as he thrust into her. Deeper and deeper, harder and faster until his hips were surging so powerfully that her breasts bounced inside her bra and her bound hands kept slapping the wall.

Only when they exploded together did he groan. A raw, primal groan that reverberated throughout the stairwell and sent chills down her spine.

And *that* was how she and Remy had kicked off their first day in London.

Shagging in a hotel stairwell.

Zandra chuckled wickedly at the memory as she strolled down the busy street, clit pulsing between her thighs. Since she'd been banished from the conference, she'd decided to treat herself to a leisurely morning of roaming London's swanky shopping districts—an activity Remy wouldn't have enjoyed anyway.

She was standing outside a boutique admiring a silk

sarong dress worn by the mannequin in the window when a man's reflection joined hers in the glass.

"Zandra?"

She turned around. Her eyes widened in stunned recognition. *"Heath?"*

He nodded slowly, staring at her.

"Oh, my goodness," she exclaimed.

They moved toward each other and hugged.

"I can't believe it's you." Heath Upshaw held Zandra at arm's length and gave her an appreciative twice-over. "You look wonderful. Absolutely wonderful."

"Thank you, Heath." Zandra wished she could return the compliment, but his handsome face had grown gaunt, the cheeks hollowed so that his gray eyes looked sunken.

She frowned, touching his face. "You've lost weight."

"Too much?"

She nodded.

He smiled ruefully. "That's because I haven't had *you* around to look after me and fatten me up."

She smiled, but only briefly. "Are you well?"

His smile dimmed. "As well as can be expected. I had colon cancer."

"Oh, Heath," Zandra whispered, stricken. "I'm so sorry."

"It's all right. It's in remission, and my prognosis is promising." One corner of his mouth turned up. "I know I don't resemble the strapping young lad you met thirteen years ago."

Zandra smiled, because they both knew he'd never been what you'd call physically imposing. He was tall, yes, but too elegantly slender to ever be considered anything that approached *strapping.*

His gray eyes roamed her face, returning her silent appraisal. "How have you been, Zandra?"

She smiled softly. "I'm well."

"I can see that. And you're in love."

His words startled her.

She stared at him. "Wh-what?"

A quiet smile touched his mouth. "Is he here?"

"Who?"

"The lucky fellow who put that glow on your face, the twinkle in your eye. The one you're in love with. Is he here with you?"

"No. I mean, um, not at the moment. He's, um, at a conference." Zandra was flustered. And stunned.

*In love with Remy?*

"Heath, I—"

"Come along," he said, tucking her hand through his arm. "Let's sit down somewhere and talk. We have a lot of catching up to do."

Zandra smiled weakly. "Ten years' worth," she murmured as they set off for the nearest café.

Heath was one of the employers she'd had while attending Oxford. They met one afternoon while she was working at a museum of sex in the East End. Heath was part of her tour group, and he'd seemed more fascinated by her than her animated spiel on ancient Japanese dildos. She was nineteen years old and no stranger to male attention, though her sexual experiences up to that point had been limited to a few unsatisfying romps with two fellow students.

Heath was an older man, thirty-four at the time. His maturity and quiet elegance had appealed to Zandra, and something about his slow smile had reminded her of Richard Gere's. When he asked her out for coffee at the end of her shift, she'd accepted.

Heath was an affluent businessman who'd lost his wife to a car accident three years earlier. Zandra could empathize with his grief, having lost her grandmother that past winter. She'd sensed that Heath, like her, felt lost and lonely more often than he admitted to others. So it was no wonder that they'd struck up an immediate friendship.

Over the next two years, he would take her to the finest restaurants, the opera, the ballet, Wimbledon tournaments, you name it. He was intelligent, cultured and worldly, and they thoroughly enjoyed each other's company.

Several months after they met, she'd quit her job at the museum to become Heath's personal assistant, earning twice what she'd been making before. She efficiently managed his busy schedule, ran his errands, even hosted dinner parties for him while juggling her academic workload. Her friends had teased her about having a sugar daddy, but she'd never accepted lavish gifts from Heath, and they weren't lovers.

At least not at first.

One evening after class she'd arrived at his town house in Belgravia to find him in his study, sobbing over his wife's picture. It had fallen off his desk, shattering the glass inside the silver frame.

Moved with compassion, Zandra had rushed to his side and folded him into her arms, holding and comforting him as he wept.

That was the night they finally became lovers.

Right there, on the plush oriental rug with the ghost of his wife watching, Heath had removed Zandra's clothes and made love to her. He was sweet and gentle, and when it was over, he'd cried some more and thanked her.

Years later when she opened her escort agency, she would reminisce about her relationship with Heath and fondly reflect that he'd been her very first client.

And now as they sat across from each other inside the quaint café, sipping tea and nibbling warm scones, she realized how happy she was to see him again. And judging by the smile wreathing his face, he felt the same.

"I didn't think I'd ever see you again," he confessed. "You stopped responding to my letters and emails."

"I know." Zandra sighed. "I'm sorry, Heath. After I returned home, I just needed time to sort through everything…get my life back on track."

His expression softened. "I'm sorry I couldn't attend your mum's funeral."

"That's all right," Zandra said quietly. "I didn't want to be there myself. Didn't want her to be gone."

Heath nodded understandingly. He knew all about that kind of grief.

Silence fell between them.

"No London fog," Zandra murmured, something they used to say to each other when it was time to change a subject that had become too maudlin.

Heath remembered, and took the hint. "Let's see. I'm forty-seven now, so that would make you—"

"Thirty-two," Zandra said wryly. "Old enough to wanna kick your ass for having the impertinence to bring up my age."

He laughed, shaking his head at her. "Still cheeky as ever."

"Damn straight." She grinned as she polished off a scone, each flaky bite filling her with nostalgia.

Heath reached across the table, wiped a dab of clotted cream from the corner of her mouth and licked his finger.

Zandra smiled at him.

He smiled back. "I kept hoping you'd return to London for good, but I knew you wouldn't."

Zandra paused, her teacup halfway to her mouth. "How did you know?"

A quiet, intuitive gleam filled his eyes. "Your heart was in Chicago. Always has been."

Zandra sipped her tea, saying nothing.

"So tell me more about him," Heath invited.

"Him?"

"You know who I'm talking about. The man you brought with you to London." Heath paused. "It's Remington Brand, isn't it?"

Zandra shot him a surprised look. "You still remember his name?"

"Of course. If it weren't for him, you might have fallen as madly in love with me as I fell for you."

Zandra slowly set her teacup down on the table. "Don't talk like that," she murmured.

"But it's the truth." Heath chuckled softly. "I remember how your face would light up whenever you talked about him. Oh, you had plenty of wonderful things to say about his family, as well. But Remington clearly brought you the most joy—and aggravation. I remember how worried you were when he joined the navy, and I remember how you grumbled and complained because he wasn't good at keeping in touch. I always knew when you'd received one of his rare letters. You'd bring it to the house with you, and during your study break, you'd sneak it out and read it with this secretive smile on your face, as if you were savoring every word. I'd stand in the doorway watching you, and I'd think to myself, 'When is this poor girl going to realize she's in love?'" Heath smiled gently. "It was only a matter of time before it happened."

Zandra brought her hands up to her cheeks. Her skin was hot and flushed.

"Look at you. You're blushing like a schoolgirl." At her affronted look, Heath laughed. "That wasn't meant as an insult, love. You were always such an old soul, Zandra. Wise and troubled beyond your years. I don't know how long you and Remington have been dating, but it's obvious that he makes you happy. Happier than I ever remember seeing you."

Zandra made no reply, picking up her tea and sipping quietly.

"You always imagined him when we made love."

Zandra nearly choked on her tea. The cup rattled into the saucer as she set it down, her eyes snapping to Heath's face.

"Wh-what did you say?"

The corners of his lips quirked with wry humor. "Did you think I didn't know that you fantasized about making love to Remington when you were with me?"

Zandra was astonished. *Had she?*

"If I did, it wasn't because you were a bad lover, Heath," she hastened to assure him. "I always enjoyed being with you."

"I know. I felt genuine passion from you." His eyes glinted. "But *he's* the one you really wanted to be shagging."

Heat rushed over Zandra, scorching her from scalp to toes. "I… It's not something I consciously thought about. I've known Remington practically all my life. He was the most important male in my universe. And as we grew older, he became…well, I guess he became, to me, the quintessential embodiment of masculinity. And he… he… *Oh, God.*" She turned and stared out the window, her face burning with mortification.

How could she have forgotten about the illicit fantasies she'd once had about Remy? How could she have forgotten that the second time she and Heath made love, she'd closed her eyes and pictured Remy rising above her, his face tender with longing as he thrust into her.

Or maybe she *hadn't* forgotten. Maybe she'd simply suppressed the memory because she was ashamed, and she was afraid to analyze the meaning of her fantasies. She was good at that. Burying memories, suppressing feelings.

Heath gave a sympathetic chuckle. "You have no reason to be embarrassed, Zandra. Although you didn't know it at the time, you were in love with Remington. So it was only natural that you'd imagine him during our lovemaking." He paused. "Now if it had been some random bloke whose name you called out, *then* I might have taken umbrage."

Zandra stared at him, aghast. "Please don't tell me I—"

"Oh, heavens, no. Nothing like that." Heath's gray eyes glinted with humor. "Well…maybe once or twice."

He laughed as Zandra groaned and covered her face with her hands.

After the barista came over and removed their empty plates, Zandra smiled ruefully at Heath. "Enough about me and my Freudian issues. How are you doing? Are you seeing anyone special?"

"Not at the moment. Oh, I've dabbled in relationships

over the years, but there's been no one special." He smiled wistfully. "You ruined me for all others, Zandra."

"I'm truly sorry to hear that," she said softly. "If there was any way for me to make it up to you, I would."

Heath reached across the table and gently took her hand.

She stared at their entwined fingers, then slowly raised her eyes to his.

There was an edge of sadness to his quiet smile. "In case my cancer comes back, and I never see you again… there is one thing you can do for me before you leave."

Zandra held his gaze. "Anything."

He hesitated for a long moment. "I need to see you with him. Hearing about him is one thing. Seeing the two of you together…that's what will finally set me free."

# *Chapter Eighteen*

It was after one when Zandra returned to 51 Buckingham Gate, a luxury hotel nestled on a secluded side street between Buckingham Palace and Westminster Cathedral. The moment she stepped from the chauffeured vehicle, the concierge materialized to take her shopping bags up to an opulently furnished presidential suite that featured beautiful artwork, a separate living and dining room, a kitchen, and views overlooking the hotel's lavishly landscaped courtyard garden.

She hadn't been back long when Remy returned from the conference. She helped him out of his suit jacket and fixed him a drink from the bar.

When he saw all the shopping bags in the room, he laughed and shook his head at her. "I guess I don't have to ask how *you* spent your morning."

She gave him a saucy grin. "Don't make fun of me. You know what a clotheshorse I am. Besides, *you're* the one who banned me from attending your panel session." Her grin widened. "How was it, by the way? Were you able to concentrate any better?"

"Not really."

"Why not?"

"Because," he murmured, leaning down to brush his lips across hers, "all I could think about was the way you looked in bed when I left this morning."

"Mmm," Zandra purred, letting her tongue touch his. "Guess that defeated the purpose of the banishment, huh?"

"Guess so." His tongue swept the underside of her upper lip before dipping inside her mouth.

Shivering with arousal, she forced herself to pull back and smile up at him. "Are you ready to go sightseeing?"

"Yeah." His eyes glinted wickedly. "But not the kind of sightseeing you're talking about."

"Oh, no," she warned laughingly, stepping away from him. "Uh-uh. We're not doing that."

"Why not?"

"Because we stayed in bed most of yesterday doing *that.*"

He wiggled his brows suggestively. "I didn't hear you complaining."

She grinned. "That's not the point, Remy. Look, while you were in the military, you never came here for pleasure. London is a great city. I want you to experience it with me."

He heaved an exaggerated sigh. "Fine. We can do the tourist thing."

"Thank you."

"Just let me catch my breath first." Ice clinked in his

glass as he sipped his scotch, then smiled at her. "Why don't you show me some of the clothes you bought."

Zandra grinned. "You mean the clothes *you* bought?" she reminded him, because even though she could more than afford her own shopping spree, Remy had insisted on spoiling her during this trip, refusing to let her pay for even a pack of gum.

"Yeah," he drawled teasingly, "let me see how you spent my hard-earned money, woman."

"Yes, sir."

Tugging his silk tie loose, Remy sat on the king-size bed and watched as Zandra modeled one designer outfit after another. She made him laugh as she strutted back and forth, struck haughty poses and dramatically executed the half pivots perfected by runway models. Remy clapped, whistled appreciatively and pretended to snap pictures of her like a fashion photog.

But when she emerged from the bathroom in nothing more than pink lace lingerie and racy six-inch stilettos, all traces of humor vanished from his face. He stared at her with naked hunger as she slinked over to him, breasts bouncing softly from the cups of her sheer bra.

"My God," he whispered.

"What's wrong?" Glancing innocently down at her body, Zandra feigned shock at discovering herself unclothed.

"Oops," she breathed in her best sex-kitten voice. "Looks like I forgot something."

Remy's eyes darkened.

Zandra gave him a coquettish smile and winked, then turned and sashayed back toward the bathroom. She didn't get very far before Remy grabbed her from behind, making her squeal with laughter as he swept her up into his arms and carried her to the bed. He lowered her to the mattress, his body following hers as he peeled her panties down her legs and over her stilettos.

"See, woman, I tried to be good, but you just had to be bad."

Zandra grinned as he unzipped his pants. "I couldn't resist."

"Neither can I," he whispered, staring into her eyes as he sank into her moist flesh and shuddered. *"Neither can I."*

Eventually they made their way out of bed and ventured out to explore the city. Since they'd gotten a late start, Zandra knew they would only have time to see a few things in order to keep their dinner reservation. But that was fine with her. They had four more days to spend together, and she intended to savor every moment.

Strolling hand in hand, they wandered from place to place enjoying the sights, sounds and smells of London.

At St. Paul's Cathedral, they spent time gazing up at the dome's interior and marveling at the stunning monochromatic mural. Then Zandra led Remy by the hand up to the Whispering Gallery. Taking advantage of the dome's unusual acoustics, they whispered romantic messages to each other that could be heard on the opposite side of the mezzanine level. This lasted until Remy's sweet nothings turned raunchy. Breathless with laughter, Zandra raced around and grabbed him, hustling him out of the historic place of worship before they got struck by lightning.

Still in a playful mood, they headed to Trafalgar Square and laughingly frolicked in the fountain, earning amused stares and smiles from passersby. Before their antics could draw attention from the boys in blue, they left and strolled to a popular adult store in Waterloo.

They roamed from one level to another, browsing through a kinky array of costumes, lubricants and sex toys. Remy followed close behind Zandra, licking the nape of her neck and sending sensual shivers through her as she handled nipple clamps, cock rings, leather handcuffs, dildos and vibrators.

"I'm gonna fuck you so good later tonight," he murmured in her ear.

"Oh, my," Zandra breathed as her nipples hardened and cream thickened between her thighs. "You are *such* a naughty boy, Remington Brand."

"And you love it."

She smiled wickedly. "You know I do."

By the time they left the store armed with a bag of goodies, she was more excited than ever about the erotic adventure she had planned for them tomorrow night.

As dusk fell, they stood on the banks of the Thames kissing and cuddling as they watched the city's bright lights streak across the gently rippling water.

Afterward they returned to the hotel, showered and donned evening wear for dinner at Clos Maggiore, an upscale French restaurant nestled in the heart of Covent Garden. They were seated inside the enchanting conservatory, which boasted an open fireplace and lush greenery beneath a twinkling canopy of starlight. It was breathtakingly romantic, with a warm summer breeze wafting over the candlelit tables and piped music playing subtly in the background.

As they dined on roasted venison fillet and succulent Charolais beef, they talked and laughed companionably. Zandra teased Remy by reeling off an exhaustive list of places they would visit and things they would do during their stay. Afternoon tea at The Ritz, tours of the National Gallery and Tower of London, a speedboat ride down the Thames, a sunset dinner on the top of Primrose Hill, the London Ghost Walk to retrace the steps of Jack the Ripper.

Remy listened with quiet amusement as she shared her fondest memories of the four years she'd resided in London. She left out any mention of Heath because she didn't want to risk making Remy jealous, and thinking about Heath reminded her of the things he'd said about her secret feelings for Remy. Feelings she'd hidden from herself for so long.

She didn't want to dwell on those thoughts any more than she already had. So she pushed them aside and focused on the here and now.

After the main course, she and Remy were served a lavender-infused crème brûlée and a decadent chocolate tiramisu. As they tasted each other's rich desserts and groaned, Zandra slipped off her stiletto heels and ran her bare toes up and down Remy's strong calf, enjoying the fine wool texture of his suit pants.

He smiled, slow and heart-stoppingly sexy. "Why, Miss Kennedy, are you playing footsie with me?" The words were teasing, but his deep voice was husky with arousal.

"I think so," she purred. "I've never done it before."

"Never done what?"

"Played footsie. Can you believe that?"

His eyes darkened. "Well, you're doing one helluva job."

Zandra smiled demurely and sipped her red wine, glancing around at the other diners. Satisfied that no one was paying attention to them, she slid her foot up Remy's leg to his hard, muscled thigh.

His sharp intake of breath gave her a wicked thrill of satisfaction. Emboldened, she rubbed her foot against the thick, rigid bulge of his erection.

He made a sound—a deep, rough sound that bordered on a growl. The eyes that met hers were smoldering.

Before she could coyly retreat, he reached beneath the table and caught her foot, trapping it against that delicious male hardness.

Her pulse jumped and raced as she stared at him. She felt reckless, naughty, heady with excitement and desire.

As his warm, strong fingers began massaging her toes, she whimpered softly with pleasure. Heat pooled in her loins, and her heart pounded so violently she had to set her glass down on the table before she dropped it.

Remy's talented fingers moved to the soles of her feet, gently kneading and caressing until it was all she could do not to moan and writhe in her chair. She squeezed her thighs together, but that did nothing to quell the lust surging through her body.

"So you've never played footsie before?" Remy asked in that low, husky rumble that always made her tingle all over.

She shook her head, not trusting her voice.

"How is that even possible, as naughty as you are?"

She could only smile.

"Has anyone ever sucked your toes before?"

"No," she whispered.

"Good." His eyes glittered fiercely. "Then I can be the first for that, too."

Zandra bit back a groan. Her nipples were achingly

hard and her clit was swollen, slick with her arousal. She wanted to come. *Needed* to come.

And then suddenly she was, staring into Remy's eyes as pleasure rolled through her…pussy muscles tightening…fingers clenching on the linen tablecloth… teeth biting down on her lip to keep herself from crying out.

Remy watched her intently, his eyes gleaming with wicked satisfaction. "Mmm. Another erogenous zone."

"That I knew nothing about," Zandra rasped.

The waiter chose that moment to appear. "More wine, ma'am?"

Zandra swallowed hard, cheeks flushed. "Yes. Please."

As he solicitously topped off her glass, she looked at Remy. As he stared back at her, she couldn't resist rubbing her foot against his bulging shaft.

She felt him shudder, saw his nostrils flare.

Looking at the waiter, he all but growled, "I'll take the check now."

Sometime later that night, Zandra awakened to find herself alone in the huge, rumpled bed. Confused and disoriented, she sat up slowly, clutching the sex-scented sheets to her naked breasts.

Glancing around the room, she saw Remy standing at the windows. His chest was bare and he wore white pajama bottoms as he stared outside, a brooding figure bathed in moonlight.

Zandra watched him for a few moments.

"Hey," she whispered.

He turned and looked at her. "Hey."

"What're you doing up? Couldn't sleep?"

He shook his head. "Sorry. Didn't mean to wake you."

"You didn't. Not directly. I sensed…that you were

gone." She looked at him, but his face was cloaked in shadows and she couldn't read his expression. But she didn't have to. She could sense the tension radiating from him. Tension and turmoil.

She frowned. "Are you okay?"

"Yeah."

She didn't believe him, and he knew it.

He held her gaze another moment, then turned back to the windows. "Get some sleep," he said gruffly. "We've got a full day tomorrow."

"I know," she drawled. "I'm the one who set up the itinerary, remember?"

He didn't respond.

She slid quietly from the bed and bent down to pick up the silk robe that Remy had peeled from her body before they made love. She slipped it on and loosely knotted the sash, then padded across the room.

Reaching Remy, she slid her arms around his back, moving her palms up to the thick pad of his pectorals. He caught her hands and brought them to his mouth, making her shiver as he tenderly brushed a kiss across her knuckles.

She closed her eyes and rested her cheek against his broad back, absorbing the heat of his skin. "What's wrong?"

"Nothing."

"Remington."

She felt his muscles tighten, and then he stepped out of her embrace and started across the room. "Come on. Let's go back to bed."

She didn't follow him. "I don't want to."

"Zandra—"

"I want to know what's bothering you. And don't tell me it's nothing because I know better."

Heaving an impatient breath, he turned back to face her. "This is supposed to be a romantic getaway—"

"And that won't change, unless you want it to."

"Damn it." He scrubbed his hands over his face and growled, "Leave it alone, Zandra."

"I can't." Her voice softened. "And neither can you."

He stared at her for a long moment, then pivoted on his heel and stalked from the bedroom.

She followed him through the darkened suite to the kitchen. She turned on the light, wincing at the sudden brightness as she watched him remove a beer from the refrigerator and twist the cap off the bottle.

"Remy—"

He tipped back the beer and drank deep.

"Something is obviously troubling you." Her voice was gentle and soothing, as if she were trying to calm a wounded but feral animal. "It's about what happened three years ago, isn't it?"

He didn't answer her.

"If it's confidentiality you're worried about—"

"No." His voice was flat. "It's not that."

"Then what is it?"

He remained silent, brushing past her to walk into the living room.

Undeterred, Zandra turned and followed him. He sat in a chair, and she knew it had been deliberate. He didn't want her sitting close to him.

Her throat tightened at the sting of his rejection.

Ignoring the plush sofa and other chairs, she lowered herself to the floor at his feet, tucking her legs under her.

She was determined to get through to him once and for all, even if it took all night.

"Talk to me, Remy," she said softly.

He sat with his back at an angle to the kitchen. The light cast shadows over his face, making it so impenetrable he might as well have been covered with the camouflage paint he'd once worn.

"I feel like you're keeping an important part of yourself from me," Zandra whispered. "And it hurts."

Something like guilt flickered in the dark eyes that met hers. "I'm sorry. I don't mean to hurt you."

"I know." She swallowed tightly and moistened her dry lips. "You were there for me after my mother died. You took leave so you could look after me, and those two weeks you were home meant *everything* to me. You brought me food and made me eat when no one else could. You comforted me, held me when I needed you to. You kept me from falling completely apart, Remy."

He leaned his head back against the chair. "Zandra—"

"Ever since you came back I've wanted to return the favor, but you haven't let me." She shook her head. "It's not fair."

He clenched his jaw, his grip tightening on the beer bottle until she thought it might shatter, slicing his hand.

She waited tensely, breath suspended in her lungs. She was surprised at just how badly she wanted him to confide in her, bare his soul.

They were quiet for several moments before he finally spoke, his voice low and remote. "The commander of my SEAL platoon was a guy named Dustin Shaughnessy. He came from a long line of naval officers dating back to his great-grandfather, who'd served in World War One and earned the Medal of Honor. Shaughnessy's grandfather and father were also decorated war heroes. If ever there was such a thing as navy royalty, Shaughnessy was it. He graduated from the Naval Academy in Annapolis, reported for duty as an ensign and was promoted to lieutenant within a year. But he never acted entitled, never lorded his family pedigree over anyone. He was a good teammate and a damn good SEAL. A frogman's frogman."

"Sounds like you had a lot of respect for him," Zandra observed quietly.

"I did. We all did. Out in the field, rank rarely ever matters. Officers and platoon leaders never have a problem taking advice from their men. We're a team, working together to achieve the same goal. I was second in charge to Shaughnessy. I was an LTJG—lieutenant junior grade. But even though he outranked me, Shaughnessy never tried to pull rank." Remy paused, his expression hardening. "Until that night in Fallujah."

He stared into the distance for several moments, lost in memories that were beyond Zandra's reach.

She waited.

He took a deep swig of his beer, as if he needed to shore up the courage to proceed with his narrative.

"Three years ago my platoon was tasked to conduct a body snatch, which is an operation to kidnap high-value enemy personnel. Our target was a Muslim cleric I'll call Jaffar. He had ties to a terrorist cell that was plotting to attack several U.S. embassies and navy warships. But Jaffar wanted no parts of the plan. He'd had some sort of spiritual reawakening, and he wanted to defect from the group. But by doing so, he would have signed his own death warrant and endangered his family. So my team was sent to Fallujah to extract him. We weren't supposed to kill him. He was wanted alive. Like I said, he was a high-value target, and we needed the intel he could provide about the terror plot."

As Remy paused to down the rest of his beer, Zandra could sense his growing tension. She braced herself for what he would reveal next.

He set the empty bottle on the floor, leaned back against the chair and started bouncing one leg up and down, an agitated gesture he probably wasn't even aware of doing. "That night we were inserted by helicopter into Jaffar's residential compound. We'd executed these kinds of operations so many times before, we could do them in our sleep. But not that night. After we dropped in from the roof of Jaffar's house, all hell broke loose."

Zandra stared at Remy's grim face, every muscle stretched taut. "What happened?"

His eyes hardened. "Shaughnessy went way off course. After we secured the target, we should have gotten the hell out. But Shaughnessy insisted on rounding up Jaffar's family members and putting them in one room. Jaffar had a pregnant wife, five children and an elderly mother. None of them were armed. By this time some of my other teammates were engaged in a gunfight with Jaffar's guards outside."

Remy shook his head. "Everything happened so damn fast. One moment I was in another room guarding Jaffar. He was rambling in Arabic, talking about Allah and the gift of redemption and second chances. He was scared, but not because I was holding a machine gun to his head. He was worried for his family, and I assured him that they wouldn't be harmed. No sooner had the words left my mouth than I heard gunshots down the hall. I put a man on Jaffar and ran to the room—" Remy broke off, rubbing his face with trembling hands.

Zandra waited, her heart pounding with dread.

He swallowed tightly. "Shaughnessy had shot and killed Jaffar's family members. All of them, including the youngest child. A four-year-old."

"Oh, my God," Zandra breathed in shock.

Remy's nostrils flared, his eyes burning with raw emotion. "I lost it. I stormed over to Shaughnessy and cracked him on the jaw with the butt of my gun. When I asked him what the fuck had happened, he said that Jaffar's family had been whispering to one another, plotting to kill him. He said the oldest son rushed him with a knife, and he was just defending himself." Remy snorted bitterly. "The kid was fourteen years old. *Fourteen.* I'd seen Shaughnessy dismantle a three-hundred-pound, AK-47–toting tango without breaking a fucking sweat, and here he wanted me to believe he'd felt threatened by a skinny teenager wielding a butter knife. I was furious. We started yelling at each other, and then I heard a scream from the doorway. An anguished, bloodcurdling scream I will never forget for as long as I live.

"Jaffar had overpowered the man guarding him and run down the hall. When he saw his family members sprawled across the floor…his pregnant wife… his children…all the blood… *Jesus,*" Remy whispered hoarsely, closing his eyes with a hard shudder.

Zandra was horror-stricken. She couldn't speak as nausea clawed at her throat.

After several moments, Remy inhaled a shaky breath and opened his eyes. "When Jaffar saw what Shaughnessy had done to his family, he tried to kill him. But as he pointed the gun at Shaughnessy, I couldn't let him do it. So I shot him without thinking twice. When he fell to the floor, I went over to check his pulse. Before he died, he looked into my eyes and he…he condemned all of our souls to hell. I was the only one who spoke Arabic, so no one else understood what he'd said. But I did, and it's haunted me ever since."

"Oh, my God, Remy." Zandra touched his thigh, feeling his muscles tighten beneath her hand. "I'm so sorry. What an unspeakable tragedy."

His jaw hardened, grief and regret stamped into his features. "It was."

Zandra rubbed his knee, trying to soothe him. "What happened after that night?"

He grimaced darkly. "The operation was a colossal clusterfuck. We'd not only lost our high-value target, we'd lost one of our own. Heads had to roll." His lips twisted bitterly. "I was a convenient sacrificial lamb."

Zandra was stunned and outraged at the injustice of it. "So that's why you were discharged."

He nodded tightly. "Shaughnessy wanted to cover his hide, so he accused me of misconduct and insubordination. Our commanding officer intervened to ensure that I received an honorable discharge."

Zandra was livid. "And what about Shaughnessy? He slaughtered eight innocent people that night, including an unborn child. Why wasn't an investigation launched? Why weren't charges brought against him?"

"The Pentagon didn't want the public to know," Remy admitted grimly.

Zandra snorted. "How fucking typical."

Remy pushed out a heavy breath. "You have to understand something. There are some classified missions that aren't disclosed to the public for years. And then there are covert operations that will never see the light of day. The Fallujah op fell into the latter category."

"So what happened to Shaughnessy? *He's* the one who went rogue and botched the mission. *He's* the reason you were forced to kill Jaffar. Did he at least get discharged?"

"No," Remy answered in a low, embittered voice. "As I explained before, Shaughnessy hailed from a long line of decorated naval officers. No one wanted to tarnish that legacy."

Zandra frowned, growing angrier by the second. "But he was obviously a loose cannon."

"That's true. He was. But he hadn't always been." A dark shadow fell over Remy's face. "Four months before the Fallujah operation, he'd lost his best friend in Afghanistan. It devastated him. That night at Jaffar's house, he looked into the faces of Jaffar's family members, and all he could see were the insurgents who'd killed his childhood friend. It was too much for him, and he snapped."

"Dear God," Zandra murmured, shaking her head at the senselessness of the carnage. One tragedy begat another tragedy, and innocent lives were destroyed. When did it ever end?

"Shaughnessy wasn't discharged," Remy continued, "but he was reassigned out of the platoon to a desk job." He paused, his eyes darkening. "Four days ago, he shot and killed himself."

Zandra gasped, staring at Remy. "Oh, my God. Why?"

He pressed his lips into a grim line. "Knowing the type of man he was, my guess is he couldn't go on living with the guilt of what he'd done that night."

Zandra felt moisture pricking her eyes. This story couldn't get any more tragic.

Remy shook his head slowly at her, his eyes haunted.

"I've killed more men than you will ever know. I've killed with guns, with bombs, with improvised weapons. I've killed with my bare hands, and I've watched men take their last breath as I shoved my knife through their heart. Fighting to win is what I was trained to do, and I did it well. But no life I've taken has ever affected me the way taking Jaffar's life did. Watching him fall next to the body of his pregnant wife…surrounded by their dead chil—" His voice hitched, and he dropped his head.

Zandra's heart constricted painfully. She pushed to her knees, wrapped her arms around his shoulders and hugged him, absorbing his pain and anguish as if it were her own.

When he lifted his head and looked at her, his eyes were bright with unshed tears, and so full of sorrow her heart broke.

"It wasn't your fault," she whispered fiercely.

His nostrils flared with suppressed emotion.

"Do you hear me?" Zandra urgently cupped his face between her hands. "It wasn't your fault, Remy."

He stared at her another moment, then made a muffled sound deep in his throat and threw his arms around her. Tears flooded her eyes. He clung tightly to her, and she clung right back. Nothing could have separated her from him at that moment.

He'd finally opened up to her, giving her the missing piece to the puzzle he'd become over the past three years. She was devastated for him. Devastated for the innocent people who'd paid the ultimate price that harrowing night. She was grateful that Remy had finally entrusted her with the painful secret that had been slowly ravaging his soul. Right then and there she vowed she'd do whatever it took to help him find peace and healing.

She didn't know how much time passed while they clutched each other. It didn't matter.

When Remy eventually drew away and exhaled a shuddering breath, she kissed his forehead and whispered, "Let's go to bed."

He nodded silently.

He helped her to her feet, then Zandra took him by the hand and gently led him back to the bedroom.

As they climbed into bed, she pulled him into the cradle of her arms. Her heart swelled to aching as he curled his big body into hers and tucked his head beneath her chin. She held him close, rubbing her cheek back and forth against his soft, low-cut hair.

They didn't speak. Words would have interfered.

But when his breathing had grown deep and even, she brushed her lips across his forehead and tenderly confessed, "I love you, Remington."

And tomorrow, when he was awake, she would tell him again.

# *Chapter Nineteen*

"Did you know that vibrators were once used by doctors to induce orgasms in female patients suffering from hysteria?"

The audience for Zandra's impromptu lecture on antique vibrators included Remy and an elderly couple wearing matching T-shirts emblazoned with the American flag, brand-new white sneakers and bulging fanny packs. The couple looked as out of place in a museum of sex as two nuns at a biker convention.

Remy, on the other hand, looked like a badass who'd feel right at home at a rowdy gathering of Hells Angels. He wore a black T-shirt that showed off his tattooed biceps, black jeans and black combat boots. His eyes glinted with wicked fascination as he watched Zandra deliver her spiel while handling the antique vibrator.

"That's right," she continued as the elderly couple exchanged shocked glances. "In Victorian times, it was believed that the way to cure any disease was to induce a crisis during the course of the illness. So if you had a fever, sweating would break the fever and you'd feel better. Well, the crisis that supposedly cured female hysteria was hysterical paroxysm—known today as an orgasm." She held up an unwieldy metal device. "Before the vibrator was invented, doctors had to use their fingers to manually massage their patients to orgasm."

The old man chortled. "Not a bad gig."

His wife shot him a lethal glare.

Smothering a grin, Zandra held out the vibrator to her. "Would you like to touch it, ma'am?"

She shrank back from Zandra, looking scandalized. "Absolutely not."

Her husband gently patted her arm, his blue eyes twinkling with laughter as he thanked Zandra for the "informative lecture."

As he and his wife shuffled off, Zandra didn't have to wonder whose idea it had been to visit a museum of sex that day. When the old man glanced over his shoulder and winked at her, she chuckled.

As she returned the antique vibrator to the glass display case, Remy sidled close and murmured in her ear, "You've been a very bad girl."

Zandra gave him a cheeky grin. "What do you mean?"

"Come on," Remy gently guffawed. "Are you gonna pretend you didn't notice the way that old dude was checking you out during your presentation? Wearing this tight little blouse and short black skirt. Hell, he probably didn't realize his old dick could still get that hard."

Zandra choked out a laugh. "Will you stop that?" she whispered, glancing around at the crowd of people browsing about with audio-guide phones pressed to their ears and studious expressions on their faces.

Remy grinned. "I'm just speaking the truth. His wife should send you a thank-you card, because if that smile on his face was any indication, they won't be needing any Viagra tonight."

"Stop it," Zandra laughingly scolded, ushering him toward the next exhibit.

"How did you remember all that stuff anyway?" Remy marveled, briefly stepping out of character. "It's been almost thirteen years since you worked here."

"I know, but I've always been good at memorization. Spend a year lecturing tourists about antique vibrators and ancient sex practices, and after a while the facts just roll off the tongue." She winked lewdly. "Pun intended."

Remy laughed.

After enjoying a day of sightseeing capped by an early dinner, they'd headed to the Institute of Sex, where Zandra had a memorable evening of role-playing planned for them.

The museum's nondescript three-story building in London's East End was off the beaten path, but its obscure location had never hurt business. If anything, it seemed to heighten the museum's risqué appeal, adding to the allure of the forbidden. Back when Zandra had worked there as a tour guide, herds of tourists had arrived daily to view sexually explicit photographs, illustrations, books, stag films and an eclectic collection of artifacts that included vintage condom tins, tokens from burlesque peep shows and prototype sex machines.

Before leaving Chicago, Zandra had contacted the museum's owner, who still remembered her fondly and had been pleased to hear from her. After Zandra explained what she wanted—sweetening the unusual request with a generous donation to the museum's coffers—the woman had graciously granted Zandra and Remy free roam of the building tonight. She'd even provided Zandra with an updated tour guide uniform to wear as part of her role-playing.

Remy was thoroughly enjoying himself—and they hadn't even gotten to the grand finale yet.

Returning to character as an irresistibly sexy stranger she'd just met, he followed her into a cool, dimly lit room that featured pornographic woodblock prints and brothel guides from eighteenth-century Japan. This, too, was one of the museum's permanent exhibits that Zandra was already familiar with.

"So," he drawled, "what's a nice girl like you doing in a place like this?"

She gave him a coy smile over her shoulder. "How do you know I'm a nice girl?"

"You mentioned earlier that you're from a small town." He raised an amused brow. "Aren't all girls from small towns nice?"

"Only the ones who stay behind," Zandra quipped.

He gave a low, husky laugh that made her nipples harden.

"As for the other part of your question," she continued challengingly, "what do you mean by 'a place like this'?"

Remy grinned, glancing around at the explicit paraphernalia on display throughout the exhibit hall. "I think that's self-explanatory."

"Oh, I see. You're one of those people who thinks this is nothing more than some raunchy sex museum, like you'd find in some red-light district. But you're wrong.

This *isn't* a sex museum. It's a museum of sex. There's a difference."

"Really?" His dark eyes glittered with genuine amusement. "Why don't you enlighten me?"

"Well, for starters, this is one of only a handful of museums in the world that takes an academic approach to sex. Our exhibits aren't designed to titillate, but to educate."

"Educate," Remy repeated thoughtfully as he wandered farther into the hall. She fell in step beside him as they walked the length of the wall, studying a series of handpainted scenes that depicted men with monstrously exaggerated penises in various sexual positions with women.

"The society was really obsessed with genitalia," Zandra explained.

"Aren't we all?" Remy mused, giving her a sidelong look that naturally made her think of *his* obsession-worthy genitals.

Ignoring the hungry throbbing of her pussy, she continued her educational spiel. "These prints are called *shunga,* which means 'spring pictures' in Japanese. Each *shunga* was mass produced to be used as masturbatory aids."

"You don't say." Remy had stopped to face her. "So they were basically like porn in those days."

"Yes. They were considered visually stimulating."

He looked at one of the prints on the wall, assessing. "Doesn't do much for me." His gaze returned to hers. "What about you?"

Zandra gave a husky laugh. "With all due respect to the artists, it takes a bit more than a kinky drawing to turn me on."

Something hot and wicked flared in Remy's eyes, and his voice dipped indecently low as he asked, "What turns you on?"

*You,* Zandra thought without hesitation. *The way you look, the way you smell, the way you say my name. The way you fuck.*

She swallowed, watching his hooded gaze follow the path of her tongue as she licked her parched lips.

He'd shifted subtly closer. His nearness, his sheer physicality, always made her acutely aware of her own body. The friction of lace against her tight nipples. The dampness of her panties between her thighs, rubbing against her clit.

"It's kind of dark in here," Remy murmured.

"To protect the art from harmful light," she explained, feeling and sounding breathless. "The room is also temperature-controlled."

"You're very good at this," Remy remarked, and Zandra suspected he was talking about her role-playing. She could definitely say the same of him.

"Good at what?" she asked.

"Your job. You really know your stuff."

"Thanks. I'm still learning."

Mischief glimmered in his eyes. "Do you have to be an expert on sex to work at a sex museum?"

"Museum of sex," she corrected with a chuckle. "And, no, you don't have to be a sex expert to work here."

"But it probably doesn't hurt."

Zandra smiled demurely. "When does it ever hurt to be an expert on anything?"

One side of his mouth lifted in a smile. "Well played."

Grinning, Zandra glanced toward the entrance to the

hall. She could see people milling around, but so far no one had ventured into the exhibit.

Deciding she and Remy had better leave before she was mistaken for a real tour guide again, she took Remy's hand and ushered him from the hall.

"I need to use the ladies' room," she told him as they headed up to the second floor of the building, which was far less populated than the first level.

Remembering what had happened the *last* time they were at a museum together, Zandra gave him a warning look. "*Don't* follow me."

He chuckled, snapping his fingers. "Damn. I was just about to do that, too."

"I know you were." She shook her head at him. "Wait for me by the Kama Sutra exhibit."

He wiggled his brows suggestively. "Is that code for—"

Zandra laughed, pointing him in the direction she wanted him to go.

Inside the clean restroom, she found the bag she'd secretly stowed earlier and quickly changed into the costume she'd bought at an adult store in Chicago.

When she emerged wearing a belted trench coat and red stiletto boots, Remy ran a slow, speculative gaze over her. Just as slowly, he smiled.

"What're you wearing under there?"

Zandra smiled mysteriously. "You'll see soon enough. Follow me."

She took his hand and guided him to a rear stairwell that led up to the third level, which the museum's owner had agreed to close to the public for the night.

Zandra's spiky heels clicked seductively against the floor as she escorted Remy down a shadowy corridor to a glass-fronted chamber, where an antique Victorian bed was on display. It was decadently draped in red silk and featured ornate medallions on the head and footboard.

"What's this room?" Remy murmured as they entered the chamber.

"This," Zandra proudly explained, "is the museum's showpiece exhibit. This bed belonged to one of the last great courtesans of Victorian London."

"Really?"

"Yes. Her name was Millicent, but everyone called her Millie. She was rumored to be the illegitimate daughter of King Edward the Seventh, but he never acknowledged her birth. She grew up to become a fashion trendsetter and one of the most beautiful women in England. Men couldn't resist her and, well, she couldn't resist them."

Remy grinned wickedly. "Sounds like my kind of woman."

Zandra smiled, sauntering over to the bed. "Some of Millie's benefactors included political leaders, intellectuals, aristocrats, even members of the British royal family."

"Yeah?"

"Mmm-hmm." Zandra seductively trailed her fingertips over the silk spread. "She embraced her sexuality and enjoyed many pleasurable liaisons in this very bed."

Remy cast an appreciative glance over the antique showpiece. "Many, huh?"

Zandra nodded, lips twitching with humor. "But she was known to be something of a control freak in bed."

"Really?" Remy looked both amused and fascinated. "How so?"

"Well—" Zandra sighed dramatically "—Millie's biggest lament in life was that she would never become queen. She was a courtesan who wanted more than anything to ascend to the throne someday. But it wasn't possible, especially since her father refused to even acknowledge her existence. It saddened and angered her. So whenever she was in bed with her lovers, she made them call her 'my queen' or 'Your Highness.' And if they didn't, she punished them in ways you can't imagine."

Remy's eyes gleamed with lascivious interest. "What kind of ways?"

Zandra smiled enigmatically. "Let's just say it kept them coming back for more."

"Damn. That good, huh?" Remy grinned, shaking his head at Zandra. "Are you making this all up?"

"Of course not. Why would you think that?"

"Beautiful woman with lousy father. Fashion trendsetter. Unconventional occupation. Lusted after by hordes of men." His mouth twitched. "Sounds like someone we both know."

Zandra gave him a blank look. "I have no idea what you're talking about."

"Uh-huh." He chuckled, pointing to the bed. "Are those the original sheets?"

"No." The museum's owner had replaced the linens for Zandra's purposes. "Anyway, what made Millie so desirable to men was that she was different from the well-bred English girls who came to London for the Season. Millie wasn't at all repressed. She was exciting, adventurous. Naughty."

"Mmm," Remy murmured. "I'm liking her more and more."

Zandra grinned. "Oh, but I don't think you could have handled a woman like her."

He arched a brow. "And why not?"

"Because you're too domineering, Remy. Too much of a control freak. You could never be…submissive in bed."

"Submissive?" he repeated.

Zandra laughed. "It even sounds foreign coming out of your mouth."

"That's not true. I can be—" he paused over the word "—submissive."

"Oh, really?"

"Really. I can be any way you want me."

"Any way, huh?"

"Any way. Anytime."

Their gazes locked in seductive challenge.

A slow smile curved Zandra's lips. "I was hoping you'd say that."

"Yeah?" His voice turned smoky. "Why's that?"

Zandra slowly unbelted and removed her trench coat, letting it fall to the floor.

Remy's eyes widened, and his jaw dropped at the sight of her body sheathed in a red satin dress that was a modern twist on Victorian-era gowns. His hungry gaze traveled over the lush mounds of her breasts spilling over the vintage corset, down to the translucent skirt that slitted up to her bare thighs.

*"Dammmnnn,"* he breathed, licking his lips. "So that's what you were hiding under that coat."

"Mmm-hmm." Zandra smiled, thoroughly enjoying his reaction. "You like?"

"Oh, I like very much," he drawled huskily, sauntering over to her. The naked heat in his gaze made her nipples tighten as her clit pulsed and throbbed.

As he reached out to touch her, she stepped back and held up a hand. "No."

He frowned. "What?"

"This will be the next phase of our role-playing," she told him. "But before I explain our new identities, I feel obligated to tell you that this chamber has a one-way mirror, which represents Millie's voyeuristic tendencies. She liked to be watched during her liaisons. Anyway, even though this floor is closed for the night, there's always the possibility of someone sneaking up here to…indulge their voyeurism." Her voice turned silky. "Do you have a problem with being watched, Remington?"

He paused, glancing across the room to the wall she'd indicated. "One-way mirror, huh?"

"Yes."

After another moment, his gaze returned to hers and narrowed. "Do *you* have a problem with being watched?"

"No." She gave him a sultry smile. "I'm going to be Millie. She got off on being watched. But if you don't, we can end the game right here."

Remy looked her over, taking in her eye-popping cleavage and deeply slitted skirt. He shook his head slowly. "If you don't have a problem with it, neither do I."

Zandra smiled with satisfaction. "Good boy."

Humor lit his eyes. "So if you're the courtesan queen," he drawled, "who am I?"

Her smile widened. "You're a brave, dashing captain in the British Army."

"Army?" Remy made a face. "How about the Royal Navy?"

She sputtered indignantly. "Look at you. Defying orders already."

He chuckled. "Sorry. But you know I'm a navy man."

"Hey, I didn't even have to put you in the military. Besides, this is supposed to be *my* fantasy. You can't just—

Oh, never mind," Zandra relented in exasperation. "You can be in the bloody Royal Navy."

"Thank you," he said with exaggerated courtesy.

"It doesn't matter anyway." Zandra licked her lips seductively. "The only thing you are tonight is my slave."

His dark eyes gleamed. "Is that so?"

"Umm-hmm," she purred, stroking his chest. "You said you can be submissive. So let's put you to the test."

"Bring it on."

"All right." She pointed. "Take off your clothes."

He grinned wickedly. "With pleasure."

She watched as he made quick work of stripping—tugging off his shirt, toeing off his boots and socks, then unzipping his jeans and shoving them down his long, powerful legs.

Holding her gaze, he slowly pushed his dark briefs down over his hips. When his huge cock bounced free—long, thick and gloriously hard—Zandra's mouth watered, and her belly quivered.

His eyes glinted at her. "What now, my queen?"

She swallowed with difficulty. "Lay down on the bed."

As he moved to do her bidding, she knelt and reached under the bed. She pulled out a small red bag containing some of the toys they'd bought at the adult store. Removing a pair of leather handcuffs, she stood and provocatively crawled onto the bed as Remy stared at her through hooded eyes.

"You know what Millie's favorite thing about this bed was?" she purred.

He shook his head.

"Being able to tie up her lovers." Zandra straddled Remy's lap, feeling his cock twitch and throb against her mound through her sheer skirt. Ignoring her own body's reaction to the delicious contact, she fastened the leather cuffs onto his wrists. His lips curved in lazy amusement as he watched her link the chain through the heavy iron bedposts.

As powerful as he was, she knew he could escape at any time without even exerting himself. So she figured she'd better give him some incentive not to.

"Don't try to pull yourself free," she warned, "or you'll damage the bed. It's an antique, worth a fortune. I don't want anything to happen to it. Do you understand?"

His eyes danced with mischief. "Yes, ma'am."

She arched a brow.

"Yes, my queen," he dutifully amended.

"That's better." She slid off his lap and ran an appreciative eye over him, enjoying the sight of him bound to the headboard. Brutally male and hers for the taking. "Mmm. I ought to tie you up more often."

He leered. "Or maybe I could tie *you* up next time?"

Zandra shot him a stern look. "Are you being impertinent?"

"No, Your Highness."

"Better not be."

Sliding off the bed, she retrieved the goody bag from the floor and set it down on the bedside table. She removed a flesh-toned dildo and stroked it, glad that she'd bypassed the brightly colored dildos at the store and selected one that looked realistic enough to suit her purposes.

She turned and slithered back onto the bed, then lay back on her elbows with her booted feet planted on the mattress. As Remy watched, she lifted the sheer skirt out of the way and slowly spread her legs, baring the smooth-shaven mound of her pussy to his dark, smoldering gaze.

He shuddered and groaned, his cock jumping against his chiseled stomach.

Enjoying his reaction, she ran the dildo up and down her labia. Her nerve endings sizzled with arousal, and moisture leaked from her sex. She circled her opening with the curved tip of the toy, then slowly slid it inside.

Her soft gasp joined Remy's agonized groan.

She stared at his strained face, the muscles pulled taut over his clenched jaw as he watched her push the dildo deeper inside her wet cunt.

With his wrists bound to the headboard, he couldn't reach down to stroke his raging erection to relieve some of the pressure. He could only watch and burn with frustration as Zandra began fucking herself with the rubber cock, moaning with pleasure.

"Damn you," he growled at her, his chest heaving as his breathing accelerated. "You're trying to kill me."

"Not at all. You'd be no good to me dead." She sat up, ripped away the skirt, spread her knees on the bed and began riding the dildo in earnest.

She thought Remy would go crazy.

"Zandra," he groaned, his hips surging off the bed. "Fuck. *Fuck.*"

"Don't call me that," she panted sharply. "I'm your queen, remember?"

"Yes…Your Highness."

"What's wrong?" she taunted wickedly. "Don't like watching me ride another cock? Hmm? It's nowhere *near* as big as yours, but—" she paused to moan as she shoved the dildo even deeper "—it feels *so* good."

Remy swore harshly, his eyes slamming shut.

"Open your eyes, slave," she commanded. "Watch what I'm doing."

When he did, the raw hunger in his gaze nearly undid her.

She rode the dildo faster, her breasts bouncing above the tight corset as her breathing escalated to match Remy's.

She couldn't take her eyes off his dick. It was impossibly hard, shooting straight into the air as if it were made of steel and not flesh and blood. A thick vein pulsed and throbbed as pearly precum erupted from the narrow slit and streamed down the sides like a bubbling volcano.

Her mouth watered, and her sex ached to be filled with him. It was all she could do not to yank out the dildo and impale herself on that monster erection of his.

She rocked her hips up and down, her pussy sucking hard on the fake phallus as fluid ran down her slit and between her buttocks.

She was on the verge of coming when Remy tugged at the leather restraints, his thick biceps bulging.

"Ah, ah, ah," she scolded breathlessly. "What did I tell you about trying to get free? You're my prisoner. I'll release you when I'm ready to release you."

His eyes flashed with savage displeasure, but he stopped moving.

"Good slave." She gave him a sultry smile. "Do you want this pussy?"

His nostrils flared. "You know I do."

"How bad do you want it?"

"Bad," he growled. "*So* fucking bad."

She smiled with satisfaction. "And you shall have it. Any way you want it."

Anticipation filled his eyes as she slowly eased the dildo out of her body. It was slick and coated with her creamy juices.

Holding Remy's gaze, she slid the rubber cock into her mouth and closed her eyes on a sultry moan of pleasure.

He made a strangled sound—half tortured groan, half violent expletive.

She laughed, deliberately licking the toy clean before reaching over to set it down on the table.

She turned back to Remy and pointed. "Slide down on the bed."

He obeyed at once, moving down so that his muscular arms were stretched over his head and he was propped slightly on the pillows.

As he watched, she climbed over him and straddled his face backward. "Eat my pussy."

The throaty command had barely been issued before he pressed his hot mouth to her drenched cunt. Her back arched, and she had to bite down hard on her lip to stop herself from crying out with ecstasy.

Her thighs shook as he nibbled at her clit, rubbing it with his lips and tongue. She shuddered deeply, reaching down to squeeze her swollen breasts through the corset as he licked and stroked the plump folds of her slit, his hot breath gusting over her slick flesh.

She tilted her ass and hips back against his face, pushing at his hungry mouth as he ate her pussy with slow, deep licks that went from her clit to her asshole. With every stroke of his tongue, her body reeled with pleasure and raw sensation. Though she tried not to moan, it felt so damn good she couldn't help herself, couldn't stop the tears that swam into her eyes. The man's oral prowess was a lethal weapon.

Seconds later she was climaxing, spasm after spasm slamming through her body and leaving her gasping. She felt the hot rush of her cum flowing out of her, shivered uncontrollably as Remy lapped it up with his tongue.

She closed her eyes and dropped her head, fighting to regain her composure before she could resume the game.

Gradually she collected herself and opened her heavy-lidded eyes.

"Very good, slave," she managed to say calmly. "I'll have to keep you around."

"Thank you, my queen." Remy's voice was so husky she heard the barely leashed control. And she knew why.

His engorged dick, glazed with precum, demanded her immediate attention.

She lowered her head, her mouth hovering tantalizingly over the rearing cock.

"Do you want me to suck you?" she purred wickedly.

A hard tremor ran through his body. "Fuck, yeah."

Her lips twitched. "Fuck, yeah, what?"

"Fuck, yeah, Your Highness."

She smiled. "It would be my pleasure."

She wrapped her fingers around the base of his cock, felt him jerk at her touch. He was so hard and engorged with blood she could feel every vein bulging out along the hot skin.

As she slowly pumped her hand up and down, he grew even thicker and harder, and precum dripped faster from the narrow slit to make her hand slick.

She leaned down and licked the glistening tip of his cock.

He groaned hoarsely, his head falling back against the pillows.

She ran her tongue down to the base and back up around the head. He shivered, his muscular thighs clenching. She closed her lips tight around the bulbous tip, then sucked her way down to his hairy groin, deep-throating him.

Remy shuddered and swore, loud and long.

Tossing her hair over one shoulder, Zandra began moving her head up and down as she sucked him. She used her tongue to trace the protruding veins, used her lips as a suction around his throbbing cockhead. She didn't neglect his engorged balls. She cupped and massaged them as her mouth milked his shaft, coating him with her saliva.

His feet twitched and his toes curled as he thrust his hips upward, driving his cock deeper inside her. His guttural sounds of pleasure excited and aroused her, made wetness leak from between her thighs.

"My queen…" he groaned in a voice so ragged with lust it sent chills through her. "Ah, *fuck*..."

As his breathing grew harsh and labored, Zandra knew he was going to explode at any moment. So she wasn't prepared when he suddenly lifted his head from the pillow and licked her soaking pussy.

She shattered at the same time that he violently ejaculated, shooting hot cream into her mouth and down the back of her throat.

She swallowed without choking, then slumped forward onto his muscular legs as he lay there gasping and shuddering. Neither could speak for several long moments.

When Zandra finally got her larynx to work again, she looked over her shoulder and demanded imperiously, "Who gave you permission to put your mouth on me again, slave?"

Remy chuckled, low and sexy. "It's called sixty-nine, Your Highness. Perhaps you have another term for it, but when two people are in this position, the general idea is to provide mutual oral pleasure."

Zandra smothered a laugh. “Don’t get smart.”

“My bad, Your Highness.”

“Yes, you are. You’re *very* bad. But I’ve decided to show you some mercy.” She climbed off him, turned around and unlocked the leather handcuffs, leaving them dangling from the headboard.

Suddenly freed from his restraints, Remy sat up and lunged toward her.

She put her hand to the wall of his chest, halting his advance. “Not so fast, slave. I’m still in command.”

His eyes glittered.

She shivered at the realization that she might as well have said “Stay” to a dangerous, bloodthirsty wolf.

She waited weakly for Remy to pounce.

But he surprised her.

“All right,” he smoothly acquiesced.

She smiled approvingly. “Good boy.”

“Can I kiss you?”

Her stomach quivered.

She bit her lip, then nodded her consent.

He leaned forward, slanting his mouth over hers. The kiss was slow and tender, such an achingly sweet counterpoint to the eroticism of their role-playing that tears stung her eyes. If she hadn’t already accepted that she loved him, she would have known in that moment.

Her lips clung to his as he slowly drew back.

They stared at each other.

Then he smiled that slow, sexy smile that always melted her insides.

“Get the nipple clamps from the bag,” she whispered.

His eyes twinkled. “Aye, my queen.”

As he moved to do as he’d been told, she admired his

firm, round butt. The man was the epitome of masculine perfection and beauty.

When he returned to her, she angled her back to him. "Undo my corset."

"With pleasure."

She held her hair out of the way as he unhooked the binding, his knuckles skimming the skin on her back as he worked quickly. When he was done, he tossed the corset aside and gripped her shoulders, turning her around on the bed.

His hands reached out and plumped her breasts, his thumbs circling her nipples until they were achingly hard.

He groaned with appreciation. "God, you have the prettiest tits, Zan— Your Highness," he caught himself.

"Thank you. Now put the clamps on me."

"Yes, ma'am."

She watched, pulse pounding erratically, as he carefully fastened the clamps onto her elongated nipples. She hissed, pain mingling with erotic pleasure.

"Are you okay?"

She nodded tightly.

He leaned down, licking her areolas to soothe the raw ache. Delicious shivers raced through her. As his lips suckled the plump swell of her breast, one then the other, she could feel the wetness of her slit, the hungry need pulsing in her clit.

She cupped his face between her hands, coaxing his gaze to hers. "I want you to fuck me from behind," she whispered.

A slow, wicked grin curved his mouth. "With pleasure."

"In the ass."

He went still, his eyes searching her face. "Are you sure?"

She lifted an imperious brow. "Are you questioning my command?"

"No, my queen," he said huskily. "I'll make love to you, any way you want me to."

Her heart skipped a thrilled beat.

Nipples throbbing from the clamps, she crawled to the table, reached inside the bag and retrieved the anal lubricant that she'd snuck into the cart yesterday when Remy wasn't looking.

He watched through heavy-lidded eyes as she poured some of the lubricant into her palms, then smoothed it over his rigid erection, making him shudder from the silky friction.

He climbed off the bed, then dragged her to the edge and set her booted feet on the floor. She spread her legs and bent forward, thrusting her ass high into the air. Remy murmured appreciatively and caressed the swell of her backside.

Glancing over her shoulder, Zandra watched as he licked his middle finger, then gently slipped it inside her hole, preparing her for his entry.

As he pushed a little deeper, she instinctively tensed.

He stopped.

"I'm kinda big," he murmured without a trace of conceit. "I don't wanna hurt you."

Her heart melted at his concern. "You won't."

"Are you sure?"

"Absolutely." She slowly gyrated against him. "Come on. Fuck me."

He used one hand to spread her ass cheeks. With the other he gripped his erection and guided the blunt head to her tight opening. She closed her eyes as he eased inside her, his thick cock stretching the tight anal muscles.

She bit her lip hard, letting herself relax to take more of his length.

"Am I hurting you?" His voice was rough.

She shook her head quickly. "Keep going," she half begged.

He moved deeper, his cock dragging against the sensitive tissue as he stretched her some more.

Suddenly he paused, gasping and shaking. "*Ahh*... you're so tight. You feel so...fucking good."

She moaned. "Don't stop. *Please* don't stop."

After another moment he began thrusting his hips, his cock slowly pumping in and out of her ass. When he reached between her thighs and rubbed her clit, she shuddered with pleasure, clenching fistfuls of the silk bedspread.

His strokes accelerated, his dick tunneling between her buttocks as he buried himself deeper inside her tight clasp.

She closed her eyes and bit her lip hard enough to draw blood.

She felt raw, wanton. Outrageously decadent.

Remy wrapped her hair around his hand, pulling her head back to growl silkily against her ear, "Am I pleasing you, Your Highness?"

"Um..."

He smacked her ass, and she cried out with pleasure. He whacked her again, harder, and this time she sobbed out, *"Yes!"*

He laughed, dark and triumphant.

She soon forgot about the role-playing, forgot about the eyes secretly watching them from the other side of the glass wall. She forgot about everything else and simply lost herself to the moment.

Lost herself to Remy.

She'd had anal sex before and had enjoyed it, but not like this. Never had it been this good. Pleasure flooded each and every nerve ending of her body. Her breasts bounced up and down as Remy fucked her deeply. With her nipples stinging from the clamps and his cock plundering her asshole, it was sensory overload.

Before long she was shaking, needing desperately to come.

And then he reached around and slid his finger into her wet pussy, filling both of her orifices.

That was all she could take.

*"Remy!"* she screamed as she climaxed, the orgasm seeming to erupt from every direction.

She felt his cock pump and jerk spasmodically. Then he shuddered, tensed and shouted her name as his hot semen burst into her, making her come even harder.

Afterward they gasped and panted together, his arm clasped tightly around her waist, clutching her to him. Her vision was blurred, and her ears were ringing from the rush of blood to her head.

"Your Highness is absolutely amazing," Remy whispered, his hot breath burning her ear.

Zandra smiled languidly. "I could say the same of you, slave."

*"Could?"*

"Mmm. Might."

She squealed as he scooped her up and dumped her onto the bed. Before she could scramble away, he swooped down on her and hauled her close so he could spoon her, their bodies sticking together with sweat.

Zandra sighed, thoroughly and deliciously sated. Belatedly remembering the nipple clamps, she reached down and unfastened them, then gently massaged her sore areolas with her fingertips.

Remy held her closer, kissing her along her ear and neck. "How long can we stay here?"

She smiled. "As long as we want."

"Mmm. That means we're staying all night then."

She laughed, turning in his arms to kiss him.

It was only then that she saw a man watching quietly from the open doorway of the chamber.

Their eyes met and held.

She glanced down at Remy. His lids were lowered as he lazily nuzzled her throat.

She lifted her gaze back to Heath.

His eyes were shining.

She blew him a kiss. A kiss farewell.

He smiled softly.

And then he was gone.

Long afterward Remy and Zandra lay quietly together. At some point he'd gotten up to remove her outrageously sexy boots so she could be more comfortable. Since then, neither of them had moved.

"I have to say," he murmured lazily, "this is the most… unusual place I've ever made love."

Zandra laughed softly. "More unusual than the ladies' room?"

He chuckled. "Oh, most definitely."

"I think I have to agree."

Remy smiled, stroking her hair. "When did you plan all this? And how?"

"That's for me to know," she said slyly, "and you never to find out."

"Why not?"

"Because you don't need to know details. It'd spoil the illusion."

"Believe me, *nothing* could spoil this."

"Doesn't matter. I'm not telling you."

He grinned. "Fine. Keep your secrets then."

"I will. After all," she murmured whimsically, "what's a woman without her secrets?"

"Hmm." Remy kissed her bare shoulder. "You're an amazing woman, Zandra Kennedy."

She sighed. "I know."

Remy reached down and smacked her on the ass.

She laughed, wriggling away from him.

He pulled her right back, burying his face in her soft hair. "I must say, Z, you'd make one *badass* queen."

She giggled. "You think so?"

"Hell, yeah. I'd do whatever you told me to."

"You should do that anyway," she quipped.

"What? *What?*"

She squealed protestingly as he rolled her over to face him, pinning her beneath his body. She stared up at him, her dark eyes glimmering with laughter.

"See," he murmured, gently brushing her hair back from her face, "I told you I could be submissive."

She snorted. "Barely."

"What's that supposed to mean?"

"Oh, come on, Remy. You know it was killing you to lay there and let me be in charge."

"That's not true," he objected.

She gave him a look.

He grinned sheepishly. "Okay, maybe a little. But only because you make me so damn hot for you. I just want to devour you every time."

"Mmm," she purred, curving her arms around his neck. "The feeling's definitely mutual."

Remy lowered his head, brushing his lips across hers. Her warm breath fanned across his face as he kissed her, sliding his tongue into her mouth. He licked the insides of her cheeks, making her moan softly with pleasure. As she twined her tongue around his, blood rushed into his dick, hardening him at once.

Zandra smiled against his mouth. "Looks like *someone's* ready for the next round."

"Hmm." Remy licked the seam of her lips. "I think that's a safe assumption."

"Good. Because I'm ready to go for a ride."

With that, Zandra pushed Remy onto his back and straddled him, her juices bathing his shaft as she ground slowly against him.

He groaned, his eyes glazed with desire as he stared up at her. She was so damn beautiful, he could have come just from looking at her.

Holding his gaze, she provocatively raised her hips above his jutting erection, then lowered herself and cried out as his cock sank deep into her wetness.

His hands went around her waist, but he didn't begin thrusting into her. He'd let her set the pace. Let her ride him with that hot, beautiful pussy of hers.

"Ohh," she moaned, exulting in the feel of him embedded deep inside her.

His mind was blown by the sight of her, head arched back, eyes closed, voluptuous breasts thrust forward. She looked like a work of art. Powerfully feminine, fiercely erotic.

She began to move on him, her pussy clenching around his shaft, gripping him in that way only she could do.

Heart knocking against his ribs, he watched her face as she fucked him slowly and tantalizingly. He memorized the flutter of her black lashes, the delicate flaring of her nostrils, the flush that heated her cheeks, the way she bit her luscious lip in ecstasy.

He savored every sigh of hers, every gasp, every moan, every whimper of his name.

And with every grinding motion of her glorious hips, she drove him closer to orgasm. Closer to paradise.

He ran his hands up and down the silky curve of her back as she rode him. He met each of her thrusts, gave them back to her. As the pressure mounted, his cock pulsed and swelled.

And then he was coming, exploding inside her at the same time that she went liquid around him, her inner muscles contracting.

They came together, long and hard, for what seemed like hours.

It was breathtakingly intense. A spiritual bonding.

When it was over she fell forward onto his chest, gasping and shivering.

He cupped the back of her head and kissed her, unleashing years of pent-up emotion and longing upon her mouth. He kissed her until she was breathless and trembling, until she had to draw back and gasp for air.

Framing her face between his hands, he gazed deep into her eyes and whispered fiercely, "I love you."

Her eyes softened with tears. "I love you, too, Remy."

He stared up at her, afraid to believe he'd heard wrong.

So she repeated herself. "I love you."

His heart soared.

"Zandra," he said, his voice husky with emotion, "you

have no idea how long I've dreamed of hearing you say that."

Surprise flickered in her eyes. "Really?"

"Really." He swallowed tightly. "I've been in love with you for…a long time."

She gazed wonderingly at him. "How long?"

"Very long."

A smile quivered on her lips. "That's…funny."

"Why?"

"Because I think I've been in love with you for a pretty long time myself."

"Really?" he whispered.

She nodded slowly. "Really."

They stared at each other.

Then Remy groaned and crushed his mouth to hers, and this time she kissed him back just as hard, just as desperately. As he rolled her onto her back, she wrapped her arms around his neck and clung to him like she never wanted—or planned—to let go.

Remy vowed right then and there to tell her the truth about his secret investigation. As soon as they returned home, he'd come clean with her.

And then he'd do everything in his damn power to convince her to spend the rest of her life with him.

## *Chapter Twenty*

If Zandra had had an inkling of the powder keg that awaited her back in Chicago, she would have insisted on remaining in London.

She should have insisted anyway. She and Remy had been having such a wonderful time together, she hadn't wanted to come home.

On the day they returned, they still couldn't get enough of each other. Remy drove Zandra home from the airport and carried her luggage inside, then wound up spending the night. They'd made love into the wee hours of the next morning and slept in late, spooned like perfect halves.

When Remy left around noon, promising to return that evening for dinner, Zandra took a hot shower and put on a halter top and jeans. She'd considered going into the office for a few hours, then changed her mind. She'd left the agency in Christine's capable hands, so there was no need for her to rush back.

Grabbing her iPad so that she could catch up on emails, Zandra made her way to the living room and turned on the television. She surfed disinterestedly through channels before settling on the noon news.

She'd just opened her email app when the newscaster announced, "In breaking developments this afternoon, just one week after announcing his bid for mayor, City Alderman Landis Kennedy has already run into a buzz saw that has his campaign in full damage control mode."

Zandra's head snapped up as the anchor continued speaking. "Kennedy's political troubles began when sources revealed that his daughter, Zandra Kennedy, is the owner of a local escort agency named Elite For You Companions. Miss Kennedy, who's been in business for five years, is considered something of a power broker on Chicago's arts scene, sought by many for her fundraising prowess."

Zandra froze, watching as photos of her at various functions flashed across the television screen.

"But raising money for charitable causes might not be Miss Kennedy's *only* passion," the news anchor continued with amused glee. "At a recent museum gala, Kennedy was spotted leaving a restroom with a man identified as powerful CEO Remington Brand."

The blood drained from Zandra's head as a picture of her and Remy filled the screen. Remy was adjusting his tie while Zandra glanced furtively around, making sure the coast was clear. Her flushed face and Remy's satisfied grin left no doubt what they'd just been doing.

"Oh, my God," Zandra whispered, her cheeks burning with humiliation at the thought of some photographer skulking in the shadows, waiting to snap the perfect scandal shot of her and Remy.

"If hooking up for tawdry trysts in public bathrooms is Miss Kennedy's idea of a good time," the snarky anchor intimated, "one can only imagine how her escorts entertain clients."

Another wave of hot shame swept over Zandra. Forking shaky fingers through her hair, she could only watch in a daze of unreality as her world was turned upside down.

When her cell phone rang, she grabbed the remote control and punched off the television. Her nerves instinctively tightened when she saw that the caller was Christine. Everything had been fine when she'd checked in with her receptionist yesterday, but she had a feeling that was about to drastically change.

"Sorry to be the bearer of bad news so soon after you've gotten home," Christine began anxiously, "but I just thought you should know that within the past hour, three clients have called and canceled dates with escorts."

"Shit." Lunging from the sofa, Zandra began pacing up and down the floor. "Did they say why?"

"No. They just said something else came up." Christine sounded distraught. "What's going on, Zandra? Are we being investigated?"

Johanna Kennedy's warning echoed tauntingly through Zandra's mind. *One day you're the toast of the town. The next day you're a pariah.*

Shaking off the thought, Zandra gritted her teeth. "I think one of my father's campaign rivals went to the media about me and the agency. I just turned on the news, and they're doing a hit piece."

"Oh, no," Christine groaned in dismay. "Just what we need."

"Tell me about it." Zandra's mind was racing. First and foremost, she needed to protect her escorts. "Listen, Chris. Reporters are probably en route to the office as we speak. I want you to send out a text and email to everyone to tell them to stay away from the office. And then I want you to transfer the phone lines to your private extension, lock up the building and go home."

"In the middle of the week?"

"Yes," Zandra said grimly. "Once the press hounds arrive, you probably won't be able to get much work done anyway."

Suddenly her apartment intercom buzzed, signaling that she had a visitor downstairs.

"I have to go, Chris. Call me when you get home."

She ended the call, then walked to the front door and nervously pressed the intercom button. "Yes?"

There was a heavy pause. "It's your father."

Her blood ran cold. He was the last person on earth she wanted to see right now.

"What do you want?"

"We need to talk," he said curtly.

"I have nothing to say to you."

"But you might be interested in hearing what *I* have to say."

Zandra frowned, staring at the intercom panel.

After several moments, he said levelly, "It's important, Zandra."

She closed her eyes and swallowed hard, then reluctantly pushed the button. "Come up."

Remy had just strolled through the door of his downtown apartment when his cell phone rang. Setting down his suitcase—he'd only needed one, unlike Zandra—he dug the phone out of his pocket and saw Duke's number.

He hit the answer button. "Talk to me."

"You owe me big-time," Duke growled.

"Why? What happened on your date?"

"It's what *didn't* happen that's got me fucked up."

Remy couldn't help chuckling wryly as he walked to the windows overlooking Lake Michigan. "You're talking in riddles, Gannon. Give me the shit straight."

Duke heaved a short, ragged breath. "The date was last night. The escort was some hot little brunette named Brigitte."

"Brigitte?" Remy frowned, not recognizing the name. Zandra must have forgotten to tell him that she'd finally hired Lena's replacement, after months of interviewing candidates and finding fault with every last one.

"Yeah, Brigitte," Duke muttered. "French spelling."

"Gotcha. So what happened?"

"I'll tell you what happened. I came on to her to see if she'd take the bait. Oh, she took it all right. Had me damn near begging for mercy by the time she got done with me."

Remy pushed out a heavy breath, disappointment washing over him. "Fuck."

"Yeah. That's *exactly* what I wanted to do. Like you wouldn't believe."

"But you didn't, right?"

"No," Duke said with grim humor. "I was a good little boy and kept my dick in my pants. And it's been punishing me ever since."

Remy's lips twitched with amusement, even as his stomach knotted at the implications of Duke's report. It only took one wayward escort to bring down Zandra and her agency. He had to warn her. And he had to come clean about what he'd been doing. He owed her the truth, and the guilt was eating him alive.

"Anyway," Duke grumbled, "I don't think I'm the right man for this job."

"Maybe not," Remy said wryly. "Or maybe it's just this one broad who pushed your buttons."

Duke snorted. "Is that supposed to make me feel better? If so, it sure as hell didn't."

Remy chuckled, perpetually amused by Duke's irascible temperament. "You can stand down, soldier. I'm putting this job on hold until further notice."

"Good. Glad to hear it. Now if it's all the same to you, Chief, I'm off to take another cold shower."

Remy chuckled. "Don't hurt yourself."

Duke muttered a dark expletive before hanging up.

Remy grinned, shoving his phone back into his pocket.

But as he stood there contemplating the shimmering blue vastness of Lake Michigan, his amusement quickly faded. He knew what he had to do, but he dreaded the hell out of it. He didn't want to hurt Zandra, especially after the amazing week they'd just spent together. She'd told him that she loved him, sending his heart into the damn stratosphere. Now that they'd reached this incredible new level in their relationship, he could never go back to being just friends with her.

Once she learned that he'd been secretly investigating her agency, he hoped and prayed that she'd understand his reasons and forgive him.

Because the alternative—living without her—was absolutely unthinkable.

Zandra didn't offer her father a drink or invite him to sit down. She barely wanted to let him through the door. Of course, once he was inside, he helped himself to a chair.

She watched as he looked around the living room, his gaze landing on her mother's paintings. Lightly at first, then returning to linger on each one. As he stared, something like pain and regret flickered in his eyes.

He'd hated being married to an artist. He'd hated having to share Autumn with her gift, resented the hours she'd spent painting instead of catering to him. He'd hated that no matter how viciously he ridiculed and brutalized her, she'd always found solace and healing through her painting. Even when he flew into a rage and maliciously destroyed her work, he couldn't destroy the beautiful imagination that would fuel the next piece. Autumn's gift was the only part of her he couldn't conquer, and he'd always known it.

After her funeral, he'd gathered all her paintings and dumped them on the front porch, then called Zandra and told her to come pick them up. It was one of the few kindnesses he'd ever shown her.

She watched now as he swallowed visibly, then dragged his gaze from the familiar artwork to look at her. His eyes were unfocused and haunted, and for a moment she couldn't tell whether he was seeing her, or her mother.

She waited for him to remember. Waited for the hatred and anger to slide back into place.

It didn't take long.

"Well," he said bitterly, "I hope you're happy."

Zandra didn't sit down. She didn't want to pretend that he was an invited guest, that this was a normal visit between a father and daughter.

She folded her arms across her chest, a defensive posture. "What the hell are you talking about?"

"Haven't you been watching the news? The very thing I tried to warn you about is happening!"

Zandra's lips twisted scornfully. "Am I supposed to care that your political campaign is in trouble? Cry me a damn river."

His face reddened with anger. "You conniving little bitch. This is exactly what you wanted to happen."

Zandra snorted. "Oh, yeah," she mocked. "I *really* wanted to have my name and photo splashed across the news so that complete strangers can be titillated by the details of my personal life."

"And whose fault is that?" Landis spat, raking her with a look of scathing contempt. "Running a prostitution ring. Screwing men in public restrooms. You're a whore. Just like your mother."

Zandra's temper exploded. "*You bastard!* Stop calling her a whore! Despite the abominable way you treated her, she was *never* unfaithful to you! It's not her fault you were too paranoid and insecure to handle being married to a beautiful woman. It's not her fault that she couldn't even make eye contact with another man without sending you into a jealous rage!"

Landis lunged to his feet and charged toward Zandra. Though her knees trembled, she stood her ground, chin raised defiantly.

He stopped just before her, jabbing his finger into her face. "You'd better mind your tongue, little girl."

"Or what?" Zandra challenged. "You gonna beat me like you did that night just because I screamed at you to stop hitting my mother? You gonna take off your belt now and whip me senseless just because I told you to stop smearing her memory with that ugly word?"

He glared at her, nostrils flaring.

Zandra didn't back down.

And then suddenly he smiled. A slow, malevolent smile that made ice congeal in her veins. "You're really feeling yourself today, aren't you? I wonder how you're going to feel when I tell you that Mayor Norwood is the one who leaked the story about you to the media."

Zandra frowned. "Why the hell should that matter to me?"

"Oh, I don't know. Maybe because your old friend Remington has been digging up dirt on you on behalf of the mayor."

Zandra's stomach lurched up into her throat. As the room spun around her, she stared at her father. "What the hell are you talking about?" she whispered faintly.

"Remington has been investigating your escort agency so the mayor can use it against me."

Zandra's hand flew to her mouth, but the cry of wounded disbelief had already escaped.

Landis smiled with vicious satisfaction. "That's right, dear daughter. Your precious childhood hero has been betraying you behind your back."

"I don't believe you," Zandra snarled.

Landis sneered. "Ask him. Ask him why he's been secretly meeting with Norwood's top campaign advisor."

It wasn't possible, Zandra told herself. Remy would never betray her like this. He couldn't.

But she suddenly remembered the secret phone call he'd taken that night at her apartment. And she'd never been able to explain his sudden interest in dating her escorts.

Still, she resisted the damning evidence before her. Resisted the inner voice that reminded her she couldn't trust her heart with any man.

She resisted all those things and lashed out at her father, "You're a damn liar."

His expression hardened. "You always think I'm lying to you."

"Because you always have."

He glared accusingly at her. "I know you still blame me for your mother's death. You suspected me of the worst from the moment I called to tell you the news. I still remember the way you carried on when you came home from England. Asking me all those questions about where I found her body, interrogating me like I was a fucking murder suspect. Hell, if that spiteful woman had left a goddamn suicide note, you would have sworn I'd forged it!"

"She did."

It took a delayed moment for her quiet words to register. When they did, Landis went completely still, his eyes narrowing on her face. "What did you say?"

Zandra calmly met his gaze. "My mother *did* leave a note. I received it after her funeral."

It gave her some satisfaction to watch the blood leach out of her father's face.

He shook his head in stunned denial. "You're lying."

"I assure you I'm not."

"She wouldn't have done that. She wouldn't have left me without saying goodbye."

Zandra sneered, driven to hurt him as much as he'd hurt her. "If she'd wanted to say goodbye, she would have left the note for you instead of me. But why would she have done that when *you're* the one she was trying to esc—"

Landis's hand shot out, delivering a vicious backhand.

Pain exploded across Zandra's cheek and down her jaw.

Refusing to cry out or show any weakness, she straightened slowly and looked him square in the eye. "Get out."

Shaken, he stared at her. "Look what you made me do."

Zandra laughed caustically. "After all these years, you're still blaming others for your cruelty. What a pathetic excuse for a man you are." She pointed to the door. "Get the hell out of my sight before I call security."

He wavered another moment, then turned and stormed out of the apartment, slamming the door behind him.

It was only then that Zandra lowered herself into the nearest chair and slowly brought her hand to her stinging cheek. It hurt, but the pain radiating through her heart had nothing to do with any blow she could ever receive from her father.

Half an hour later, she was on her way out the door when Remy showed up.

She was wearing wide-lens sunglasses, so he couldn't see the swelling flesh around her upper cheek.

"Hey." He smiled, backing her into the apartment. "Looks like I caught you just in time."

She frowned. "I'm really gonna have to talk to the concierge about letting you up without my permission."

Remy's smile faltered. "What's wrong?"

"You obviously haven't been watching the news," Zandra snapped.

"I haven't. After I got home, I took a shower and had

some phone calls to return." He searched her taut face. "Why? What's going on?"

She took a deep breath that burned, then blurted out, "Have you been investigating my escort agency?"

He was taken aback. "Who told you that?"

"Don't worry about it. Just answer the damn question."

His guilty expression spoke volumes before he answered quietly, "Yes."

The floor tilted beneath Zandra's feet. She'd wanted him to deny it. Had fervently prayed that he *would* deny it.

Reeling with shock and confusion, she stared at him. "How…how could you?"

Remy looked as if he were in acute pain. "It's not what you think."

"Then what is it, Remington?" she demanded furiously. "Help me understand how you could go behind my back to investigate my agency."

He swallowed hard. "Can we just sit down and—"

*"You son of a bitch!"* she exploded, ripping off her sunglasses. "How could you do this to me? I trusted you!"

Remy froze, staring at her in shocked horror.

Too late, she remembered her injured cheek.

"What happened to you?" Remy whispered.

Zandra didn't respond.

As he reached out to touch her face, she jerked her head back and demanded, "Don't."

The savage fury that hardened his eyes chilled her to the bone. "Goddamn it, Zandra," he growled. "Who hit you?"

She scowled. "Don't change the sub—"

"Who. Hit. You?"

She hesitated, alarmed by the lethal menace in his voice. “It was my father.”

Remy’s face contorted with rage.

Zandra gulped hard. “Look—”

Without another word, Remy pivoted sharply on his heel and stalked off.

## *Chapter Twenty-One*

"Where's Kennedy?" Remy snarled, barging his way past the startled butler who opened the door to him.

"Is Mr. Kennedy expecting you?"

Ignoring the snooty old man, Remy strode through the cavernous foyer of the sprawling mansion, his boots crashing against the polished hardwood floor. As his thunderous gaze swung toward the sweeping staircase, the butler started forward indignantly.

"Sir, Mr. Kennedy is not avail—"

Hearing the sound of voices raised in argument, Remy took off down the arched hall, following the commotion to the open doorway of a huge, wood-paneled library.

Landis Kennedy stood by the fireplace shouting and waving a leather-bound book at a visibly distressed servant.

The butler came up behind Remy. "Sir, I must ask you to leave this moment."

Kennedy and the red-faced servant whipped their heads toward the door. When Kennedy saw Remy standing there, his eyes bulged in shock.

"What the hell are you—"

Remy shot a hard glance at the servant. "Leave."

The woman took one look at his ominous expression and scurried across the room. She gave him a wide berth as she went out the door and closed it behind her, taking the sputtering butler with her.

As Remy looked at Zandra's father, a crimson haze settled over his vision. He cracked his knuckles, his lips curling back over his teeth in a snarl.

Kennedy eyed him nervously. "Now just hold on, Remington—"

As Remy lunged forward, Kennedy's eyes flew wide with panic. He dropped the book and turned to run toward the terrace doors, but Remy was already upon him.

The first blow he landed struck Kennedy's left cheek and snapped his head back. Before the man could draw breath to cry out, Remy punched him again, smashing his fist deeper into skin and bone.

Kennedy screamed and doubled over, clutching his broken nose.

Remy could have snapped his sorry neck and been done with it. But he was too enraged to offer swift mercy. He wanted Kennedy to suffer, wanted him to feel the pain of every punishing blow Remy delivered.

So he hit him with two more uppercuts that dropped Kennedy to his knees, gurgling in agony. And then he swung a roundhouse kick into the man's stomach, driving him backward.

As Kennedy toppled to the wood floor and lay there groaning, Remy crouched over his prone body and whipped out his KA-BAR knife. The steel blade caught the light as his hand slashed down, bringing the razor-sharp edge to Kennedy's throat.

"Oh, God. *Oh, Jesus.*" Kennedy stared up at him, his eyes so wide with terror that Remy could see the whites around his pupils. Blood gushed from his nose and a gash in his cheek, and his lips quivered piteously.

"Please," he whimpered. "Please don't kill me."

Remy pressed the deadly blade into the man's flesh, drawing a thin ridge of blood. With one flick of his wrist he could sever Kennedy's carotid artery and end his miserable life.

Tears spilled from the man's eyes as blood soaked into the collar of his white shirt. "P-please d-don't do this, Remington," he stammered pleadingly. "Y-you know th-this isn't wh-what she'd want."

Remy stared down at him, violence pumping hot and thick through his veins.

Relief flickered in Kennedy's eyes as Remy slowly removed the knife from his throat. He brought it to his mouth, closing his eyes as he licked the stained blade.

"I've been craving your blood all my life, old man. It tastes even better than I always imagined."

Opening his eyes, he stared into Kennedy's horror-stricken face.

A small, feral smile curved Remy's mouth.

Slowly, deliberately, he ran the tip of the blade from Kennedy's throat down to his rib cage, stopping at his pounding heart.

When a pungent odor filled his nostrils, he glanced down and saw a dark stain spreading across the front of Kennedy's pants. The fucking coward had pissed on himself.

Remy smiled narrowly, looking into the man's eyes. Shame had now joined the fear.

"Give me one damn reason I shouldn't gut you right now, you pathetic son of a bitch."

Kennedy whimpered. "I—I didn't mean to hit her. Sh-she provoked me."

"Wrong answer!"

"Please don't do this, son—"

"I'm not your damn son! And you'd better be glad I'm not, 'cause I'd have killed you after the *first* time you put a hand on my mother."

Kennedy gulped audibly. "Be reasonable, Remington. You're trespassing on my property. The police are probably on their way right now. You wouldn't get away with killing me."

"You'd be amazed what I can get away with," Remy snarled, slicing the blade of his knife through two of Kennedy's shirt buttons. When the man whimpered, Remy sneered contemptuously. "You sniveling little piece of shit. You like pounding on helpless women? You like taking out your frustrations on people who can't fight back? That shit ends today, you hear me? Today is the last fucking day you will *ever* terrorize—"

"Remy" came a quiet voice from across the room.

He tensed, then glanced over his shoulder to see Zandra and her stepmother hovering in the doorway.

Johanna Kennedy looked stunned and horrified, while Zandra's expression was indiscernible behind the sunglasses she wore.

"Let him go, Remy," she said softly. "Please."

He clenched his jaw, turning back to Kennedy. The man had the relieved look of a condemned prisoner who'd narrowly escaped a one-way ticket to the execution chamber.

*Not so fucking fast.*

Viciously grabbing the man's chin with one hand, Remy commanded, "Take a good look at your daughter."

Kennedy obediently looked across the room at Zandra.

"Every time you think of her from now on," Remy snarled, "I want you to remember her as the angel of mercy who saved your sorry hide today. But understand this. If you ever come anywhere near her again, if you even *think* about contacting her, I will take great pleasure in disemboweling you. That's not an empty threat, motherfucker. That's a promise."

A fresh wave of terror swam into Kennedy's eyes.

"Now say thank you to your daughter."

The man gulped hard and looked at Zandra. "Th-thank you."

She smiled contemptuously. "I didn't do it for you. I did it for Remy. Because as despicable as you are, you're not worth him losing a piece of his soul for ending your miserable life." She looked at Remy, and though he couldn't see her eyes, he knew they were full of the same tender compassion that had unraveled him that night in London.

He swallowed tightly, then sheathed his knife and stretched to his feet. Skewering his urine-soaked nemesis with one last lethal glare, Remy pivoted and strode from the room.

As he neared the doorway, Johanna stared up at him with a mixture of fear and fascination.

He spared her a curt nod before turning his attention to Zandra.

Without a word, she took his hand and led him down the hall, past the whispering servants and out the front door.

Her driver stood by the Phantom, which was parked in the circular brick driveway behind Remy's black Escalade. The man nodded a greeting to Remy, who nodded back.

In silence he and Zandra started down the front steps. As soon as they reached the bottom, she released his hand and stepped back.

Dread tightened his throat. "Zandra—"

"Thank you for coming to my defense like that," she said in a low voice. "You didn't have to, but I appreciate it."

He shook his head at her. "You don't have to thank me. You know I'd do anything for you."

She smiled bitterly. "Except be truthful with me, right?"

Remy flinched, the salvo hitting him square in the chest. "I didn't mean to hurt you, baby. I was just trying to protect you—"

"By going behind my back to investigate my agency?"

"I had my reasons for doing that, if you'd just let me explain—"

She held up a hand. "This isn't the time or place."

"Then I'll follow you back to your apartment and we can talk there."

"I don't think so," Zandra said tightly. "I'm not ready to hear whatever you have to say. Honestly, I don't even know that it would make any difference. You betrayed my trust, Remy. As far as I'm concerned, there's never a good reason for doing that to someone you claim to love."

Her words couldn't have hurt him more if she'd taken a serrated knife to his heart. He stared miserably at her, wanting to touch her. To stroke her face, feather his fingers over her cheek and soothe her bruised skin. But he knew she'd reject his touch, and he couldn't handle that.

Still, he had to get through to her.

"I wasn't conspiring with the mayor. You may not remember this," he rushed on as Zandra opened her mouth to interrupt him, "but Norwood's senior advisor is my former CO. Keegan came to me a few weeks ago and warned me that the mayor was planning to investigate your agency so he'd have ammunition to use against your father. Keegan wanted to hire me for the job so I'd be able to warn you if there was any trouble." Remy paused, his expression turning grim. "You need to know that one of your escorts failed the test."

Zandra visibly tensed. "Who?"

"Brigitte."

"Brigitte?" she repeated blankly.

"Yeah. Is she new?"

"No. I don't have a—" Suddenly the confusion cleared from Zandra's face, and she heaved an exasperated breath. "That wasn't one of my escorts. That was Skylar."

Remy frowned. "Your *friend* Skylar?"

"Yes. She was impersonating one of my girls. Long story," she added with an impatient wave of her hand. "The point is, your mole—"

Remy winced at the biting accusation in her voice.

"—didn't expose anything more than the fact that Skylar has a weakness for hot guys." She smirked. "It's a flaw we both possess, unfortunately."

Guilt assailed Remy. "Zandra—"

She pushed her sunglasses up on her nose, reinforcing the barrier between them. "We'd better leave before my father or Johanna call the police."

Remy scowled. “Let them. I don’t give a fuck.”

“I do.” Her lips twisted cynically. “God knows I have enough damage control to tackle without adding an arrest to my troubles.”

Remy felt another stab of guilt. “Zandra—”

“Go home, Remington. There’s nothing left to say.” With that, she turned and walked to her waiting car. When Norman opened the back door for her, she hesitated.

Remy held his breath.

After another moment, she lowered herself into the backseat, dashing his hopes.

“Damn it.” Clenching his jaw, he started determinedly toward the vehicle. He couldn’t just let her leave like this. “Zandra, wait, damn it—”

Norman closed the door, then stood there protectively as if to say, *If you wanna get to her, you’re gonna have to go through me.*

Remy held the older man’s stern gaze for a tense moment, then scowled and backed down. He couldn’t very well fault the man for doing his job, especially when Remy was the one who’d interviewed and hired him in the first place.

“Take care of her, Norman,” he growled.

“Yes, sir. You know I always do.”

After the Phantom pulled off, Remy climbed into his truck, slammed the door and roared away from the mansion, determined to get some answers from Keegan.

Robyn, Racquel, Lena, Morgan and Skylar converged upon Zandra’s penthouse that evening. They surrounded her with their arms wrapped around her waist, their eyes full of gentle concern and righteous anger as they fussed over her bruised cheek and hissed scathing invectives at her father.

Since Cora was on vacation, Robyn bustled into the kitchen and whipped up a chicken casserole that soon had the whole apartment smelling like heaven. Under normal circumstances Zandra would have been the first in line to get a helping, but tonight her voracious appetite was nowhere to be found. She had to be prodded and bullied into eating the modest portion that Robyn served her, then she'd curled up on the sofa with her legs pulled up to her chest. Someone draped a warm blanket over her at some point, and a glass of red wine on the table beckoned her to sip and soothe her frayed nerves.

Though no one turned on the television, the conversation centered around the story that had headlined the day's local news broadcasts. The women were so outraged at the injustice Zandra had suffered, she wouldn't have been surprised if they simultaneously broke into a chorus of Helen Reddy's rallying anthem "I Am Woman."

Throughout the spirited discussion, they cast worried glances at Zandra as she sat with her head leaning back against the sofa, staring vacantly at the ceiling. They weren't used to seeing her like this. They were used to her being a tough, feisty fighter—the first to smear on the war paint and charge into battle.

But Zandra didn't have much fight in her tonight. She felt like she'd been ambushed, because she'd never seen Remy's betrayal coming.

He knew better than anyone how much her escort agency meant to her. When she'd decided to open Elite For You Companions, he was the first person she'd told, and over the years he'd been her sounding board when things didn't always go smoothly. Yet none of that had mattered to him when he'd decided to conduct his secret investigation.

And that, more than being publicly humiliated or losing clients, was what devastated Zandra the most.

"Honey, do you want to go lie down in your room?" Skylar asked, gently touching Zandra's knee.

She shook her head, trying to smile. "I'm fine."

Lena frowned sympathetically. "Sweetie, we can all see that you're *not* fine."

Zandra made no reply. She hadn't told them about Remy's role in this whole nightmare. The pain of his betrayal was too raw, and she didn't feel comfortable bashing him around his sisters.

Especially when Robyn curved an arm around her and gently guided Zandra's head down to her warm shoulder. "Everything's gonna be all right," she murmured soothingly, comforting Zandra as she'd done in those dark, disorienting days following her mother's death. "You'll get through this, too."

Zandra wished she could share Robyn's optimism. But the truth was that even if her agency came through the scandal unscathed, her relationship with Remy would never be the same again.

Racquel glanced around at everyone and frowned. "We need to do damage control. Where should we start?"

Skylar's lips tightened with anger. "I know where *I'd* like to start. By digging up some dirt on that smart-ass news anchor at Channel Five. She seemed to take just a *little* too much satisfaction in repeatedly flashing that picture of Zandra and Remy."

Zandra grimaced as the others grumbled in agreement.

"She's just doing the mayor's bidding," Morgan said with grim pragmatism. "He's obviously the one who leaked the story to the press. He has the most incentive to eliminate his strongest competitors as quickly as possible. If that means going after his rival's daughter, so be it. That's what politicians call collateral damage."

"Bastard," Skylar hissed furiously. "All of them."

"They *can* be pretty despicable," Robyn agreed, gently stroking Zandra's hair.

"You won't get any argument from me," Morgan asserted. "But like it or not, ladies, that's how the game is played. When Zandra's father held his press conference to announce his candidacy, he portrayed himself as an upstanding city council member, a pillar of the community, a family man—"

Several rude snorts peppered the room.

"—and a devout Christian. He all but declared himself on par with the Pope. Going after Zandra's escort agency and sullying her reputation is the perfect way to attack her father's character and integrity, even his parenting skills."

"Of which he has none," Zandra muttered caustically.

This elicited angry murmurs of agreement.

Morgan grimaced at Zandra. "Unfortunately, your father and his people are probably gearing up right now to throw you under the bus."

Zandra smiled bitterly. "It wouldn't surprise me."

Racquel scowled. "That's really fucked up. Hasn't he done enough to her?"

"You would think," Robyn said with withering scorn.

Lena frowned at Morgan. "So what you're saying is that Zandra could be fending off attacks from the mayor *and* her father?"

Morgan nodded grimly. "I'm afraid so."

Robyn and Racquel sucked their teeth in disgust.

"If those sons of bitches want a war," Skylar snarled, her eyes glinting fiercely, "I say we give them one."

As the others got fired up, Zandra could feel her fighting spirit clawing back to the surface. After her mother died, she'd sworn never to be a victim to any man, for any reason. Wallowing in self-pity and despair was a surefire way to remain trampled upon.

"In order for Zandra to get ahead of this story," Morgan said decisively, "she has to seize control of the media narrative."

Lifting her head from Robyn's shoulder, Zandra met Morgan's gaze. "All right, Miss PR Guru. You've got my attention. Just how do I go about seizing control of the media narrative?"

Morgan's expression softened, her eyes touching on Zandra's bruised cheek. "By finally breaking your silence and telling the world the truth."

## *Chapter Twenty-Two*

Three days later, Zandra stared out over a sea of reporters who'd gathered for her scheduled press conference. The bright glare of their cameras made her grateful for the dark sunglasses that concealed her eyes.

As she surveyed the large crowd, nervous apprehension fluttered deep in her stomach. There were local reporters, as well as reporters from national cable networks. Morgan had rightly predicted that this story would generate national interest. It was a slow summer news cycle, and something about Chicago politics had always captured the public's imagination.

But not everyone assembled was a member of the press. Zandra's courage was bolstered by the presence of supporters that included Skylar, Lena and the Brands, who'd always been there for her.

And then there was Remy.

When their eyes met, Zandra's heart twisted painfully.

She hadn't spoken to him since she'd left him standing outside her father's house. He'd called her, but she hadn't answered the phone. He'd emailed her, but she hadn't opened the message.

Looking into his dark eyes, she could see that he was as miserable and heartbroken as she was. But now was not the time to dwell on regret, to mourn what could have been.

Dragging her gaze from his, Zandra watched as Morgan—her newly hired publicist—strode confidently to the podium and read the opening statement she and Zandra had prepared.

After she finished speaking, all eyes were on Zandra.

Taking a deep breath, she looked out into the audience. "Thank you all for coming. The first thing I'd like to do is acknowledge the nine individuals sharing the stage with me this morning." She looked up and down the table, meeting the eyes of each escort flanking her on both sides. "I'm damn proud of these women. Before today, many of them hadn't told their families, friends or colleagues that they moonlight as professional escorts. It took strength, courage and conviction for them to come forward today to stand with me. I'm tremendously grateful for their support, and I'm honored to not only call them friends, but sisters."

Touched by her heartfelt words, the women smiled endearingly and blew kisses at her. Claudia, seated beside Zandra, squeezed her hand and mouthed encouragingly, *Give 'em hell.*

Shoulders squared, jaw set with steely determination, Zandra turned her head to address the crowd. "I'd like to start off by addressing the growing allegations that my escort agency, Elite For You Companions, is a brothel.

It's not. Let me repeat that for anyone who might not have heard me the first time. I'm not running a prostitution ring. My escorts are paid to provide companionship to clients, not sex. If Mayor Norwood would like to verify that claim, he doesn't have to resort to hiring private investigators. If his wife doesn't object, he's more than welcome to set up dates with any of the women up here. Although," Zandra added dryly, "after the way he's behaved, he might not get a very warm reception."

Laughter swept through the audience.

"Miss Kennedy," challenged one local reporter, "I think it's admirable that you speak so highly of your escorts, and you insist that they're not having sexual relations with clients. But with all due respect, what else would you be expected to say? You're not exactly going to stand up there and admit to any illegal activity that could send you to prison."

"You're right," Zandra said smoothly. "I wouldn't."

"So you can understand why someone like me might take your claims of legitimacy with a grain of salt."

"Someone like you?" Zandra raked the man with a coolly dismissive glance. "Yes."

He frowned, not knowing whether he'd just been vindicated or insulted.

"Miss Kennedy," shouted another reporter, "you seemed to suggest that Mayor Norwood engaged in underhanded behavior for political gain. Do you think he deserves to be reelected?"

"That's for the voters to decide," Zandra said mildly. "I don't have an agenda. I'm not a politician, nor am I affiliated with any campaign. But the mayor brought me into this when he decided to use me as a political pawn.

He was sadly mistaken if he thought his attacks on my reputation and business would go unchallenged."

"Since you brought up your reputation, Miss Kennedy, would you like to address the elephant in the room?"

Zandra glanced toward the snide voice. Her favorite reporter again.

He smirked. "By now we've all seen the photo of you leaving a public restroom with Remington Brand. What do you have to say about that?"

Zandra gave him a look of amused disbelief. "Have you *seen* Remington Brand?"

The room erupted with feminine laughter and lusty whistles.

Remy looked adorably embarrassed as his brothers teased him and playfully slapped him on the back.

The reporter frowned disparagingly at Zandra. "Come on, Miss Kennedy. As the owner of an escort agency, surely you can agree that your public conduct is a reflection of your business and your escorts?"

Zandra heaved a sigh of resignation. "Look, if it makes you feel better to call me a slut, a whore, a madam, then do what you must. If it makes you feel morally superior, or if it'll help you sleep better at night, then by all means get out the pitchforks and burn me at the stake. I can't concern myself with your opinion of me or what I do. *I* know what kind of business I'm running and the caliber of women working for me, and that's all that matters."

As murmurs of approval went around the room, the rebuked man turned a deep shade of red. Zandra hoped she'd shut him up for good this time.

"Any particular reason you're wearing sunglasses, Miss Kennedy?" a reporter from the *Tribune* inquired curiously.

It was the question Zandra had been dreading, though she'd come prepared to answer it.

She glanced at Morgan, who gave her a subtle nod of encouragement.

She hesitated another moment, then slowly reached up and removed the sunglasses.

A collective gasp swept through the crowd when her bruised cheek was revealed. The shiner had darkened to purple over the past three days, and probably looked worse than it felt. She'd considered applying concealer that morning, but had changed her mind.

She'd spent her whole life hiding, trying to mask the scars of her past. Her mother had suffered in silence until the day she died.

No more hiding. No more silence.

"What happened to your face, Miss Kennedy?" the reporters shouted simultaneously.

Zandra smiled sadly. "I had a painful encounter with the past."

"Could you elaborate?"

As an expectant hush fell over the room, she took a deep breath and forged ahead. "Since my father's campaign surrogates have been making the rounds to put a revisionist spin on the nature of our estrangement, I thought it was time for me to tell my side of the story. Contrary to what you may have heard, I didn't stop speaking to my father because he disapproved of my escort agency. He was out of my life long before the business even opened."

She paused for a moment, meeting Remy's gaze. The tender ferocity in his eyes brought an ache to her throat, forcing her to swallow hard before she glanced away and continued speaking. "I grew up in a house ruled by fear. Not fear of the violence that plagued my neighborhood. Fear of violence from my own father. He verbally and physically abused my mother, and because of that, I grew up afraid of him. I feared the sight of his car pulling into the driveway. The thump of his footsteps. The sound of his voice. As long as he was around, I knew that my mother wasn't safe from his anger, and I never felt safe either."

She paused to sip from the glass of water that had been poured before the press conference began. The room was deafeningly silent. So silent she could hear herself swallow.

Her hand trembled slightly as she set the glass down, but her voice was steady as she resumed speaking. "In my father's house, femininity was something to be ashamed of, and beauty was a curse. He demanded modesty from me and my mother. Modesty to the point of invisibility. Not only should women not be seen, they shouldn't be heard. It wasn't until I left home for college that I realized just how warped this was, how dangerously oppressive.

"When I decided to open an escort agency, one of my goals was to ensure that the women I hired would be seen *and* heard. They aren't arm candy. They're strong, intelligent, capable women with voices that matter. I'm proud of them, and if my agency were to be shut down tomorrow, I'd have no regrets about the way I ran the business. If my father wants to publicly scold me for running what he deems a brothel…well," she murmured, touching her bruised cheek, "I'll let others decide whose sins are greater."

At the end of her speech, a low murmur of sympathy ran through the audience. She could feel an undercurrent of shock and anger, could see several female reporters dabbing at the corners of their eyes.

"I just have to say something."

Everyone turned to stare at Claudia, whose blue eyes were glistening with tears. She picked up Zandra's hand and held it as she solemnly addressed the crowd. "Zandra is a very private person, so I know how difficult it was for her to share what she just did. The painful experience she so eloquently spoke of was my reality for the eight years I was married. My husband beat me, and he made me feel worthless and unattractive because I wasn't a perfect size four…or six…or— Well, I think you guys get the point."

This drew appreciative chuckles that brought some levity to the room.

"Anyway," the petite blonde went on, "my husband preyed on my fears and insecurities and convinced me that he was the only man who would ever want me. We have two daughters, and when my oldest started having body-image issues—" Claudia's voice hitched, and she rapidly blinked back tears and inhaled a shaky breath before continuing "—it broke my heart, but it was part of the wakeup call I'd been needing. When I finally found the courage to take my girls and leave their father, I honestly didn't know whether we could make it on our own."

She turned to Zandra, warm gratitude shimmering in her eyes. "This young lady was my advocate when no one else cared. Becoming one of her escorts created opportunities for me I wouldn't have had. And you know what? No client has ever made me feel less than beautiful for not being a perfect size four. So I just want to thank you, Zandra, for giving me the fresh start I desperately needed."

Humbled by the moving tribute, Zandra squeezed Claudia's hand and mouthed, *Thank you.*

As the two women turned back to the audience, Zandra said quietly, "I hope that the stories we've shared today will help others come forward. If you've never been a victim of abuse, you might not understand just how paralyzing fear can be, and how it can keep people trapped in destructive relationships. My mother lived in constant fear of my father, and she suffered until the day she took her own life."

Zandra paused, her voice thickening with emotion. "Growing up, I was very fortunate to have the love and support of a very special family—" She met the caring gazes of each member of the Brand clan "—and to them I am eternally grateful. It's too late for my mother, but if this message helps anyone out there who has been suffering in silence, then maybe Autumn Kennedy's death wasn't in vain."

As the press conference ended, someone began clapping.

Zandra looked out into the audience.

It was Remy, standing on his feet, his eyes glowing with fierce pride and adoration.

Her heart lurched into her throat.

Then others started clapping, and within moments the applause had swelled to a thunderous roar.

As Zandra exchanged quiet, triumphant smiles with the other women on the stage, she allowed herself to believe that everything would be okay from now on.

Even though she knew better.

Several hours after the press conference, Zandra received an email from Heath.

Just saw the video. You were positively amazing. Couldn't be more proud. I'm coming to Chicago on business next month. If you're not available for dinner—and I suspect you're not—perhaps you could put me in touch with the cheeky blonde. You know I've always had a fondness for feisty women.

A delighted grin swept across Zandra's face. Without thinking twice, she wrote back, Claudia is indeed feisty. And you're going to love her....

# *Chapter Twenty-Three*

Three days later, Landis Kennedy issued a statement announcing his withdrawal from the mayoral race. The decision came as no surprise to anyone who'd watched or heard about Zandra's emotional press conference. Her revelations about her father's history of violence had, as one political analyst put it, "singlehandedly demolished the shortest-lived campaign" Chicagoans had ever seen.

An hour after Landis made his announcement, Johanna Kennedy filed for divorce. After the news broke, she sent Zandra a cryptic text message. Just three words that spoke chilling volumes: You were right.

Later that morning, Zandra was in her office when Christine sauntered through the doorway. "She is woman, hear her roar."

Zandra glanced up distractedly from the email message she'd been composing on her computer. "Hmm?"

"That was the headline from the latest editorial about

you," Christine explained, lowering herself into the chair across from Zandra's desk. Her manicured fingers slid across her smartphone, scrolling through pages. "These are just some of the other headlines that have graced articles about you, and I admit some are more corny than clever. Zandra: Warrior Princess. A Daughter's Triumphant Vengeance. The Slap Heard Around the World. Bullies Beware. Hell Hath No Fury Like a Madam Scorned." Christine paused with a chuckle. "The girls are getting some great press, too. Oh, and they've been dubbed *Zandra's Angels.*"

Zandra made a pained face. "Hadn't heard *that* one."

Christine grinned. "Three days later, you're still one of the top trending topics on Twitter, and your Google ranking is even higher than that *other* famous Kennedy."

Zandra shook her head, lamenting the societal tendency to sensationalize any story, no matter how tragic or deeply personal. But she'd understood what came with the territory when she'd agreed to hold the press conference. She'd forfeited any expectation of privacy the moment she'd looked into those cameras and invited the world into her life. But she had no regrets. Not if her actions helped other victims.

"You're being hailed as a feminist heroine," Christine said warmly.

Zandra heaved a sigh. "I'm not a heroine."

But apparently others thought so. Since the press conference, she'd been flooded with calls and invitations for speaking engagements. She'd been contacted by every organization under the sun, from battered women's shelters to civil rights groups.

It was both humbling and overwhelming.

Which was another reason she needed to get away.

To that end, she was taking a month-long sabbatical to St. Lucia. Her flight was scheduled to depart in three hours, but she still had one last important thing to do before she left.

Christine winked at her. "Are you sure you don't want to stick around and bask in your new celebrity status?"

"I'm sure," Zandra said wryly.

Christine's expression softened. "Thanks for entrusting the agency to me while you're gone."

Zandra smiled. "You've been with me from the beginning, and you love this agency as much as I do. Who else would I leave in charge?"

"Not Morgan, thank God." Christine gave a mock shudder. "Love her, but she's bossy as hell."

Zandra laughed.

After the press conference, Morgan had resigned from her job to officially become Zandra's publicist. She'd be earning more than she had ever imagined, which would enable her to save money toward opening her public relations business.

"Well, I'd better get back to the phone," Christine said, rising from the chair. "We've been getting nonstop calls, and not just from reporters. The girls are in demand even more than ever. We'd better hire Lena's replacement soon."

"I know," Zandra agreed with a sigh. "I'm working on it."

After Christine left, Zandra returned her attention to her unfinished email.

It was the most difficult message she'd ever had to compose, because she knew how much pain she would cause by sending it.

But she had to. Or at least that's what she'd been telling herself.

Zandra hesitated another moment, then resumed typing.

Ten minutes later, eyes brimming with tears, she stopped and read over what she'd written.

Rem,

I wanted you to know that I've rented a beach house on St. Lucia, where I'll be spending the rest of the summer. By the time you receive this message, I'll already be gone. I planned it that way. Only a few people know where I'm going, and I considered swearing them to secrecy so you wouldn't follow me. But I knew that was pointless because you'd crack them too easily.

My mother used to say that she and I were nothing alike, and that was a source of great relief to her. But maybe she was wrong. Maybe we're more alike than she ever thought. Maybe I'm a coward for sending you this letter after I've already skipped town. But I didn't want to see you, Remy. I didn't want you to try to talk me out of leaving. And I was afraid that if we talked, I might have said things I'd later regret.

Let me savor that last image of you, standing and applauding at the end of the press conference.

Please don't come to me. So much has happened. I need time and distance to process everything. I think you understand that better than anyone.

I love you, Remy. No matter what happens between us, my love for you will never change.

Be well,<br>
Z

Zandra stared at the blurred words on the screen, her hand hovering over the mouse.

*Am I doing the right thing?* she wondered for the umpteenth time. *Am I?*

After the press conference, she'd seen Remy only briefly because he'd had to catch a flight to Mexico. He'd only be gone a few days, he'd told her, but he wanted them to get together and talk when he got back.

She hadn't refused. But as she'd watched him leave, she already knew she would be gone when he came home.

Zandra closed her eyes, sighing heavily. Fatigue had settled between her shoulder blades, weighing her down. Spending a month on a tropical island would do her mind and body good. Her heart…well, her broken heart was a different ailment that only time could cure.

After wavering another moment, she scheduled the email to be delivered after she was safely on the plane. Out of reach.

Swallowing a hard lump that had lodged in her throat, she shut down the computer and grabbed her purse and attaché case.

She paused at the door, glancing around the office to make sure she hadn't forgotten anything.

Then she turned off the light and walked out.

Remy sat behind his desk, the glow from the computer screen the room's only illumination.

He'd never felt more acutely alone than he did that night.

Because Zandra was gone.

She'd left him.

Just walked out of his life with no warning.

Upon returning from Monterrey that afternoon, he'd intended to drive over to her apartment and talk to her, make her see that they belonged together and could get past any obstacle.

He'd needed to stop by the office first and take care of a few things. But an hour later, just as he was getting ready to leave, he'd received her email message.

And his world came crashing down.

Remy took a swig of beer, swallowed bitterly as his eyes returned to the glowing computer screen.

He read her letter again, each word carving deeper into his heart.

She'd asked him not to go to her. She might as well have told him to stop breathing. Even her closing salutation wounded him. *Be well?* How the fuck did she expect him to do that when she'd just jammed a stake through his heart?

*You brought this on yourself,* his conscience reminded him. *You have no one but yourself to blame.*

After settling the score with Kennedy last week, Remy had driven straight to Keegan's office to get some answers. The commander had been deeply apologetic and incensed, explaining that Norwood had gone behind his back and asked one of his campaign staffers to spy on Zandra. Threatened by Kennedy's growing popularity and promising poll numbers, Norwood then decided to preemptively leak the story about Zandra.

The mayor's underhanded tactics, coupled with his obvious lack of trust in Keegan, had prompted the commander to resign in angry disgust. But this news brought Remy no consolation.

He'd tried to protect the woman he loved from scandal, and it had all blown up in his face. He'd deceived her and betrayed her trust, and that was something he'd have to live with for the rest of his life.

A life that Zandra had just walked out of. Possibly for good.

Remy gripped the beer bottle, then lifted and hurled it against the nearest wall.

As glass and foam exploded, he dropped his head into his hands and closed his eyes.

*God,* he prayed like never before, *let her come back. Please let her come back to me.*

# *Chapter Twenty-Four*

"So when are you going to tell me the *real* reason you skipped town?" Skylar demanded.

Zandra sighed, glancing around the bustling terminal of the Hartsfield–Jackson International Airport in Atlanta. She'd been flipping through the latest issue of *Vogue* while she waited out her layover when her cell phone rang.

She shouldn't have answered it. She wasn't in the mood to be grilled.

"Hello?" Skylar prompted. "Are you there?"

"Actually, the reception's been kind of spotty. So if we get disconnected—"

"Nice try. You're not getting off this phone until you tell me what's really going on with you."

Zandra frowned. "Why do I have to have a reason to visit St. Lucia? It's a beautiful island—"

"That you already visited this summer," Skylar interjected. "*And* you just returned from London not too long ago."

"So what? I didn't realize I had to justify the number of vacations I take every year."

"Don't do that. You know that's not what I meant."

Zandra sighed. "I know. I—" She broke off as her gaze landed on a tall, dark and unbelievably gorgeous man sauntering through the busy airport, sipping from a tall cup of coffee. "Hey, I think that's Michael Wolf."

*"What?"* Skylar squealed excitedly. "The celebrity chef?"

"Yeah. I think that's him."

"Oh, my God! Are you serious? Don't tease me, Zandra. You know how much I love Michael Wolf. You *have* to get his autograph for me."

Zandra chuckled dryly. "I know, or you'd never forgive me." She lifted her sunglasses, peering closer at the approaching man. "Hmm. On second thought…I don't think it's him."

"Really?" Skylar sounded deflated. "Are you sure?"

"Yeah. I think it's his brother…or one of his cousins. They all look just alike."

"I know," Skylar breathed. "Every time he has them on his show, I have wet dreams afterward. God, they're gorgeous. And when they huddle together at the end of the episode, put their heads back and howl? I need a defibrillator when they do that."

Zandra chuckled, holding the phone away from her ear as Skylar let out a piercing howl that sounded *nothing* like the sexy rumble unleashed by the members of the Wolf Pack, as they were popularly dubbed.

As the man drew nearer, Zandra rifled through her

memory bank, trying to recall names. Manning maybe? Marcus? Montana?

As if sensing her stare, the man's dark eyes shifted to the right and met Zandra's.

As he sauntered past her gate, he winked.

Zandra quickly snapped her sunglasses back into place and ducked her head over her magazine. She felt so foolish she couldn't help giggling.

"What's so funny?" Skylar asked curiously.

"Nothing," Zandra muttered. "You've got me acting like an idiot over here."

"Oh, I think you can manage that just fine on your own."

Zandra frowned. "What's that supposed to mean?"

Skylar countered with a question of her own. "Did something happen between you and Remy?"

Zandra closed her eyes, heaving a deep sigh. "How many times are you going to ask me that question?"

"As many times as it takes until you answer it."

Zandra shook her head in frustration.

She still hadn't told any of her friends about Remy's betrayal. She didn't want to be pitied, didn't want anyone hovering worriedly over her. She didn't want to be given false reassurances, nor did she want to be told that she'd overreacted.

And maybe some small part of her wanted to protect Remy from censure.

Either way, she wasn't ready to share what had happened. So Skylar would just have to accept that.

"It's complicated, Sky," Zandra said quietly. "That's all I can really say for now."

Her friend sighed resignedly. "Well, that's more than

you've admitted up to this point. So I guess we're making progress."

Zandra smiled ruefully. "When I'm ready to talk, I'll let you know."

"You promise?"

"I promise."

"Okay. Because you know I'm here for you if you need me."

"I know," Zandra said warmly. "And I appreciate that."

"Hey, that's what friends are for. Speaking of which, I still haven't told you how my date went with that hot guy I met at your office. In all the chaos of the past week, it kind of got lost in the shuffle."

Zandra grimaced, guilt washing over her. Since she hadn't told Skylar about Remy's secret investigation, she couldn't very well tell her that the man she'd gone out with wasn't who he'd claimed to be.

"Maybe it's best that I don't tell you anyway," Skylar continued sheepishly. "I, uh, wasn't on my best behavior that night."

*I know,* Zandra mused grimly.

"So," Skylar said casually, "I was just wondering whether he'd called the agency to, you know, set up another date. I know that's how it works, right? Your escorts don't personally follow-up with clients, do they?"

Zandra sighed heavily. "No," she answered. "They don't. And no, he hasn't called again."

"Oh." Skylar sounded so disappointed that Zandra's heart twisted.

*Damn Remy and his duplicity.*

"It doesn't mean he didn't have a good time," she assured her friend. "Clients don't always call back right after a date. These guys are really busy. For all we know, he's out of the country on business."

"Of course," Skylar said quickly. "That's what I was thinking, too. Not that I've been dwelling on it or anything. I was just curious."

"I know." Zandra glanced around as her fellow passengers began gathering their things and powering down electronic devices. "Listen, Sky, they're boarding for my flight now, so I'd better go."

"Oh, okay. Well, have a safe trip, and remember I'm just a phone call away if you need me."

"Thanks, Sky." Zandra smiled. "Enjoy the rest of your summer and stay out of trouble."

Skylar chuckled impishly. "I'll try."

"Try harder."

"Yes, ma'am."

Before Zandra ended the call, Skylar said, "Zandra?"

"Yeah?"

Her friend's voice was gentle. "Whatever it is you're running away from? It'll still be here when you get home. So don't run too long."

Over the next two weeks, Zandra licked her wounds in the peaceful solitude of a cozy cottage overlooking the same beach she and Remy's family had visited during the previous trip to St. Lucia.

As one day blended into another, she tried to pretend that everything was normal. She ventured into town and bought artwork from local vendors to decorate the cottage. She took bus tours of the island, or went exploring on her own. She shopped at the food market, and cooked more than she had in years.

But when she ate on the terrace beneath a canopy of

stars, she wished Remy were sharing the meal with her. When she went sailing and snorkeling, she longed for his company each time. When she headed down to the beach, lay in the shade and tried to lose herself in a book, her mind always wandered back to Remy, remembering the way he'd playfully tossed her into the water that long-ago afternoon.

One day as she watched a young couple build a sandcastle with their small child, she became so emotional that she had to get up and leave.

Coming back to St. Lucia, she soon realized, was like returning to the scene of a beautiful crime. Everywhere she looked she saw reminders of Remy, and she had to ask herself whether she'd subconsciously chosen to subject herself to these memories, the way she periodically read her mother's suicide note. It was as though she found catharsis in self-punishment.

She was thinking of Remy late one afternoon as she walked along the shore of the empty beach, letting the waves wash over her feet, enjoying the warm sand between her toes. She squatted to pick up a shimmering shard of coral. As the foamy water lapped at her ankles and a gentle breeze sifted through her hair, she closed her eyes.

When she opened them and saw Remy walking toward her, a choked sob rushed up her throat. She thought she must be hallucinating. That she'd conjured him from a bottomless well of longing.

So she snapped her eyelids shut, kept them screwed together and slowly counted to ten. Then she carefully peeled them open.

He was still there.

And coming closer.

As she stared, the sight of him sauntering across the sugary sand took her breath away. He looked heart-stoppingly handsome in his white navy dress uniform. The one he swore he'd never wear again.

When he reached her, she got unsteadily to her feet.

"What are you doing here?" she asked in a choked whisper.

His dark eyes glinted at her. "You didn't really think I could stay away, did you?"

She made a muffled sound, torn between laughter and exasperation. "You never could follow orders."

His lips curved. "No, my queen."

"Oh, God." Her fingers trembled against her lips at the memory his words had evoked. "Remy…I—" She broke off, her voice strangling on another sob.

He gently stroked her hair, his eyes tracing her features. "I had to come, Zandra. Being apart from you was killing me."

*I know the feeling,* she thought.

"How have you been?" he asked quietly.

"Um. I've been better." She looked him over, shaking her head slowly. "You're wearing your old uniform… How did you know?"

His expression softened. "Your mother told me."

She stared up at him, stunned. "My…mother?"

"Yeah." A shadow of a smile touched his lips. "It was on your prom night, after you left the house. She pulled me aside and told me about your bonding ritual, how you two would watch *An Officer and a Gentleman* together and cry afterward. She joked that any man who wanted your hand would have to show up wearing a navy uniform."

"She told you that?" Zandra whispered brokenly.

"Yeah." His voice was husky with emotion. "She must have known…long before we did."

As tears welled in Zandra's eyes, Remy pulled her into his arms, tucked her head beneath his chin and held her tight as she wept into his chest.

She almost imagined she could feel her mother standing beside her, whispering the words from her letter. *Never be afraid to open your heart. The right man will know how to take care of it.*

Remy was that man. And her mother had realized it years ago.

Long moments afterward, Zandra lifted her damp face to his. "I missed you," she whispered.

"God, I missed you, too," Remy groaned, kissing her forehead and her closed eyelids. "I couldn't get here fast enough."

She smiled. "I'm glad you came."

"Are you?"

She nodded as he lovingly brushed the tears from her cheeks. "I really am."

He shook his head at her. "I'm so sorry I hurt you, Zandra," he said thickly, stroking her windswept hair off her face. "I tried like hell to convince myself I was doing the right thing, but instead I betrayed your trust."

She swallowed. "I never expected that from you. I felt blindsided."

"I know, baby. Not a day goes by that I don't regret what I did. Do you think…do you think you can ever forgive me?"

She stared into his eyes, saw his anguish and remorse, and knew there was nothing she could ever refuse him.

She reached up and touched his cheek. "I think I already have."

He turned his face and pressed a kiss to her palm, his eyes closed in an expression of infinite gratitude that clutched at her heart.

"I'm staying here for two more weeks," she murmured.

As he opened his eyes and looked at her, she added almost shyly, "You're more than welcome to stay, too. If you'd like."

His gaze softened. "Oh, I'd like. I'd like very much."

She smiled.

He leaned his forehead against hers, and they looked into each other's moist eyes.

"I love you so much," Remy said fervently.

"I love you, too."

"I *need* you."

"I need you, too."

Cupping her face between his hands, Remy said in an achingly raw voice, "I can't live without you, Z. Please don't make me have to."

Her throat tightened. "I won't."

"Then marry me."

Even as rapture burst inside her, she couldn't resist arching a brow at him. "Are you asking or telling me?"

"Both." His eyes glittered. "Because I'm not taking no for an answer. In fact—"

She watched as he reached inside his pocket and removed a small black velvet pouch that she recognized, having purchased jewelry from Tiffany's.

He said, "I'll give you the box later. It wouldn't fit in my pocket."

"Oh, my God," Zandra breathed as he removed an exquisite princess-cut engagement ring. "Remy…"

As he held up the ring, the five-carat diamond caught and reflected the sunlight.

Zandra beamed.

Remy chuckled at her, tweaking her nose. "You were always such a girl."

She grinned, not denying it. "It's a gorgeous ring, Remy."

"I'm glad you like it. I can't wait to put it on your finger."

She held out a trembling hand.

"Ah, ah, ah," he murmured. "Not so fast."

"Don't play with me, Rem."

"I'm not. But you haven't given me an answer yet."

"Does it matter?" she teased. "You said you weren't taking no for an answer."

"I want to hear you say the word." He held up the ring. "Do you want it?"

She gazed into his eyes. "Not as much as I want the man holding it."

A look of tender euphoria swept over his face. "God, I love you," he whispered.

"Ditto." She paused. "And my answer is yes."

"Yes?"

She smiled. "Yes."

Tears misted her eyes as he slid the ring onto her finger. Then he hauled her into his arms, lifted her off the sand and spun her around. She laughed joyously, clinging to his neck as the ocean breeze danced through her hair.

Remy held on to her, his hands curving under her bottom as she wrapped her legs around his waist. Their lips met hotly, sealing the deal.

Even as the frothy waves washed over Remy's feet, soaking the bottom of his pants, he didn't stop kissing Zandra, didn't release her mouth or uncurl his tongue from hers. As the kiss intensified, heat surged through her, hardening her nipples and dampening her panties beneath her sundress. She moaned with pleasure, tightening her thighs around him.

It was only when they heard whistles that they broke apart and glanced around to see a couple strolling past, grinning broadly at them.

"Go, Navy," the man cheered encouragingly.

Remy laughed as Zandra blushed.

"I guess we should, ah, take this reunion inside the house," she suggested.

Remy grinned. "Where is it?"

She pointed across the beach.

As he turned and started toward the white cottage, she marveled at the strength of his arms. She knew he could carry her up and down the entire length of the beach without ever faltering.

Smiling at the thought, she tenderly framed his face between her hands. He'd been a constant in her life, his role evolving over the years. Protector, hero, friend, lover. It was only natural that he now become her husband.

Glancing around the palm-fringed beach, she remembered, once again, that this was where it all began.

They'd come full circle.

"This is perfect," Remy murmured, gazing around with the same sense of wonder she felt.

"Yes, it is," she said softly. "It couldn't be more perfect."

"We should find a minister to marry us right here on the beach."

Her pulse leaped. "Ooh, how romantic."

"This week."

*"This week?"*

"Why not? We're both here."

"That's true," Zandra smilingly agreed, fingering the gold rank insignia on his breast pocket, "but if we eloped and deprived your mother and Grandma Eleanor of planning our wedding, they'd kill us. And you know it."

"Yeah, I know," Remy grumbled. "Damn."

Zandra laughed, leaning down to nip at his jaw. "But that doesn't mean we can't get married here. Just not this week."

"Soon, though. I don't want a long engagement. I've waited long enough."

"Aye aye, sir." Zandra smiled, nibbling his lower lip. "I'm coming off the Pill."

He stared into her eyes. "You are?"

She nodded. "I want babies. Lots of them. Like your family."

His gaze was fiercely tender. "Nothing would make me happier."

"Good." She smiled dreamily as he nuzzled her throat. "You're going to teach them how to swim like you taught me—minus the taunting."

He laughed. "Yes, ma'am. No taunting the tadpoles."

"That's right. And we're going to bring them here every summer. We'll take them snorkeling, and we'll frolic on the beach and build sandcastles with them."

"Mmm. Sounds like an absolutely beautiful plan." He feathered kisses over the flesh above her breasts, sending hot flickers of desire through her. She closed her eyes, already anticipating the endless nights of passion that awaited them.

"I want to make love at sunrise," she breathed as they reached the cottage, where his suitcase waited on the porch. "I want to feel you deep inside me as the sky blushes."

Remy shuddered with pleasure. “Any way you want it, my queen,” he whispered against her parted lips. “Any way you want it….”

* * * * *